"So what are you wearing in bed?" Jack's voice was like silk on the cell phone.

Raine smiled. "Flannel pajama shorts and a top. Cushy socks. Not exactly Victoria's Secret, but soft and warm."

"Very nice... But I want to know what secrets you're hiding *under* that flannel."

Raine felt rather than saw the heated flush on her body. Her breathing was erratic. "Maybe we should just talk...."

She could almost see his naughty grin as he spoke. "Just relax and have fun. I want you to slip out of your clothing. And pretend I'm there with you...watching."

Talking online had been so much easier. Now he was asking her to do something wildly new and incredibly daring.

"Raine, you make me so hot. I want to touch you."

She pictured Jack on the other end of the phone, desiring her. Fear and feminine power warred in her mind, and in her heart.

She took a deep breath. "I'm naked now, and I'm under the covers thinking about you. I want to wrap my hands around you. Slide my mouth over you. I want to taste you...."

A strong groan of masculine appreciation came over the line.

Dear Reader,

The thrill of publishing my first romance novel is almost beyond words! I'm so happy to be able to share Jack and Raine's story with you. Writing for Blaze is a dream come true. I hope to write many more books in the future, but this first one—like a first love, first child or first house—will always be extra special.

Jack and Raine's story is also very dear to me because it springs from my own experience meeting my husband on the Internet. That happened more than ten years ago, and while our story was *very* different from Jack and Raine's, the magic of meeting someone in this particular way always stayed with me and was a source of inspiration for this book.

I hope you enjoy reading *Virtually Perfect* as much as I enjoyed writing it! And don't forget to visit my Web site, www.samanthahunter.com.

Best wishes,

Samantha Hunter

VIRTUALLY PERFECT

Samantha Hunter

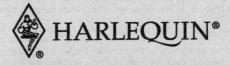

HARLEQUIN®

TORONTO • NEW YORK • LONDON
AMSTERDAM • PARIS • SYDNEY • HAMBURG
STOCKHOLM • ATHENS • TOKYO • MILAN • MADRID
PRAGUE • WARSAW • BUDAPEST • AUCKLAND

Many thanks to Cara Summers,
from whom I've learned so much. Your insight and good humor
added so much joy to the writing of this book!

For my husband, Mike:
technical consultant, brainstorming partner and
the love of my life. You're everything to me.

ISBN 0-373-79146-1

VIRTUALLY PERFECT

Copyright © 2004 by Samantha Hunter.

1

NORMALLY, RAINE COVINGTON would've enjoyed a stroll on a snowy evening. Though Salem was renown to tourists as "Witch City" for its gruesome persecution of women and men accused of witchcraft, the town had more than the history of its witch trials and occult legends to offer. It was a quaint New England coastal town, but in many ways it was also a developing metropolis.

She'd always felt comforted by the homey, narrow streets and historic Federal-style homes huddled up against each other. Right now, however, she couldn't enjoy any of it. She was too preoccupied figuring out some way to escape Jerry Donnelly who was by her side, nudging into her suggestively from time to time. She clenched her jaw, didn't say a word and walked a little faster.

Jerry was a freelance graphic artist she'd met at an office lunch given in appreciation of freelance workers. He'd seemed nice enough then. Yeah, *nice*—they were all "nice" until they were trying to slide their hand up your leg under the dinner table. He had beachboy-blond hair and soft, brown eyes that gave him an innocent look that she'd found attractive. It hadn't taken much time alone with him to discover that he was anything but.

When he'd suggested dessert-to-go so they could enjoy it in

more interesting ways, she officially called time and asked to go home. Who the heck suggested something like that two hours after meeting someone on a first date? Well, apparently Jerry did. And she had the feeling he didn't take rejection easily.

They were finally here. On the sidewalk in front of her house. The porch light warmed the step, and she gazed at the brick-red door wistfully—escape was so close at hand. Jerry moved closer, going for the kill, and Raine, trying to avoid a confrontation, did the only thing she could think of.

"Oh, God!" She doubled at the waist and held her stomach hard, contorting her face in what she hoped looked like a very painful expression. Startled, Jerry stepped back.

"Um…uh…what? What's the matter?"

She threw a little heavy breathing into the mix, and winced up at him, backing away slowly. He started to follow, but she held a hand out, motioning him to stay away as she inched toward the porch.

"Oh, Jerry, I'm so sorry, but I have to get inside quick. Something bad…stomach cramps…night!"

"But you seemed fine a moment ago…."

His voice trailed off behind her. Without a glance back, Raine closed the door behind her with a blustery sigh of relief, leaning back against it as if the devil himself were on the other side. It wasn't her most elegant escape, but at least it had worked.

Resting her head against the door, she let the emotions roll over her. Annoyance, relief—and ah, there it was—disappointment. Her familiar friend. All she wanted was some good company, a little romance, and, if she was lucky, halfway decent sex. When it came to men, those things were getting increasingly hard to find.

There was only one man whom she missed when she didn't get to see him after so much as a single day. Only one who popped up in her thoughts and made her smile, and who didn't disappoint.

Rider.

Not even bothering to change, she grabbed her laptop and plopped down on the sofa, a soft shiver of anticipation taking the edge off an otherwise miserable night. The screen glowed, and she tapped at the keyboard, hoping she hadn't missed him.

She hadn't! He was there! He saw her logon immediately. She smiled wider, watching his words appear across the screen. He had been waiting. For her.

"Hey, beautiful, I thought you might not be by tonight. Working late?"

"No, was just out for a while."

"Hot date?"

"No. Boring, boring night."

She lied, not knowing exactly why she didn't want to tell him she had been out with someone.

"Nilla, maybe it's time to spice it up a little."

"I think we have been quite spicy enough lately."

Nilla—her pseudonym. She hadn't been able to think of anything else when she had registered on the site, and had been eating vanilla cookies at the time. So much for her creativity.

"Oh, I don't know. Depends on your taste. I like things a little on the hot side."

She grinned, her fingers racing over the keyboard.

"Hold on, tiger. Let me get a glass of wine and change into something more...comfortable. I'll be right back."

Jumping up off the sofa, she headed into the bedroom to change. She had been talking with Rider—not his real name, of course—online for a little more than a month. They had met online at RomanceMUD, an interactive virtual world. She'd been researching Internet romances for her most recent column in *Real Woman* magazine, which was just hitting its stride as one of the leading women's magazines in the U.S.

Over the last decade, she had literally grown with the magazine, which had recently relocated to a bigger and more prestigious building overlooking Salem Harbor to house its ever-expanding staff, now topping two hundred. She'd started as a freelance writer right out of college. The job had really just fallen into her lap and she took it for some income while figuring out what to do next. Then as more and more magazine pieces came her way, she discovered a knack for writing; she loved the work. Eventually she was hired for a permanent position.

She was the head writer for the Lifestyles beat, which covered everything from raising children to fashion. She provided editorial input and was deeply involved in planning each issue's content. She hired freelancers for most of the articles, but the core element of the section was her relationships column. It had begun as an advice-type column and had blossomed into longer pieces of social commentary. She wrote about all kinds of relationship issues, including friends, siblings, marriage, sex, same-sex families, and working parents.

Pouring herself a glass of merlot she thought about how some things never changed: jealously, passion, misunderstanding, loneliness.

Since more and more readers were writing in with questions about Internet romance, she'd pitched a series of columns exploring love and sex on the Internet—and here she was right smack in the middle of it herself.

She had started off the series by writing about Internet dating services that had emerged over the past two or three years. Plenty of people used the formal services, but since the majority of her readers had "just met" someone online, she'd been wandering through chat rooms and virtual erotic playgrounds to see what she found "out there."

Raine had joined the RomanceMUD site on impulse, and there she'd met Rider. They'd clicked immediately. With him, she felt that little hint of something special she had been missing with the men she'd dated.

Padding back to the sofa, she sat, lugged her laptop up close to her and stared at the screen. What was he doing right now? What was he thinking?

She was coming to understand more and more about what attracted women to men on the Net. She and Rider talked about everything. They shared intimate fantasies without the disappointments and expectations that often plagued relationships. He could be intense and romantic, and he was always amazingly sexy. It was a compelling combination.

She was sure that in real life, Rider, like all men, probably left the toilet seat up and his beard shavings in the sink. He would make promises he didn't keep and would glaze over when you talked about things that mattered to you. Online, she didn't have to worry about any of that. If she wanted to, she could just hit the off button and he would be gone. The perfect man.

He had started out being part of her research project. An experiment. But things had changed, and she felt that they were becoming, well, close. They talked every night, long discussions that kept her up into the morning hours. She was starting to feel as if she knew him, and he her.

Their online talks were always varied. Sometimes it was casual conversation; sometimes it was very *intimate* conversation. At first it was awkward, writing out her innermost feelings on her laptop's screen. But then it became more like they were weaving their own little world. As if she was the heroine in her own romance novel. She didn't have the chance—or the nerve—to be as bold, funny or daring in real life as she could be online. But here, all inhibitions were lifted without risk. What could be better? She shook her head briskly, shaking herself out of her thoughts, and typed.

"Hey, sorry I took so long. I'm back. So, have you thought about joining up with another game?"

"No, I think I am done with that for now—this was just a whim to keep me amused while work was slow. I think I would rather take a dip into reality for a while. How about you?"

Grunting in annoyance, she had hoped he would drop the issue, as she'd obviously ignored it several times before. Another infuriating male trait—if it wasn't what they wanted to hear, they refused to get the message when it was offered loud and clear.

Rider had been hinting about taking things to the next step, referring to real life a little too often, and she wasn't big on that idea. However, she knew from her previous research and interviews that this was also the key moment that came about in every Internet romance: should we or shouldn't we? Fish or cut bait. And she had no idea what to do.

"Still there, Nilla?"

She typed a smile into existence for him.

"Yes, I'm still here. Just caught up in thought. Sorry."

She watched the words appear on the screen that glowed in the darkness of her room.

"What are you thinking about?"
"About being a 'whim that has kept you amused while you have been at work.' I think my ego just dropped a few notches."
"The *game* was a whim to keep me amused at work. You are something else entirely."
"Oh, and what would that be?"

Nilla held her breath as she sat back, sorry she had asked that question, but it had just flown from her fingertips.

I smooth your hair from your face, and look in your eyes. I slip my hands up the back of your shirt, and rub your bare shoulder blades, then pull you closer to me. "I don't know, I am still trying to get a handle on it myself.

But it's something special. I'm intrigued by you. That doesn't happen too often, for me at least."

Raine sighed and closed her eyes. She never would have believed it if she hadn't experienced it herself. It was amazing how erotic, how amazingly vivid the words could be, typed across the screen. There was no sound, yet she could hear each word as if he was whispering it in her ear.

She felt her back arch a little as if she really was being pulled closer to him, and she imagined she could feel his warm breath on her face. Then again, maybe she had just gone without real sex for so long, lame as it usually was, that she was like tinder to a spark—even a virtual one.

JACK SAT BACK and waited to see how she would respond to his request. *C'mon, Nilla, sweetheart, talk to me.* He couldn't get over the effect this woman had on him. He was hypnotized. He hadn't understood why for weeks he would rather be here, sitting on his sofa with a beer and a hard-on, typing pages and pages of conversation, having virtual sex and whatever else they came up with, instead of going out and bringing home a real live woman who could do more than just get him completely hot and then leave him to take care of it by himself.

He was getting impatient with the whole situation; it wasn't his usual style. Nothing about this was his usual style. He wasn't a party animal but he'd had a healthy social life that had gone to the dogs lately. He liked to go out, meet women, hang with his friends and have a good time. He hadn't been with anyone exclusive in a while, but maybe that was because he was spending way too much time sitting in front of his laptop.

His pal Greg had called him to go out twice in the last two weeks, and he had made excuses. He said he had to work, when the truth was he really didn't want to miss time with Nilla.

He muttered to himself, "I must be crazy. Getting desperate in my old age." Of course, thirty-four wasn't exactly ancient. The lines appearing on the screen erased his thoughts.

I am sighing as I press into you. I pick up your shirt at its edges, peel it up over your skin, up over your head, and nestle my face against your chest, sucking on your skin, biting you lightly.

Jack sighed, feeling a surge of arousal. Hey, he was human. Having a woman say things like that was the next best thing to being there. The next best thing. But not the best thing. He ignored the doubt that was chipping away at him, and started to respond in kind, when another line appeared, and then another…

I slide my hands down your stomach and wrap my fingers around your erection, squeezing and stroking, loving the feel of you in my hand. "Rider, I want you…I want to make you crazy…."

He felt his heart pound and shook his head, surprised that this was affecting him so deeply. He had been using online networks before most people knew networks existed. His dad had helped him build his own computer, and he'd "talked" to people on the old, slow FIDOnet bulletin boards in the eighties when he was just a kid.

He had literally grown up with the Internet, and it had always been a part of his life—but it had never, ever, been like this. This was a whole new world, a different kind of reality. His jaw clenched as he pounded out the words to her.

"You've made me crazy every night, and a good part of every day, for weeks now. I want you to make me crazy for real, Nilla. I want to do the same to you."

Nothing. The cursor hung like heavy silence between them.

"Hmm, Rider. Are you okay? You don't seem like yourself tonight."

Jack shook his head and ran his hands over his face. It was all he could do not to track her down in real life. During the day, he would think of her, something they'd shared, something she'd said, and feel immediately aroused, which wasn't always convenient. When he wasn't losing sleep, he dreamed of her at night. Of knowing her. Finding her.

He was an Internet security expert. He certainly had the skills to find her, to get past the pseudonym and find out who she really was. Hell, at his level of expertise, locating her wouldn't even be a challenge. Even though they used generic e-mails with pseudonyms, it was a simple matter of finding her network address, locating her service provider and making some phone calls.

What most people didn't understand in the miraculous age of the Internet was that the most common method of hacking wasn't done with computers, but by finding out the information you needed the old-fashioned way: talking to people who could tell you what you needed to know.

Most people were afraid of putting their credit card number online, but didn't think twice about handing it over to a waiter who disappeared with it for five minutes. It never failed to amaze him, but those curious social and psychological traits made his work interesting. Computers, he knew, were all about the people sitting in front of them.

A few keystrokes, a few casual requests, and he could know who she was, where she lived and worked, and probably anything else he wanted to know in just a few hours. But he wouldn't do it, though he damned his sense of ethics to hell. His job was to enforce the rules, not break them himself. Though he was desperately tempted.

"Nilla, baby, I am in knots. That's the problem. You tie mo up."

"We could certainly try that, if you want."

Jack nearly broke into a sweat. She could do this to him just with the words. What would the reality be like? There was some kind of wild connection between them, though he didn't know how it happened, or what to do about it.

He reached down, slid his hand over his crotch, felt the stiffness pushing at the seam of his jeans and dropped his head back, the sharp edge of need burning through him. But this time, it just wasn't right. He was sitting on his sofa in the dark. Again. Alone.

No. No more of this.

This wasn't what he wanted, how he operated. It just wasn't enough anymore, not nearly enough. He sometimes felt as if he lived in front of the screen—it was where he worked, kept up on current events, had his morning coffee and sometimes his dinner—but he was damned if he was going to have his sex life there, too! He typed impatiently this time.

"Nilla, I want to meet you. We need to meet. For real."
"Not a good idea. I could be fat, bald and seventy-five years old, for all you know."

He let out a heavy breath. She was trying to deflect him. Disappointment doused arousal as he realized she wasn't as avid to make that connection as he was.

"Nilla, we're two healthy adults who are driving each other crazy and then ending up in bed alone every night. I want to kiss you. I want to stop imagining and pretending. I want to see what color your eyes are. What's wrong with that?"
"I don't know, Rider. We don't know each other well enough. This is just a game. I like it this way."
"It stopped being a game a while ago. For me, anyway. Think about what we could be missing."
"Like I said, it could be all lies, Rider. How can we know? We are creating a kind of fiction here, right? That's what this place is for, not truth. But at least here we know that outright. Why do you want to complicate this?"
"Have you lied to me, Nilla?"

He held his breath for the few long seconds the screen remained blank.

"No, but I haven't told you the truth, either. You don't really know anything about me. Not really. I don't want you to know."

"What I know is that there is something in you that speaks to something in me. I know you are smart, funny and passionate. I know your politics and your beliefs, but I don't know the shape of your face, the scent of you, the sound of your voice. And I want to. I didn't go looking for this, for you, but now I can't settle for words on a screen."

"Hold on. This is getting too intense, Rider. I need to think."

Jack's shoulders slumped and he rubbed his tired eyes, shoving the computer back on the table. He wandered into the kitchen to get another beer. He had pushed the issue, and he was going to lose her. Though he felt ridiculous getting all worked up over a name on a screen, that idea really hurt.

RAINE CLOSED HER EYES and let out a frustrated sigh. Since they'd never even mentioned meeting in person, they'd had openly shared their thoughts and feelings, developing a high level of intimacy fairly quickly, something she had never actually had happen in a so-called normal relationship. She wasn't sure she believed it could happen in a normal, real relationship.

She had never known a man could share this way, communicate feelings and thoughts the way Rider did. It certainly had never happened to her. If he was like this in real life… She blew out a breath and dropped her head back, amazed at the possibilities. But that was unlikely—this was fantasy. In real life, everything would be exposed, all the faults and awkwardness, all the things that got in the way.

She wished she could meet a man who would not leave her

hopes in shambles, but she couldn't bring herself to believe he really existed. She steadied herself, and wrote carefully.

"Rider, you're right, this has been special. And if we meet, it might all just evaporate in a big cloud of disappointment. Here we can say, do, be anything we want. We get to be larger than life, but in real life we would probably just bore each other senseless. Or worse."

"I don't think so, Nilla. And what if we didn't? But so what if we did? What's to lose?"

"I don't know, Rider. I don't want to lose this. I enjoy what I've had. You. Here."

"Nilla, this is not real—we're just two strangers sitting in front of a computer every night, having to face being alone when the screen clicks off. I want to know you. I want you to know me, for real."

Raine felt a dark cloud of frustration descend around her as she read his next words.

"We have to meet, or I'm out. I'm done."

She gaped, the ultimatum slamming into her like a hard, cold wind.

"I have to think about it, Rider. Please, I have to think. I'll meet you here tomorrow night and we can talk about it some more, okay?" I kiss you softly, press my lips to yours. Goodbye.

"Wait!... Don't go..."

She turned the computer off, ruthlessly cutting the connection.

Collapsing on the soft cushions, she groaned in frustration—this night was just not going well. She had always looked forward to these times with Rider. Meeting him had made her typically quiet evenings exciting.

Though physically it *was* difficult to be so consistently aroused by someone who could never be there to actually help you release those passions, for her it had been wonderful just to be able to *feel* them—to walk around basking in the glow of it, to dream of it at night, and to be blissfully unafraid of the pain or disappointment that inevitably followed when you dared those things in real life.

Though she didn't feel so great at the moment. It was distressing to realize that this wonderful interlude she had discovered and enjoyed was coming to an end. He wanted more, and she did not believe there could be more. She would not be meeting Rider the next evening, for talk or anything else. He would not stop pushing her, and she knew she would not hold out against him in the long run. And that would be an awful mistake.

She knew exactly what she had to do to get some distance on this situation, to grab control of it and put it behind her. First, she could never meet with him again, obviously. Next, she had to write about it. She had experienced Internet romance, right? She had faced the tough decision, and she had made it. Now it was time to share what she had learned with her readers. Only then could she move on and forget all this. Hauling herself upright, she grabbed her laptop again. She opened a blank word-processing page and went to work.

2

"WELL, THIS ISN'T a bad start, but we need more."

Raine resisted the urge to roll her eyes, and stared at Duane, her managing editor, straight in the eye. She liked him, though grudgingly at times such as now.

"I need to add in the research, get some outside interviews. That should round it off. This is just the first draft, obviously."

Duane nodded and set the draft of the article she had been up nearly all night writing on the desk between them. She could've had his job if she had wanted it, but she liked being a writer. Duane was a good manager, and oddly, he seemed to enjoy it.

He was twenty-eight, almost four years younger than her, fresh out of graduate school, and on the job for a year. He was cute in a frat-boy kind of way, with shaggy dark brown hair and bright-blue eyes. Half the women in the building were gaga for him. Raine just couldn't work up that kind of enthusiasm, though she had come to respect him as an editor.

He had one of those low-key, soft-spoken, intensely focused personalities that could be deceptive at first. But when the chips were down, or when he wanted things to go his way, he would wield his will like a sword. So far, he'd kept the ship on course, and skillfully managed a diverse group of writers at the magazine. But at the moment, Raine wasn't in the mood to be managed.

"C'mon, Raine. You know as well as I do what you have to do here to make this article pop. The real meat of it is in the move from online to real life. You need to meet him. This is too good to pass up. See it through."

She just glared, and her voice was stiff and caustic when she spoke. "Is that an order? Just how far would you like me to take this, Duane?"

"I'm not saying you have to marry the guy, or do more than have a cup of coffee with him. But you have already invested all this time in establishing a connection with him, right? And how can you answer the questions that are facing readers if you haven't really put yourself in their place?" His eyes narrowed thoughtfully, and she resisted the urge to squirm under his gaze.

"This isn't a real romance, is it? You have chalked this up as research?"

She closed her eyes and thought of all she had left out of the draft—if only Duane knew the connections she had "established" with Rider. She'd left out most of the intimate material and had written up the experience as a light flirtation, a dalliance. She wasn't about to expose the reality—or herself—like that for the sake of a column. But deep down, she knew that Duane was right, and just for the moment, she hated him for it.

She nodded. "More or less. But he is a nice person, as far as I know, and you can't just play with people's feelings, Duane. He's not just a lab rat for the article."

Nodding again, Duane quirked an eyebrow.

"If the safety aspect of it is worrying you, we can help with that. I don't expect you to go out and meet some creep by yourself."

"He's *not* a creep." She felt a headache fuzz her thoughts. "At least, I don't think so."

"Okay, but that's what we need to know. And what you need to find out." He picked up the draft and handed it back to her. "You pitched this, you make it work. Meet the guy, then take another stab at it. This could be a killer story, Raine, but you have to see it through."

"I THINK HE LOOKS LIKE Superman." Gwen sighed dreamily, watching a man who stared intently at a computer on a desk directly across from them.

Raine snorted and put sugar in her coffee. "That's Jackson Harris. I think everyone calls him Jack, though. He is the ultimate in computer gurus, from what Duane says. Been here about six months."

Raine didn't add that the new guy seemed to have taken a dislike to her on sight, for reasons she couldn't fathom. He seemed friendly enough with everyone else, but gave her the cold shoulder. The few times they'd crossed paths he hadn't even returned her hallway acknowledgments. So she'd stopped offering them. She only knew his name because he had been introduced to everyone upon his hiring.

"He's a computer geek—that would make him a lot more like Clark Kent, right?" Raine didn't bother holding back on the sarcasm.

Gwen stuck out her tongue. "Kent *was* Superman—and those dark glasses he always wore were so sexy. Anyway— that guy would look great in a tight blue bodysuit. How the heck did I miss him? This place is hiring one buff guy after another, first Duane, now Jack. I love working here."

"Please. Spare me."

Gwen just shrugged and continued to watch Jack work. "So what's the news on Jerry?"

Raine rolled her eyes and leaned back against the kitchen counter in the employees' lounge at the end of the hall. The staff often worked late hours, especially on a deadline. Having a full, stocked kitchen available was one of the luxuries that made the company worth working for.

"It was ridiculous. Terrible. He was like a dog in heat—it was crazy, I don't think I did anything to lead him on. In fact, quite the opposite."

"Yeah, the buzz is he wasn't all too happy about it, either. Did you guys argue?"

Raine expelled a disgusted breath. Word traveled fast. Jerry must not have bought the stomachache defense. Oh well.

"No, no arguing. But I was barely able to eat because I had to keep stopping him from mauling me under the table at the restaurant. He couldn't even hold a conversation. Everything—and I do mean *everything*, had to come back to sex. And it wasn't just talk, he has hands like an octopus. So, when we got back to my place, I pretended I had to throw up to escape the good-night grope. Or worse, him wanting to come in."

"Hey, that's a new one! I don't know if he bought your excuse though."

"Yeah, well, whatever. I have a whole repertoire of techniques to get away from men at the end of dates. I'll scratch that one off my list."

"Maybe you should be thinking about things to do to get them into bed at the end of dates."

Raine snorted. "All I would have to do to get Jerry into bed is breathe. There's no point."

Gwen's jaw dropped in shock. "Wow, you really have forgotten, haven't you? Jerry aside, orgasms are the point, girlie!"

Raine sipped her coffee and muttered over the top of her cup, "Really? I've never known a man who thought so."

She turned and headed back to her office. Gwen followed, slipping into Raine's office before she could close the door.

"Gwen, really, I have work…"

"Whoa—hold on. Are you trying to say you have *never*, you know—that you haven't had…"

"An orgasm. Yes, I have. Plenty. Just not with a guy." She sighed. "They haven't got the faintest clue. I mean, I don't want to have to tell someone what to do. Women shouldn't have to come with an instruction booklet."

"You should use that line in a column. Clever." Gwen grinned.

"Yeah, right. Sometimes I wish I was a lesbian, maybe a woman would be better at it. That's my curse—I'm stuck with men."

Gwen sighed and dropped down in the cushy chair in the corner of the office, ignoring the impatient looks Raine was sending her way. When Gwen was intent on a visit, there just was no stopping her.

"Oh now, it'll happen one of these days. But geez, I can't believe you are what…thirty-two?" She ignored the glare Raine shot at her. "And you haven't had one tiny tingle with a guy? I guess I can see why you don't want to bother anymore, but you know you have to keep on trying. Sitting at home in front of your computer certainly isn't going to help things any."

"I never should have told you about that. Let's just drop it.

That whole thing is coming back to bite me in the butt now, big-time."

"Why? Are things going downhill? Is the prince turning into a frog?"

Raine sighed and knew Gwen would not go away, and she would not be able to get any work done until she dealt with it.

"No. I don't know. Rider's getting too pushy, so I ended it. I wanted it over with." She sat back, staring out the window at the dark gray clouds forming in the sky over the shops lining Pickering Wharf's crescent-shaped streets. "But, Duane, in his ultimate wisdom, doesn't want it over with. He says the article won't fly unless I 'see it through.'"

She screwed up her eyes and did a shabby Duane imitation on the last three words. "But I don't want to see it through. I want to see it over."

"Why? The computer guy sounds hot from everything you've said."

"Yeah, well, he wants to meet, and I don't want to—end of story."

Gwen pursed her lips and considered that for a few seconds. "Maybe you should meet him."

"Are you in cahoots with Duane? Why on earth would I want to do that?"

"Maybe he would be the one to, you know…"

"Gwen, it can't all be about that. And most likely, it wouldn't happen. Hot online and hot in real life are two entirely different things. Besides, my luck isn't exactly good lately."

"How can you know that until you meet him? You two seem to have such chemistry. I talk to lots of people online, you know I have all my pagan discussion groups, and we have a good time, but it's not like anything you have been describing."

Raine sighed. "Well, yeah, I didn't count on it, it just happened. If we meet, all of that chemistry could go up in smoke."

"So then, what do you have to lose?"

"Now you sound just like him."

"Well, you know, I don't think you should just dismiss it. You don't have to get serious, but you can, you know, just take him for a test drive, so to speak. All in the name of research." Gwen's naughty grin almost had Raine's own lips twitching.

"Not my style, Gwen, you know that. I'm tired of test drives. I think I am just going to take a break from men for a while."

"You have been on a break from men for about ten years, by the sound of it. You need a man—a real one—who can flip your lid, so…"

"…to speak, yeah, I got it, Gwen. Stop."

The warning tone made Gwen sigh and shake her head at Raine. Raine watched her pop up from the chair and felt a twinge of envy. Gwen was intelligent, quirky and an annoyingly eternal optimist.

As the main health and fitness writer for the magazine, Gwen had a body that wouldn't quit and a lively attitude that drew everyone to her. She and Raine should not have been compatible at all, but they'd become very close over the past few years. Gwen changed her hair color weekly; right now it was platinum-blond with some red and green streaks for the holidays. Thanksgiving had just passed and Christmas was only a month away. Gwen was all sparkly. Raine supposed Gwen made everyone who came into contact with her feel a little sparkly, too.

Today she was slinking around in snug black leggings and a fitted black sweater. She wore at least a dozen silver pentacle earrings and little jingle bells on the toes of her short, stylish boots. It didn't surprise Raine one bit that Gwen mixed her Wiccan jewelry with her Christmas decorations—Gwen celebrated everything—and at least the jingle let you know when she was coming.

Men tripped over each other when Gwen walked by, not that she noticed. Love 'em and if it's good, love 'em some more and see what happens was Gwen's philosophy. She just tripped through life and "trusted the universe"—as she was always advising Raine to do. And she was a good friend. Suddenly Raine felt like queen bitch. Expelling a heavy breath, she tried to make nice.

"Gwen, I'm sorry, I'm just frustrated with Duane and this whole article thing and I want to get it over with and—"

"No problem, sweetie. I have to get back to work, too. Oh crikey—he's coming this way!"

"Who?"

"Clark!"

Raine puzzled for a moment and then saw Jack Harris appear in the doorway. He would make a lousy Clark Kent was her first thought. His hair was not black, but more of a chestnutty auburn, and his eyes were not blue, but brown. He had a good build: tall, lanky, muscular and thin. Like a cowboy.

She frowned; he wasn't dressed for the office. True, the magazine had a fairly relaxed dress code, but Raine valued a professional appearance. Jack did not look very professional in tight jeans and a black cotton, button-up shirt. His hair was a little too long, curling around the collar a bit; he needed a haircut, she thought. No, he did not resemble Superman one single bit. He said something but she missed it, and blinked at him, returning to the moment.

"Hmm?"

"I need to look at your computer. It will only take a few minutes."

"Why?"

"Routine. We've set up a new security system and need to make sure everything is working."

"Well, okay." She rolled her eyes at Gwen, who was unabashedly checking out his butt as he walked into the office. As Raine passed by him to get to the other side of the desk, she couldn't help but notice that he smelled great, like sand and sea.

She looked up, and locked glances with him, then tilted her head a bit, narrowing her eyes and studying him intently. She froze on the spot. Something itched at the back of her mind but she couldn't reach it. Something familiar. His eyes cooled and took on an unfriendly edge that made him look decidedly un–Clark Kent like. He cleared his throat.

"Excuse me."

She raised a dismissive eyebrow and slid past, following Gwen out the door.

"God, isn't he *hot?*" Gwen gave a dramatic little demonstration of being weak in the knees as she walked down the hallway.

Raine blinked. "Jack? I guess. Though there *was* something about him… I think I have seen him somewhere, but I'm not sure."

"Well, it's a small town. You may have seen him around before and just not thought about it."

"Yeah, maybe. There was something about his eyes. I just can't figure out why he seemed vaguely familiar."

"Oh well, you'll remember. Anyway, okay, back to Rider—I think you should meet him, just for kicks."

Raine rubbed her temples. "Gwen, I think I am getting too old to do things just for kicks."

"You're thirty-two, not eighty. Not that being eighty should stop you, you know, if you were. Just imagine, if he is even *half* of how you described him online in the flesh—so to speak."

Raine could imagine. Imagination wasn't the problem; reality was the problem. It never lived up. But still, what if it did? How could she ever know if it was worth the risk? She heaved a sigh and looked back down the hall toward Duane's office. Even if she didn't want to meet Rider, she felt outvoted by people who wanted her to do it. But what did she *want*?

"I need to get back to work. I guess I have some major revisions to do on this article."

"Okay, well, but think more about meeting him, anyway—it could be the chance of a lifetime."

JACK SWORE PROFUSELY at the computer as he tapped keys and compared what he was seeing on Raine Covington's computer to what he was checking on his laptop. Something just wouldn't take and he couldn't figure out why. He changed the setting on the firewall—the device that kept the network safe—for this particular computer, and it would click off again the minute it rebooted. That just shouldn't be happening.

He was going to have to take a deeper look to find out what the bug was. It would take some time and digging. Usually this was the part of his job as Network Security Administrator that he liked best—prying open the mysteries of the wires, swimming down into the information flows, right into the nervous system of the machine, and figuring it out. He could get lost in there for hours, forget to eat, and not care.

But now he felt the pressure of time. The last thing he wanted was to spend more time in Raine Covington's office, so he would have to come in during the evening or on the weekend. It galled him how she had looked at him as if he were a bug on a microscope slide, and then dismissed him like one, too. It even bothered him that it galled him—everything about her was annoying.

He'd remembered her right away when he had seen her name on the employee list. She, apparently, did not recognize him. That was really not a surprise, but it was what rankled most, in spite of himself. Some things you carried with you, whether you liked it or not.

She'd barely noticed he was alive when they were in high school together, though he shouldn't take that too personally—that was how she was with everyone. He'd thought she was the most beautiful girl in school, but her personality was far from attractive.

Living in a mansion in an exclusive neighborhood in the Connecticut countryside outside Essex, she rarely socialized with anyone at the school, and in fact, looked miserable most of the time. She obviously detested coming to school with the common folk. It hadn't been a slum, for God's sake—Eaton Marsh was a well-respected private school.

He had first noticed her in their sophomore year. He had watched her, considered talking to her, practiced what he would say—had a mad crush on her. She was beautiful then; she was drop-dead gorgeous now. But she had the same imperious attitude—that had not changed.

His parents weren't anywhere near as wealthy as hers.

They worked hard maintaining a small bed-and-breakfast in Essex, and it was a life they enjoyed. He had been raised in a home that was open to visitors nine months out of every year, and he'd loved it. His parents were warm, friendly people who'd encouraged him to interact with the visitors at the inn, who were often treated more like family than guests. Through those experiences, he had developed confidence and social skills that many young people lacked. None of it was enough to deal with the likes of Raine Covington, though.

But it was a small world, and now here they were again, and still, when she looked at him, she just saw through him as if he wasn't even there. At least he didn't have a crush on her anymore. Though he did feel a little rush of heat when she brushed past him—she was incredibly soft, and smelled like heaven. Flowers and citrus. He closed his eyes and shook his head. She may be a snob, but she was a gorgeous one.

"Is there a problem?"

He snapped his head up, eyes wide-open at her voice. She stood directly in front of the desk, watching him closely.

"A small one. I'll look into it later."

"From the way you were sitting there shaking your head, it looked like a lost cause."

He stared at her then, and he felt something pull deep down inside his stomach. Emotions crowded in, confusing him. How could he still want her after all these years? Because he wasn't blind, that's why. God, she was hot.

Idiot. He didn't want her—he didn't even know her. It was Nilla, his phantom online lover who had his head, and his hormones, all worked up. Raine just happened to be there, a warm body for him to focus all his frustration on. Nothing more.

"Yeah, I guess you could say that."

"So it *is* serious? I have a lot of work on that computer—I can't afford for it to die on me. It's been acting up lately, so if you could see that whatever is wrong is fixed, that would help."

"It won't die on you," he said. "Just a minor security problem that has nothing to do with everyday functioning. We'll figure it out another time, but I will have to get back into your computer."

Her lips pursed, and he realized how much those delicate, arching eyebrows contributed to her expressions. At the moment telling him she was inconvenienced and displeased.

"I have an article due soon, I can't afford to have these problems keep coming up, and I will be working long hours in here—"

He cut her off, his voice cold. "Don't worry, I won't interrupt your very important work, Ms. Covington."

She couldn't miss the sarcasm, and she felt heat stain her cheeks. He was angry, and she had no idea why he should be. Maybe he was just having a bad day, or was generally rude. Maybe that's why they kept him in the basement, she thought with a little sneer. She wasn't sure she cared, but right now she wanted him out of her office.

"Fine. Thank you. That's all then." She dismissed him curtly with those few words and went to move around her desk, when she ran into him again, directly on the spot she had bumped into him the first time. She made a mental note to move her desk over so she could widen that space.

Now he narrowed his eyes, pinning her with a glare. "If you want to be formal, *Mr.* Harris is acceptable, and if you want to be friendly—although I can't imagine it—then it's Jack. Jack Harris. But don't talk to me like I'm one of the servants of the manor, Ms. Covington."

He was taken aback to see those cool green eyes flare, and for a moment he was curious to see what would follow. Had he finally gotten a rise out of the cool Raine Covington? Then he saw the puzzlement, and the searching—it was amazing how you could see the mind functioning behind someone's eyes. She whispered his name, more to herself than him.

"Jack Harris." She shook herself, and blinked. "I'm sorry." She diverted her eyes, looking down. "I just thought maybe we had met before."

"No, I can safely say we've never met."

He had just watched her from afar; they never *had* actually spoken. Right now, this minute, he found himself closer to her than he ever had been, practically pressed up against her slim, soft form twice within an hour. He shifted a little, trying to slide by, and it just happened that his shoulder brushed one of the soft mounds under her sweater. He saw her eyes widen, and felt a little jab of heat himself. Looking down, he saw a nipple bud tightly beneath the soft material, and felt a masculine surge of satisfaction. Oh, yeah, she definitely noticed he was there.

"Um…" She was flustered, he noted, and trying to move past. Getting a grip, he ignored his moment of insanity and walked around to the front of the desk.

What had gotten into him? Sheesh, she would have him up on charges of sexual harassment, and she wouldn't be far off the mark. He also felt…guilty? Shaking his head again, he knew he had made the right decision about meeting Nilla or breaking it off. Now he was actually feeling guilty about having a response to another woman behind the back of his virtual lover? This was ridiculous. He had to get his life back. He had to have sex. With a real woman. Clearing his throat, he modulated his voice to be cool and professional.

"What kinds of other problems have you been having?"

"I came in on Monday, and for some reason, all my article files had been erased. I had backups of most of them, but it put me behind because—"

"Where did you have them stored?"

Bristling at his interruption, her eyes went glacial.

"I always keep my active folder on the desktop, so I can have quick access to it."

"Maybe you deleted your files by mistake. Folders and files don't usually delete themselves."

"No, they don't. But neither did I. Something happened, and they were gone."

He sighed. It was never anyone's fault when something happened to their computer. "Anything else?"

"Yes, last week I could barely get anything done. My computer kept freezing up, and was very slow. I had to keep shutting it down and restarting. Then it just snapped out of it and was fine."

"Sounds like minor stuff. Probably won't happen again. I'll send a tech up to look at it later."

With that, he gathered up his laptop and walked out of the office, leaving her feeling abruptly dismissed. Raine sat down in her chair and let out a breath it seemed she had been holding the entire time he had been in the office. What a strange conversation. Why did he dislike her so much? And why had her body leaped in response to such a casual, accidental touch? It was horribly embarrassing, especially with him.

She tried to forget it. Maybe he hadn't even noticed. He was in no small hurry to get out of her office, so she wouldn't have to worry about it again. Shaking off the uncomfortable feeling, she checked her in box, and saw the e-mail pop up on her screen. From Rider. No subject line. Opening it, she saw only one word.

Please.

The decision to meet Rider was becoming a vague possibility in her mind. She kept trying to push down the sense of anticipation, of hope that this time—this man—could be different, but it kept emerging, especially after talking to Gwen. How could she use this as research when she was so obviously losing her objectivity? What if he *was* just the way he was online? Could she do this? Should she? Her stomach fluttered thinking of it.

What if meeting him turned out to be a total bomb? What if he was crazy, or even worse, married? But in her gut she knew neither one would be true. He would be great. And she would be…well, she wasn't exactly chopped liver, but she also wasn't the adventure girl that she had come across as online. In fact, far from it.

But she had always thought, with the right man, someone whom she could open up with, someone who would care, maybe things could be different. Maybe *she* could be different. At the worst, the spark would fizzle when they actually met, and that would not be a tragedy.

All in all, she led a pretty normal, sane and sometimes boring life. Could she live up to the sexual fantasies they had shared online? Her sex life had ranged from mildly interesting to nonexistent.

But maybe it wouldn't even come to that. All she had to do was meet him. That was all.

Her readers had been sending her tons of similar questions

and stories about their Internet romances and how to handle them. And now here she was, like so many of her readers, wondering what to do. Take the chance? What was life without a little risk, right? How could she ever really know unless she took the leap? She would just control the risk, make sure things didn't go any direction she didn't want them to go. Maybe. Maybe she could risk it. One more time.

JACK SHOOK OFF his aggravation, catching a coffee at the cafeteria and heading back downstairs to the Batcave, as they affectionately referred to the subterranean floor of the office building.

He tried to ignore the anxiety of wondering what Nilla was doing at this very second, what she was wearing, if she was thinking of him, if she was considering making *them* a reality.

The incident with Raine only had his body more fired up, and he hoped something would happen soon, or he was either going to have to dig into his address book, which he was loath to do. They were women he had dated, and whom he liked. He wouldn't feel right using one of them to work off the hots he had gotten from someone else. It was more likely he was facing several weeks of cold showers until he got over this.

Never again would he get involved in an online love affair. It was just too hard on the body. He slid a furtive glance at his e-mail. He couldn't believe it, but his heart actually flipped when he saw an e-mail from her. Sent only moments ago.

He stared at it for a few moments, then opened it. One word.

Okay.

Hot damn! He thought his face would split from grinning, and all of his aggravation was lost in a consuming sense of anticipation. He was caught unawares by the person standing behind him.

"Uh, sir? Sir?"

Jack spun around in his chair, realizing he probably looked as if he had won the lottery, and not really caring. One of his guys, Neal Scott, was standing in the doorway behind him. Taking a breath, he got his excitement under control and put his professional face on, though he couldn't quell the buzz of anticipation that was running through his blood.

"What's up, Neal? Sorry, I just, um, just got some good news."

"Oh, that's good, sir."

"Please don't call me sir, Neal. Jack is fine."

"Okay, um, sir, Jack. You asked me to stop by to look at the security bug you were dealing with."

Jack watched the young man in the office. Neal was a great worker, and a nice kid, if a little shy. Jack knew he was in his twenties, but there was just something about him that made him seem much younger. Neal kept to himself a lot, but Jack had been including him more, trying to draw him out a little, and it was working. Neal was loosening up a lot, and had even gone out with a bunch of them a few times.

Jack liked the kid and thought he could really be an asset to the company. Hell, Neal seemed to do nothing but work— he had been in his office most of the weekend, which Jack had seen when reviewing the security logs.

He was smarter than hell, too, but he didn't have much confidence, and was generally overlooked by management. So, Jack had been giving him some more challenging jobs, bringing him along slowly. He pulled a chair up and gestured for Neal to sit down.

"Yeah, take a look at this. It's been giving me a headache all day."

Neal squinted behind the thick, black-framed glasses he always wore and read the screen full of numbers and symbols quickly and with interest.

"Yeah. There. I see it. Might be a worm."

"I've tried to close it down about ten times, but it keeps popping open. You are a much slicker programmer than I am, can you work on it?"

"Yeah, sure."

Neal got up to leave and Jack shook his head.

"Hey, Neal. I see you were here all weekend?"

"Um, yeah." Neal creased his forehead and then pushed his glasses up.

"I appreciate initiative, and you're doing a great job—but don't get burnt out—there's more to life than work."

Neal nodded, and headed to the door.

Jack sat back and flipped the e-mail from Nilla back on screen, smiling broadly again. He knew he wouldn't be spending *his* weekend at work. With any luck, he would be spending it making a fantasy come true.

3

RAINE DASHED THROUGH her apartment door and almost dropped the pizza she'd grabbed on the way home. She was giddy with nerves. She didn't want to think about why the change in her decision to talk to Rider tonight had such an effect on her mood. After all, she was just going to talk to him. If anything didn't hit her right, she would call it quits and that would be that. She would remain in control of the situation.

Forgetting the pizza on the entry table, she made a beeline to her computer and logged on. Connection time was slow, and she jittered on the sofa, wiggling her fingers in the air over the keys, going crazy waiting for the screen to tell her she was ready to go. "C'mon, c'mon!… There, good!"

A few quick keystrokes and she was in. She looked at the list of players logged in, and his name was not there. Damn!

She fell back against the cushions, closed her eyes, and let out a frustrated breath. It was only seven; it was early yet. She thought about the pizza, but wasn't hungry now. She put a hand over her eyes. Was she crazy? Maybe it was better this way; maybe she had made the wrong decision. This could be her reprieve. Then she peeked through two fingers and sneaked a look at the screen, smiling widely.

"Wake up, hot stuff. You beat me here. Your e-mail made my day." I kiss you warmly.

Raine watched the cursor blink, and felt as she typed that every line was rewriting her life in ways she couldn't even imagine. She hoped it was for the better.

I kiss you back. "You're pretty easy to please."
"Generally. But you seem particularly good at it."

Raine held her breath, and typed, before she could change her mind.

"We need to talk more about what we want out of this whole thing."
"Well, how can we know until we meet? Maybe nothing, maybe we end up married with five kids, who knows?"

Raine felt her jaw tense, and responded bluntly.

"You see, that's it, Rider. I don't want a house and five kids. I don't want anyone pushing me. That is why I'm not sure this is a good idea."
"Okay, well, I wasn't proposing marriage there, just saying that we can't possibly know what we want, or what this will be."

Raine pressed on, screwing up the courage to say what she really meant.

"Yes, we can—we can say what we want it to be, we can say what we will do, and what we won't—what things are possible, and what things are not. So there are no un-reasonable expectations, and no one gets hurt."

"Okay, not getting hurt is good. So you want rules?"

"I suppose...sort of. Yes."

"What rules do you want?"

Raine considered, and typed slowly.

"All right. First of all, maybe both or either of us may not be interested right away. At that point, maybe we have a nice dinner and part ways."

"Okay, I'd say that's a given."

"And if we do like each other, if we are just as attracted as we are here, we can just let it be what it is—it doesn't have to get weighed down with all the emotional baggage, promises of forever."

"Nilla, are you saying you only want to have a no-strings relationship?"

"Are you saying that you wouldn't be interested in that?"

Jack sat back and thought. What was she offering him? No-strings sex if they hit it off? Or was she saying it could never lead to anything else? Something itched at the back of his mind, and he turned cautious.

"Nilla, are you married? Or involved in some way that would keep you from having a committed relationship with me?"

"Oh no...no! Geez, Rider, do you think women can't pur-sue simple, uncomplicated lives? I am just saying, you and I can avoid messy emotional entanglements. Because we have met here, and we have already shared so much…I just think we should be clear about our expectations."

Jack considered that. He wasn't in love with her, he knew that. But he was intrigued by her, and he thought there was more than sex going on between them. Less than love, more than sex. Something in between. That seemed to be what she wanted. He wasn't going to look a gift horse in the mouth. He wasn't looking for commitment, either, though he was open to the possibilities.

"I think I understand. We can see if we are even attracted to each other, and go from there, gorgeous."

"You don't know if I am gorgeous or not. I could look like a frog."

That had crossed his mind. He didn't think so, but no matter what reptile, bird or fish she might resemble, if she could do half the things to him in real life that she could online, it would be worth finding out.

"Mmm. I like frogs. Especially their legs. Very tasty."

"Well, then, I suppose we have to talk about this, set something up?"

"I guess for starters, what is your real name, Nilla?"

"Let's not share too much here—we can find out names and those kinds of details when we meet. Tell me what you'll wear, so I can recognize you. We can meet at a restaurant or something. Plus, I may bring a friend, if you don't mind."

Jack felt a stab of disappointment, but realized she was going by the book, and he was glad for it. It was smarter not to share names just yet or share any physical details about herself. Anyone could easily locate you that way, or simply go about prying into your life.

"Sounds good. I'm thirty-four, about six foot, one-ninety, and I'll wear jeans, a brown leather jacket and a Red Sox cap. That's pretty much what I wear everywhere. Friends are fine. Maybe I'll bring one, too. Your turn."

Raine stared at the screen and felt her mouth go dry, her imagination filling in the rest of the details. So far, this was sounding very, *very* good. And he hadn't balked at meeting in a public place, or with friends—that was a good sign. Then she laughed.

"Okay, well. I just turned thirty-two last month. I don't know what I'll be wearing, but I'll put a rose in my hair, so you'll know me that way."

"When? Make it soon."

Raine smiled at the sexual intensity he could communicate in so few words, and began to feel a deep sense of anticipation soak into her, right to the bone.

"Yes, soon. But I don't even know where you live. Red Sox cap? Are you in the northeast?"

"Yep, live north of Boston. On the coast, just below Gloucester."

Raine practically fell over in shock. They were neighbors! She'd figured he was in the same time zone because they were always online at the same times, but she hadn't thought he would be that close. That could end up being either a very good—or a very bad—thing. For now she would go with it being good.

"Hey, looks like we're neighbors. I live in Salem, a bit of a drive, but not too far."

"Less than an hour's drive. I commute to work every day, so that is no problem at all. I can leave now, be there by ten."

Raine felt her heart pound and almost told him to come.

"Tempting as that is, I think we should wait. But this makes it more convenient, at least. I'm glad. I thought you might be far away."

"It wouldn't matter. I would come anyway."

Raine shivered and took the leap.

"How about this Saturday night, seven, at the bar in La Luna, on Pickering Wharf. It's a nice place but not too formal. Great food, if nothing else works out."

"Okay. Let's make it six—we'll have a drink before dinner."

Raine watched the words travel across the screen and could hardly believe it. They were going to meet, to really meet. *In person. For real.*

I stare into your luscious brown eyes. "Okay. So, in three days we'll know."

I pull you close to me. "It seems like forever. Are you sure you don't want me to drive up tonight?"

I run my fingers through your hair. "No, I am sorely tempted, but this is probably a better idea. And remember, it is just dinner—we can opt out at any time."

Jack knew it was the right thing, though he was so hot for her he could barely imagine not touching her, or making some of what they had shared a reality. But she was providing an out for him, too. Just in case. And when he got there, if things were good, who knew what could happen? He had a feeling about this; he was willing to just go with it.

"Agreed. Just dinner—unless you beg me to go back to your place and engage in illicit activities."

"You never know. Maybe it will be *you* doing the begging."

Jack smiled. Desire raced through his blood and flowed through his fingers out into the words.

"I'd beg for you, Nilla, you can count on it. I'd like to drop to my knees in front of you, kiss your feet, taste the skin on the back of your knee, and then work my way up, slowly, taste you, run my tongue over you until you come with my mouth on you, until we are *both* begging. And that's only the beginning."

"Um, I am not sure this is a good idea...."

Raine swallowed, and tried to focus as her breath became shallow. The hunger she had been feeling for weeks was suddenly a little frightening. This wasn't a game anymore; it was real. He was real. They were going to sit across a table from one another and have dinner and talk, and all that while they would both be remembering the secrets that had passed between them. She closed her eyes and tried to settle herself.

"Why not?"

"I don't think we should really discuss this, considering..."

"Nilla, tell me how you feel, how your body feels right now...."

Raine tried to think, and quell the heat pounding through her bloodstream. She wanted to back off, and knew she should, but sheer desire weakened her. She knew what she wanted, and reached down for the courage to ask him for it.

"Rider, your number. Give me your number."

"What?"

"Your phone number, Rider, tell me. I'll call you. I need to...hear you."

Jack was shocked speechless as he contemplated her request. No, not a request, a demand. The idea of actually talking to her stole his breath, and he didn't bother thinking about it, but just responded.

"Oh, yeah, sweetheart, yes. Here."

Jack typed in his cell phone number.

"I'll call you in a little while. I just want to shower and change out of my work clothes."

Work clothes? He smiled knowingly, pure masculine satisfaction pooling in his heart. She had come directly to find him. He acknowledged her message, and signed off.

His house was suddenly incredibly still and quiet, and he could hear his own heart pounding. The wind howled outside the windows, and minutes slowed down as if he was drugged, the feeling of waiting for the phone to ring weighing down on him. God, she had taken him by surprise.

She was changing. She was taking a shower. He closed his eyes and imagined the hot water running over her naked, soft skin. Then she would put on…what? His imagination nearly drove him mad. By the time the phone rang, he had imagined her in everything from black dominatrix leather to pink lace—and then in nothing at all. His mind went still. He pressed the talk button, and was relieved to discover his voice actually worked.

"Nilla."

Raine thought for sure she would pass out just hearing him say her name—well, her screen name, but the same difference. Low and smooth, it slid over her like hot lava, and she tried to sound calm in response.

"Hey, Rider."

Her voice was like whiskey, hot and golden. He closed his eyes and let it ease over him for a moment before speaking again.

"It's much like I imagined it would be."

"What's that?"

"Your voice." He settled more comfortably into the chair, and smiled into the phone. "When we talked online, sometimes I imagined I could hear you, but the real thing is a million times better."

Raine smiled. "It is. I love hearing you too." She took a deep breath, trying to calm her nerves. "This is pretty intense."

"Something tells me it's about to get even more intense, Nilla."

Raine felt weird being called by her pseudonym, and almost caved to the temptation to tell him her real name, but held back. That could wait. For now, this was good. She laughed, and almost didn't recognize the husky, sexy sound of her own voice.

"Could be."

"Um, Nilla, not to be too cliché, but exactly what did you change into?"

She laughed. "Rider, are you *actually* asking me what I am wearing?"

He laughed, too, a warm, husky, *sexy* laugh.

"You bet I am. You can't leave a guy hanging like that and not expect him to go half-mad with wondering. Tell me, Nilla."

Raine looked down, and nervously smoothed her hand up and down over her thigh.

"It's no big deal…usually when I get home from work I shower and change into my comfortable clothes."

"Tell me about them."

Raine smiled, and shook her head. This was crazy. She had thought calling him might add the edge of reality and stem the passion that was quickly getting out of control online.

She couldn't have been more wrong. Voice to voice, they were spontaneously combusting. She took a breath, and spoke, feeling a little silly, but pressed on anyway, remembering that Nilla would have no problem responding to this request.

"Flannel pajama shorts and a top. Cushy socks. Not exactly Victoria's Secret, but soft, warm, and comfortable."

Jack chuckled, intrigued by the thought of her cuddled in flannel, the cotton sliding against warm, soft skin, clean and smelling of soap and powder. The slight edge of shyness that came through her voice made him want to break through, to make her lose control and tell him what he wanted to hear.

"I wish I could smell you. I want to slide my hands along your skin, touching you. I want to know what secrets you are keeping under that flannel."

Raine felt rather than saw the flush work its way over her body, his voice setting off pins and needles of passion on her skin. She tried to speak normally, but her breath caught, betraying her response.

"Rider, I think we should just talk, we probably shouldn't..."

She could almost see his naughty grin as he spoke. "That's what makes it so much fun, Nilla. Forget the shoulds and shouldn'ts for a minute. Just relax. It's just me—Rider. Do something for me?"

"What?"

"Touch yourself—and tell me what you feel."

Okay, stop the bus!

She was not prepared for this! Nothing in thirty-two years prepared her for this onslaught of what she *wanted* to do, which was completely in conflict with what she didn't know if she even *could* do.

He was asking her to share something wildly new, and for her, something incredibly daring. It had been easy online. This was different. Way different. She closed her eyes, and couldn't think of a single way to respond. He spoke again.

"It's all right—we'll go at whatever pace you want. It's just that you are driving me crazy. The sound of your voice."

"Me? What did I do?"

"Nilla, don't you know? You turn me inside out." The words ground out of him and shocked her—frustration, desire, and control that came across clearly in his voice made Raine feel a bit faint. "Just hearing your voice has me close to coming, all I would have to do is touch myself. God, Nilla, tell me you want me to."

Raine squeezed her eyes shut and almost dropped the phone, fumbling to catch it, and wished she had bought the speakerphone she had seen on sale a few weeks earlier. She was in a sexual twilight zone, nothing was real, and everything seemed to be magnified, every touch, every sound, every thought.

She pictured him as he existed in her imagination, sitting on the other end of the phone, needing her, wanting her. Fear and feminine power warred in her mind, and in her heart. She took a deep breath, and she let herself slide out of reality.

"Yes. Yes, Rider, I want you to touch yourself, to make yourself come. I want to help you, to be part of it."

Jack slid one hand under the thick cotton of his robe, and let his head fall back on the chair as he slid his fingers over his swollen penis, rubbing his thumb over the dew that had accumulated at the head. He squeezed, sucking in a sharp breath, slowing himself down before it was all over too fast.

"Tell me, Nilla, talk to me…I'm aching for you…."

Raine turned off her light and quickly slid out of her clothes. She didn't—wouldn't—think about this. She just wanted to experience this moment of absolute letting go. She slipped back on her bed, not needing the covers. Her body was white hot and ready to go. She felt awkward as she spoke, but just said what she felt.

"I'm naked, Rider, I took my clothes off, and I'm on top of my covers, thinking of you and what you are doing. I wish I was touching you. I wish I could wrap my hands around you. Slide my mouth over you. I want to taste you."

She heard no words in response, just a masculine groan of appreciation. Still a little unsure, but encouraged, she continued.

"I'm touching my knee, running my fingers over the hollows in the back. The skin there is smooth, and so amazingly sensitive…up the inside of my thigh…I'm so hot, Rider, I'm wet already…just thinking about you, what you are doing…."

"Jesus, Nilla, I want you, baby, please, I need this, don't stop…."

"Tell me what you want, Rider, tell me where you want me to touch, where you would touch me."

"Lick your fingers, make them wet, then run them over your stomach. Think of me kissing you there."

She did as he said, and arched up toward the little paths of fire that danced along her skin, imagining his touch.

The small, kittenish sigh that traveled across the line made him smile, and he refocused, running his hand over himself slowly, imagining her hands, and what they were doing, what he could make them do.

"Nilla, cup your breasts, your beautiful breasts. Are they aroused?"

"Oh yes, Rider…oh, that feels so good. I want to come…come with me…."

"Hey, not so fast," he purred into the phone, gaining control from her loss of it. "We have time…roll over on your stomach, Nilla."

Almost drowning in swells of excitement, she mindlessly

rolled over, and set the phone on the bed. She rested her head on the receiver, freeing her hands.

"There, Nilla?"

"Mmm, hmm."

"Good…the blankets are so soft, so warm from the heat of your body. Imagine me, Nilla, behind you—I want to rub myself on you, slide my cock along where you're melting for me. Do that, Nilla, touch yourself there, and think of me pushing inside, sliding into your heat. I'm so hard, so damned hard for you. I wish I could be inside you, Nilla."

He was quickly losing the ability to talk at all, spurred on by her increasingly passionate sighs and moans. He heard her chanting his name into the phone, and pumped himself harder, faster, feeling the blood pool in his lower stomach, his body going taut as he neared the edge.

"Nilla, now…stay with me…I'm almost there, Nilla!"

She had never been so gloriously lost in her life, consumed by the voice on the phone, the hands on her body that barely seemed to be her own. She could only think of him, his voice, his hands, somehow at once bringing himself, and her, to pleasure, and she slid her fingers inside herself, finding the sensitive spot she knew would send her over, her cries filling the room and traveling over the line to touch him on the other side.

"Rider, yes…oooooh! Oh, God…"

Jack nearly dropped the phone as he listened to her give in to the throes, his taut body bowing as he fell sharply into his own release.

Raine smiled, listening to his guttural, animal sounds, wishing she could see his face right at the most intimate moment. She basked in hearing him lost in his own orgasm as the pulsing warmth of hers receded. Lying in the darkness, spent, her heart pounding against the softness of the cover, she murmured gentle encouragements, just sounds. His breath was still labored, then slowed; he was saying her name into the phone over and over again. Her body cooled, and she pulled the covers up over her, turning onto her back. She couldn't stop smiling.

"Rider?"

"Mmm. Nilla. Not quite back yet, sweetheart."

She smiled, and kicked her feet on the bed a little, feeling amazing and powerful and feminine. Her body felt wired and relaxed simultaneously, and she couldn't believe she had just had phone sex—really, really amazing phone sex. She laughed delightedly, making him smile.

"What's so funny?"

"Nothing… I just feel so incredible. That was so much fun—I have never done that before."

"Me neither. You inspire me."

"Maybe we shouldn't meet, maybe we should just do this."

"No way, Nilla—no way are you getting out of this. Not now."

Jack lay back, eyes closed. His body was a mass of conflict, at once sated and yet begging for more—for her, for real. Three more days.

"Yeah. And if this thing works out, Nilla, as they say, you ain't seen nothin' yet."

4

RAINE WATCHED Gwen crease her forehead as she studied the tarot cards she'd laid out in front of her on the table. Gwen had arrived at the door to drag her out for lunch. Gwen's hair was freshly colored with purple highlights and glitter eye shadow to match. Raine was just happy the Goth days were over; she preferred Gwen colorful and upbeat.

They sat in high-backed booth seats at a favorite diner overlooking Salem's pedestrian mall, soup bowls and coffee cups pushed to the side while Gwen turned out cards. Raine looked out the partially fogged window, watching people scurrying in and out of shops, rushing to get their Christmas shopping done.

Everything was decorated and cheerful. The sun shone brightly off the snow, almost blinding her with the glare. She was meeting Rider tonight, and the brightness of the day seemed like a good omen.

Gwen insisted on doing tarot readings for her once a month. Raine never so much as read the astrology forecasts in the newspaper, but today she was grateful for the distraction. It was a day for new adventures, and Gwen had shown up with her cards, so now the two sat eating lunch and peering into Raine's immediate future. Raine munched her tuna sandwich absently and looked on.

"So, what's the verdict?"

"First, the Chariot—that figures—he is traveling to see you, that's kind of obvious. But the card is about being balanced, in control. It suggests a sense of purpose and direction. It's a strong card. Maybe a very confident man who knows what he wants, or could be you trying to control the situation, which isn't necessarily a bad thing, just something to think about. And—" she pointed to the next card "—then you have the Ace of Wands—kind of a sexy card, eh?"

Raine peered at the card that showed a club, or tree branch—a very *erotic*-looking tree branch—standing straight up against a sky, surrounded by ivy and flowers, and nodded. Really, it did look like an erection. Or maybe she just had penises on the brain. She shook her head.

"That one's usually about new beginnings, creativity and sexuality. Good sign for getting laid." Gwen grinned and pointed to the next card, which depicted a castle-type building with flames flying out of it, and people being tossed out of the windows into the crashing seas below.

"Hmm, this one might be a problem."

"Looks ominous." Raine wiggled her eyebrows dramatically.

"Can be, but it's more about life shaking us up, throwing us on our asses when we need it. There could be something really unexpected that will happen tonight. Could be good, or not so good. You had better just keep your radar sharp."

"For what? A sexy guy with a big stick and a nice car who is going to surprise me somehow?" Raine smiled naughtily, and Gwen gave a hearty laugh.

"Good one. Let's hope so. Now it gets interesting. This chick here—" she pointed to a picture of a woman standing blindfolded in the middle of a circle of swords "—the Eight of Swords, she is imprisoned by something—see how the swords do not circle her tightly? There are ways she could free herself if she wanted to. The blindfold suggests she may not be seeing things clearly."

"Or maybe it means he is going to blindfold me."

"I never looked at it that way. Hmm…and tie you up…"

"I was kidding, Gwen."

"Hey, I'm not judging—everyone is into their own thing." She ducked as Raine took a playful swat at her, and went on.

"But seriously, the cards can mean different things to different people—it's obvious what's on *your* mind." She grinned cheekily. "Okay, then you have these last three. The Devil is what challenges you—not the devil like hellfire and brimstone, but this card can be a lot of things—obsession, darkness, or being hounded or harassed in some way. The Two of Cups follows, a card signifying what you should strive for, a meeting of the minds, coming together, emotional healing. Finally, the Four of Wands is your destination card—where you could end up—a very nice, a happy, successful card, celebrations and accomplishments. Maybe marriage. Kids, you know, the whole ten yards."

"Bite me, Gwen."

"Sorry, I couldn't help myself." She grinned, summing up. "So, the Tower and the Devil are still giving it all a pretty interesting slant, kind of intense—will be interesting to see what *that* is about, though sometimes it is nothing. I draw the Tower every month when I am PMSing." She pursed her lips and looked up at Raine.

"As for the rest, looks like maybe you have some bumps in the road, a few explosions along the way—hey! I wonder if the Tower could be about orgasms? You know, lightning striking? Like getting thrown from the heights and into the waves of passion? I never thought about that—I like it! That would kinda mesh with what you see in the eight."

"Well, it would be nice if you're right about the orgasms." Raine laughed and slid off the seat, thinking about her experience with Rider two nights before. She hadn't told Gwen about that. "But I need to think about what to wear. Come help me, okay?"

Grabbing the check, she went to the counter to pay. Gwen left the tip on the table and followed her out the door into the brisk, bright air. "Okay, what to wear? Exactly how crazy do you want to make him on the first date?"

RAINE SAT on a stool at the bar feeling jittery and unsure. She swirled the little plastic stick around in her Manhattan, her hands cold even though heat from the whiskey had worked its way through her bloodstream and softly smudged her eyes and cheeks.

It was a little after six—this wasn't a good sign. Maybe he had changed his mind, maybe he had arrived, seen her, and just left without a word—he might have considered fantasy a better deal than the reality. She made a point of turning her back to the door. She didn't want to know when. If.

She looked down at her boots, swinging her foot. The soft black leather caressed her calf. The gray wool skirt had seemed sensible and still sexy, warm enough for the weather, exposing just a little leg between midthigh where the top of the boot met her knee. The deep green cashmere sweater was nice but not revealing, at least not in the obvious sense, though it clung to curves in all the right places and had attracted more than one admiring look when she had slipped off her jacket at the door. Gwen said the color emphasized her eyes, making them look like crystal-clear jade.

Raine took Gwen seriously, which not everyone did, at least at first. But Gwen was smart, and she had style. The two women had a deep respect for each other and that had been the basis of their friendship almost from the start. Gwen was really the first close friend Raine had ever had, and Raine thought of her almost like a sister, though she never told Gwen that. She wasn't one for gushing her emotions all over the place. When it came to her own life, she was never quite sure where the lines were between people, what was allowed and what wasn't. So she tried to err on the safe side.

Raising her fingers to the small pink rosebud that was clipped into her hair, she tried not to look at her watch yet again. Her nerves settled, her hopes started to fade, and she felt a little like a fool. Ten more minutes, and she would go home and forget about this for good.

JACK CURSED the weather. The drive had been much nastier than he had anticipated. The winter storm that passed by the night before had cleared out to sea, but it had left the roads slick and dangerous. Everyone was trying to get somewhere for the weekend, and he was caught in one traffic jam after another.

His feet were freezing, and as much as he was looking forward to meeting Nilla—to put it mildly—he was very focused on getting warm. If getting warm with Nilla was in the cards, even better. But for the moment, he was so cold even thinking about that didn't warm him enough. A few miles back, a college student—driving too fast and too confidently for the conditions—had spun off the road into a snowbank, directly in front of him.

The kid was not hurt, but was not getting out of his predicament alone, so Jack climbed into snow up to his thighs to help dig the car out. He lost his beloved Red Sox cap in the wind, watching it whirl away into darkness. Jack sent the kid off again with a growling warning about driving more slowly before he killed someone else or himself.

Though he had managed to brush off most of the snow, his pants were still a little damp. He was tired, hungry, and he seriously needed a drink.

He spotted the restaurant and pulled into the first available parking space. The place was hopping, even at this early hour. He glanced at his watch. He was only fifteen minutes late, not too bad, all things considered. He took a deep breath and closed his eyes, glad to shut the engine off and concentrate on why he was here.

Reaching for the flowers he had brought with him, he shook off the agitation of the drive. His jacket was covered with salt and sludge, so he left it in the back seat and grabbed a fleece he had lying there.

The night was clear and cold, and his heart was thudding deeply in his chest as he approached the restaurant. This was it. In another minute he would be looking at, handing these flowers to—touching—the woman who had been the focus of his dreams, waking and sleeping, for the last month. He steadied his breathing and walked through the restaurant door.

He spotted her immediately, from the back. Seated at the bar, she was turned about three-quarters away from him, blond hair flowing down her back, a pink rosebud tucked sweetly behind her ear. Not white for purity, not red for passion, but something in between.

Jack watched quietly as she leaned forward and laughed

quietly with the bartender, who was pouring her another drink. The soft line of her jaw entranced him, and he stared, losing all sense of time or place. He frowned for a moment, feeling a prick of recognition, but ignored it.

He forgot that he was cold, hungry and tired as he took in the graceful curve of her neck, the slope of her shoulder and the way her hair tumbled down over the womanly shape of her back. He flexed his fingers, imagining wrapping his fingers into it, getting tangled in all those silken strands.

His mouth went dry as he followed the length of her body. She sat saucily on the stool, legs crossed at her very beautiful knees, the black leather boots offering only a hint of leg, making him lick his lips. Thank you, heaven.

The bartender walked away, leaving her with her drink, and he saw her look at her watch, and observed how her shoulders lifted and fell slightly in what must have been a sigh. Taking a deep breath for courage, he stepped forward, quickly covering the space between them.

He stopped and caught his breath when she suddenly spun around and slipped down off the stool, face-to-face with him. He stood stock-still, disbelieving, his brain and body frozen in shock. It was only a matter of seconds, but it seemed like seasons passed. She looked at him squarely.

"Oh. Jack. Hi."

She didn't appear shocked to see him, though she was less than thrilled, obviously. He realized she had no idea that he was there to see her. He didn't—couldn't—say anything. He watched her lean over, grab her purse, then her jacket. She looked miserable. She thought she'd been stood up.

Conflict raged as he realized his out—he could let her think that her date was not coming, and just walk away. But when he saw the disappointment in her face, he couldn't do it. Not that the alternative was going to get a much better response.

"Um…yeah…" He had never been so truly lost for what to say. It was a cruel trick of the universe that the woman he had been dreaming about, sharing such intimacies with— hell, getting off on the phone with—was *her.*

His brain still refused to process this new situation, but as she walked past him toward the door, he spontaneously reached out and grabbed her arm. She turned and looked at him, confused, and maybe a little peeved.

"Excuse me?"

There was only one way to deal with this, he figured. Jump right in. "I'm sorry I'm late." His slightly strangled voice did not sound like his own. He tried to smile, but it didn't quite work.

She looked at him as if he had lost his mind and removed his hand from her sleeve.

"Jack, I have no idea what you are talking about, but it looks like you have a date." She tilted her head at the flowers. "If you're late, you'd better get moving. Good night." She turned toward the door again.

He sighed, and took the leap. "You're right. I do have a date. With you. *Nilla.*"

She stopped and turned slowly to face him. He watched disbelief, and then shock, cross her features. She had such an expressive face. Not saying anything, she just stared at him, her cheeks reddening. She dropped her purse, and looked as if she wanted to slap him.

"You! Is this some kind of joke?"

"No. No joke. I'm Rider, and you, apparently, are Nilla."

She just stared, and Jack took her elbow, steering her to the bar again, to sit.

"Let go of me!"

"Fine. This is not exactly what I expected, either, believe me."

She was still too horrified to really hear him or process what he was saying to her—this was the man she'd had been sharing her intimate fantasies with? Jack, the guy from her office, was the mystery man she had phone sex with?

Her heart sank into a pit of humiliation. She had helped him have an orgasm over the phone the same day they had exchanged swipes just a few hours earlier in her office! How could this be? He must have known. He must have set her up somehow; this must be an office prank. Her fingers tightened painfully on the edge of the bar.

"Can I get you another drink? I could sure use one." His voice was resigned.

"I don't think so."

"Have it your way."

He signaled the bartender and ordered a brandy, and they both sat there silently, looking dumbfounded. When she spoke, her voice was accusing.

"Why aren't you wearing the clothes you said you would? The Red Sox hat, leather jacket? Were you trying to trick me?"

"Hardly. I had some trouble on the road, lost my hat and ruined my jacket. What do you take me for, anyway?"

"I don't know what to think about this. I mean you…we…"

He watched the emotions play over her face, and felt like a cad, even though he had not done anything wrong. He sipped his brandy, trying to think of what to do next.

"We have reservations. What do you say we make peace, laugh it off, and go have dinner? We could at least talk about it. You have to admit, this is one hell of a coincidence."

"I'm going home." She got up, walked toward the door then

outside. How could she stay? How could she let him see how devastated she was? She would not—*not*—let a single tear escape, though it seemed as if several thousand of them were threatening.

"Hey, you forgot this." He was there again, right beside her in the parking lot, and she slid a quick look to see him handing her purse over. She hadn't even realized she had dropped it. She reached out for it blindly, feeling the dam behind her eyes burst. She would not let him see her this way. She would never give him the satisfaction of knowing how much she had been looking forward to this. She hadn't even realized that herself.

Jack frowned. He was ready to go wallow in disappointment and beer for the rest of the evening, but the stiffness of her shoulders, the angle of her face—as if she couldn't even look at him—it was just too much.

He stepped around and took her shoulders in a firm grip, turning her toward him. The distressed sound she made concerned him, and he turned her face up to his, surprised to see fat tears streaming down her pale cheeks. She looked so sad it just about ripped his heart out.

She tried to turn away, but he wouldn't let her. He pulled her close against him and rocked her gently. She trembled in his arms, and he pulled back to look at her again, watching as snowflakes fell, melting with the tears that were staining her skin.

Even now, she was the most beautiful woman he had ever seen, and though he didn't want to acknowledge it, something tugged deep inside him. She was his lover, his Nilla, after all.

He spoke, his eyes glued to hers, his voice rough.

"I'm so sorry this is such a disappointment for you, Raine. Really. But it is just a coincidence. I promise. No tricks."

Puzzlement and distress mixed for a moment, and she couldn't take her eyes off his face. Then, realizing her position, she broke away and turned toward the car, but felt his hand on her arm again. Looking up, she saw his mouth set in a grim line, but his eyes were warm as they moved over her.

"C'mere. You can't drive in this condition."

Her eyes widened as she felt the warmth of his fingers stroke her damp cheek, and her mind seemed to disengage in response to the unexpected gentleness; her breath caught. He was very close—how did he get so close?—everything about him was hot, solid and male. His eyes were like magnets.

She heard him say her name as he moved in closer, but it was as if she was in a dream, frozen and unable to move. The flowers he had been carrying all this time fell onto the fresh blanket of snow at their feet. She knew this shouldn't be happening, though somehow it was. She shouldn't be allowing it to happen, but she had been waiting for so long.

His large hand had solidly planted itself on the small of her back, supporting her, pulling her in just a bit closer. Her eyes held to his, and she shivered, though she wasn't cold.

He said her name again, and tilted his forehead against hers, their bodies pressed close, snow swirling all around them. The hand that had been on her shoulder fell to his side and found her fingers, stroked them, then wrapped them in his. Pulling her palm up to lay flat against his chest, their hands pressed between them, he angled his head and lowered his lips to hers.

"Nilla."

She didn't breathe, didn't respond. He pressed his mouth on hers, then just rubbed gently back and forth, not so much an embrace as a greeting. He kissed each corner of her mouth, and she leaned toward him, seeking more. He pressed her closer, and she could feel the hardness of his chest and his heart pounding underneath the fleece.

Of its own volition, her other hand touched his face, passed gently over the heat emanating from his skin. He tested, lightly sliding his tongue along her lips, wetting them. Melting against him, her fingers slid upward, burying her fingers in his hair as his lips pursued the kiss, nibbling hers, sucking her lower lip into his mouth, teasing it with his tongue. She felt her knees weaken, and opened for him, giving him full access to explore the insides of her mouth, and heard him groan inside of her as the kiss turned scorching.

Never, in recent memory—hell, in her entire life—had she been kissed like this. It wasn't really even a kiss, it was too consuming to be called that sweet of a thing. Her body was burning and aroused just from the crushing of his lips on hers, the feel of his tongue teasing the roof of her mouth, the gentle scraping of his teeth on her lip. God, she was raw, and didn't realize how needy she was.

When he sought her tongue, wrapped his lips around it and sucked it into his mouth, she moaned as she felt herself go hot and slick, knotted and ready. His hands were wrapped in her hair and she lost herself in tasting him. They blended, pressing into each other, stumbling back against the car.

Jack hadn't intended to become so encompassed by the kiss; touch her just once, he had taunted himself, just to know what it would be like, just for a moment. Just to comfort. But by God she was sweet, the way her hands had fisted into his shirt beneath his jacket, and now how they splayed across his chest, fingering his nipple absently, sending waves of desire pulsing through him. He couldn't get deep enough into her mouth…he wanted to drown in the honey he found there.

After all the time, all the talk, all the imagining, he was desperate for her as he had never been for anyone before in his life. They twisted again, dancing around each other as the snow fell in a thick curtain around them. He found himself pushed back against the car, her lips never leaving his as they switched positions.

She was demanding from him now, meeting fire with fire. He moaned into her mouth, and let her have him, let her have anything she wanted. He smiled and encouraged her as her hands moved down and closed firmly on his butt, grinding him against her until he was sure he was going to come.

He had never been this hot with a woman before, and didn't know it would be so intoxicating. He wanted to forget control and just be consumed. Her tongue lapped at his like a cat with milk, her fingers kneading him, and he wished he could feel more of her flesh against his. He breathed her name raggedly, dangerously close to the edge as she pressed her hip against his straining erection. He pulled back, his voice rough.

"Let's go."

"Where?" Her heart was pounding so hard she could barely hear him, and she stayed leaning into him, afraid her knees would not support her.

"Anywhere. Anywhere we can be alone."

5

WARINESS STARTED to edge into her mind, but he stemmed it, kissing her hard, then pulling her close, his mouth by her ear.

"Just for now, let's forget everything else. I want you. I want you *now*. We've waited too long. Thought about it too much. Just this once. Let's just take what we both want."

Beyond thought, Raine nodded, and fumbled for the keys in her purse, somehow managing with shaking hands to press the button that unlocked her car. He took the keys and opened the door.

"I can drive."

"Listen, you've had a few drinks and no food, and a shock to boot. Just tell me where."

She walked to the passenger's side, numb and on fire at the same time. Somewhere, deep inside her brain, she was thinking something wasn't quite right, and she shouldn't be doing this…should she? But the way he was looking at her when she slid into the car next to him blotted out reasonable thoughts. Never had a man looked at her in just that way— with that hungry, starving, I-want-to-eat-you-alive look that Jack was giving her now.

She wanted him, too. He was right. They had waited a long time. In an urgent whisper, she told him how to drive to her place, and in a few minutes, like magic, they were there, and she was stepping out into the cold in front of her home.

Everything still had that dreamlike quality, and when he came around the car and took her hand, she closed her eyes, not wanting the spell to break. *Don't think too much—don't think at all—just let this happen.* She felt a sharp tug on her hand, and she was facing him, in front of her door. His voice was quiet, his eyes intense.

"I want you like hell. But I'll give you a chance to change your mind now. I'll go, if you want."

She looked him square in the eye, ignoring any voice in her head that told her one-night stands were not her thing. That she would have to work in the same office with this man on Monday. That she didn't even really know him.

"No. I…I want this, too. I've wondered if…what it would be like to really…know you."

He smiled, quick and sharp, and handed her the keys so she could open the door.

"Me, too." He watched her slip the key into the lock, and felt his breath catch as she opened the door. His body was tight with anticipation, and he could sense her next to him as they stepped into the darkness.

Before she could reach for the light on the table beside the entry, he moved quickly, pressing her back to the door and burying his face in her neck, inhaling her scent, biting the soft skin behind her ear. When she shivered, he couldn't help but moan against her soft, feverish skin.

He moved his lips gently from ear to cheek to lips again, sliding his mouth over hers while he unbuttoned her coat and slid it to the floor. His hands spanned her rib cage, molded her to him, and he bit her bottom lip, sliding his tongue across it before kissing her hungrily. He was so lost in the fog of lust they had created that he barely felt her pushing the coat off his shoulders, her voice husky and suggestive.

"Let's get more comfortable."

He nodded, and stepped away—sensed more than saw her move. Suddenly the light was on, and he briefly noted their surroundings. Comfortable. Homey. Warm. In his passion-fogged brain, something wasn't clicking. Looking around, he tried to figure it out as he picked up his coat and threw it over a chair. But this was not the time for thinking. When he saw her beckoning him in stocking feet, her hair mussed from his hands, her cheeks hot with desire, he could only stare and wonder if this was really happening. She stood next to a doorway across the room—her bedroom, he assumed—and smiled at him.

It was all the invitation he needed. Crossing the room, he framed her face in his hands and worked his mouth over hers until they were both so weak with need they stumbled into the dark room barely paying attention to where they were going, stopping only when Raine felt the bed push against the back of her knees.

God, Jack felt so good. He smelled so good. She blocked all logical thought and concentrated only on the want, the ravenous need, that was burning within her. *More.* She must have more of him. All of him. Running her hands up under his shirt, she gloried in his hot, firm, male skin, working her hands through the hair on his chest and pushing his shirt up and over his head.

At some point, he worked his own hands up under her sweater, lifting it off, and she heard him moan in male appreciation as his hands moved back down and closed over her breasts, weighing the fullness of them in his hands, pinching the turgid nipples between his thumb and forefinger. She cried out in sheer pleasure as her knees buckled. He caught her, lowering her gently to the bed. He stood in front of her, taking a moment to unbuckle his belt and slide off his pants, never letting his eyes leave hers.

Raine thought she would melt from the intensity of his gaze. He was beautiful…male, sculpted, and just *beautiful*. His eyes were almost black with desire, and she felt the gush of passion between her legs as he stripped in front of her. Her eyes roved over him and lingered on his desperately erect penis. *Beautiful*. The word became a chant in her mind.

She sat up and touched him tentatively, running her hand over his hard length, and then leaned forward to kiss him in that very spot, darting her tongue out for a taste. His breath contracted sharply, and his hands were on her shoulders then, pushing her away gently.

She looked up, and he smiled down at her, his face ruddy with desire, his voice strained. "Do that and it will be over before we've begun. And one of us still has too many clothes on."

She stood, finding herself unbearably close to him, wrapped in the heat that was pulsing out from his body. As if they could not bear to be separate, not even slightly, they quickly disposed of the rest of her clothes, until she was naked in front of him, flesh to flesh. His eyes devoured her as hungrily as hers had him.

"You're like a goddess. You're not even real—you can't be." He touched her hair almost reverently, and she was lost. Sliding back, she sat up on the pillows. Feeling wanton and wanted, she lifted an arm over her head and let one bent knee fall to the side. His eyes fixed on the patch of sandy-blond hair and the wet, pink folds she exposed, and he licked his lips.

"I'm very real. Join me?"

"Oh yeah."

Then he was next to her, and they wound around each other. Raine ran her hands down his back, exploring the muscles, gripping on to his rock-hard buttocks. She shifted to maneuver his cock between her thighs, then pressed him between them. Jack growled in pleasure, rubbing himself along the silky pocket of skin, and bracing on one elbow, dipped to draw one breast into his mouth, suckling and teasing her until she was writhing and he could feel her nails digging into his back.

He felt her teeth on his shoulder, and sparks of pleasure sizzled in his brain. Sliding one hand down, he found the juncture of her sex and purred into her mouth as he touched her.

"You're so wet—like hot, wet silk…"

"Jack…please…I want you. Now."

She shifted again, bringing him up closer to where she needed him to be, wanting him inside, but he drew back, his breathing labored, sweat gleaming on his forehead.

"Protection…in my wallet…"

She smiled, and drew him back to her, opening her thighs and cradling him.

"All set." She patted her hip, and showed him the transparent birth control patch. "Don't worry."

He nodded and braced himself over her, rubbing the hot tip of his desire along her wetness, causing her to arch her back in response. She sought him, and he found her, enveloping himself in one deep thrust.

Her eyes widened with a shock of pleasure, and then closed again as small sighs of need escaped her lips. He fisted his hands into the sheets, remembering when he had made her come on the phone, how she had made those same noises then.

Her quick pants and needy moans had driven him over the brink then, and they were threatening to this time, as well.

It had been a while, and he knew he wouldn't last long, but he wanted her to share the pleasure with him. Withdrawing slowly, he balanced back on his knees. Then placed his hands underneath her hips, he pulled her up toward him, moving his hand between her legs. He rubbed her hot, tight nub expertly with his fingers while still shallowly thrusting into her.

Her face contorted in desire, and she pushed forward, trying to take him deeper. He moved up over her, wanting to be next to her when they both fell. Thrusting deeply, taking what they both needed, he increased the rhythm. Sliding his hands up behind her head and into her hair, he whispered to her as he felt his own peak close at hand.

"Come, Nilla, I want you to come with me…."

The dull ache of loss consumed her as she sensed her body's hesitation, an all-too-familiar sensation, and suddenly hot tears spilled out before she could stop them. Unable to stop his body's reaction though he detected the faint change in hers, he poured himself into her, searing pleasure wracking his body.

Catching his breath, he felt her tense beneath him, and lifted himself, shocked to see her crying, her face turned from his.

"Raine, did I hurt you? Jesus, Oh God…I'm so sorry…." He sat up, confused, and tried to gather her to him. She pushed farther to the other side of the bed, and he didn't know what to do.

Raine closed her eyes, humiliated. She was hurting, but not in the way he thought, so she struggled to speak. Her voice, when she spoke, was low and miserable, confirming his worst fears.

"No, no, you didn't hurt me."

He sat up and scooted to the other side of the bed so he

could see her. Her face was turned into the pillow. At a loss, he stroked her hair.

"Then what? What happened? Talk to me...."

She sighed and worked up the courage to meet his eyes. He was concerned, that was clear, so she sought to comfort him.

"It's no big deal, forget it. I'm sorry. I hope I didn't ruin it for you, at the end—" She stopped as she saw awareness dawn on his face, and her humiliation doubled.

"No, no, you didn't ruin anything." As he reached for her, she drew back.

"But it *is* a big deal, Raine. It's important that both of us find equal pleasure and we didn't—something happened there that chilled you—what? Was it something I did? Said?"

Raine sat up, and tugged the blanket up in front of her defensively. "It's nothing, okay? It's nothing you did. I just never come, not like that, so don't worry about it." She offered him a wan smile. "I'm just a little frustrated, that's all."

Jack watched her, her face masking hurt, her eyes shadowed. He remembered how pliant and hot she had been in his arms. This woman couldn't have orgasms? That was hard to believe.

"But that night on the phone, you...?"

Her cheeks went hot. "Yes, that was different."

He nodded slowly, understanding. "You just have problems experiencing orgasm with someone, with intercourse."

She felt like a fool, like a failure, but nodded. A big part of it, she knew, had been that he had not used her real name when he'd spoken to her, but she would burn in hell before she'd admit that to him. It took only that moment to break the spell, to cool the pleasure she was eagerly hoping to attain, just once, with someone who had excited her beyond knowing. But then again, she probably wouldn't have made it anyway—she never did.

She knew it was her long history of not knowing how to open up that was to blame, but she didn't know what to do about it. The thought made her even more miserable. All this time she'd hoped it was the fault of lousy lovers, but she couldn't say that was true of Jack. It was just her.

She practically jumped out of her skin when he shifted over and sat beside her, placing her head on his shoulder. She stiffened and resisted, but then gave in to the comfort of it. Why not?

His voice was gentle, but with some lightness.

"I wish you had told me that. You know, there are things we can do. That was a bit…rushed. I thought you were with me. I'm sorry."

She shook her head. "It was good. Really. I told you, I don't usually even get that excited. It's just me. Really, I'd rather drop it." Her voice took on an edge, but he didn't want to drop the subject, not yet.

"It's nothing to be ashamed of, Raine. A lot of women can't have orgasms that way, but they can have them other ways— have you ever tried?"

She shrugged noncommittally, and wondered why he just would not let the subject drop; the other men she had been with hadn't cared overmuch, but Jack seemed determined to pursue the issue. She tried to sit up, to get some distance, but his arm tightened around her, so she gave up the struggle and buried her face in his shoulder instead, to avoid that penetrating gaze. She sighed against his skin, her tongue darting out unconsciously to catch the salty taste of his skin on her lips.

"I haven't had any adventurous love affairs, sex has been fairly routine, I suppose. Nothing out of the ordinary."

"What has the ordinary been? Maybe we should try something a little *extra*ordinary?" Surprisingly, he felt a warm hum in his loins again, thinking of it. This woman seemed to inspire him.

"Um, no…I'm fine. Really. I think maybe we should just call it a night."

"Well, it's up to you, I suppose. You know what you want, right?"

He turned a little, his face in her hair, and ran his tongue along the shell of her ear, and felt her quiver. Sliding a hand up to her breast, Jack kneaded gently, then ran his tongue from the curve of her ear down to her jaw, hungering for her again. He captured her mouth before she could say anything, and kissed her deeply, seductively.

Raine felt herself float away on the kiss. While it still had the edge of passion—she could tell he wanted her again—he took his time, plundering deeper, not ending the kiss until they were both gasping for breath. He settled her back on the pillows, shifted over her, kissing her everywhere, his breath feathering her sensitive skin.

"But Raine…maybe you want me to do this? Just a little?" He caught her nipple in his teeth and flicked his tongue over it lightly. She whimpered and managed to speak.

"Maybe…a little."

She couldn't take much more. He'd had her in such a state of arousal the crash had been almost too much to take. But even if final completion was not a possibility, the way he made her feel along the way was too good to stop. She couldn't say no to how he was touching her. She gave herself over to him, he could do anything he wanted.

He ran his tongue over her stomach in the most erotic patterns, her supersensitive skin responding achingly to his light touch. Then he burned paths up and down her thighs as he stroked them.

"God, you're gorgeous. You are so much more than I ever imagined…. Remember when I wrote about doing this to you online? How I wanted to taste you?"

He moved up over her and looked. She was like an angel of desire, her skin flushed with passion, arms thrown to the side, hair tangled and splayed over the pillow. When he moved his hand up between her thighs to insert a finger, then two, into her heat, he was gratified to find she was still wet; she moaned and ground against him, and he sighed in awe. She was so responsive.

He kissed her breasts again, and feathered his lips down her stomach. Nudging her knees apart, he lay between them. He didn't rush, but lifted her leg, trailing his tongue along her instep, to her ankle, and then kissed her knees, tracing his tongue up the inside of her leg to the sensitive crease where hip met thigh, and kissed her there, biting lightly, feeling her strain and stretch underneath him.

"Is this the usual, Raine? The ordinary?"

She heard him, his voice hot and teasing, and she struggled for clarity against the onslaught of passion, and faintly shook her head from side to side. "Um, no…nothing usual about this."

"Good. Tell me if anything gets…boring. Tell me anything you want, just like you did online. I'm Rider, Raine—you can tell me anything." He grinned and bit her neatly on the thigh, and she cried out the "okay" that started as a whisper and ended in a moan.

Parting the flesh that concealed her clit, he rubbed his thumb over it and then took her in his mouth, sucking hard, then softly, lapping his tongue over her, then stroking long, hot sweeps from that sensitive nub to her vagina with his tongue, gratified by her increased sounds of arousal, the tightening of her thighs on his shoulders. Backing off for a moment, he looked up at her, and felt desire rip through his own body, but he quelled it. This time was for her.

"Raine, touch yourself, sweetheart."

Her forehead creased. "Hmm?"

"Touch your breasts, Raine…do whatever feels right…it's okay…anything is okay."

Raine was unsure about this request, but as he closed his mouth over her again and his tongue was making those long, hot trips back and forth along her most sensitive areas, she lifted her own hands to her breasts, and ran her palms lightly over her nipples, so hard and stiff they were almost sore, and arched her back reflexively.

The world hazed when he grabbed her cheeks in both hands, squeezed and opened her wider, penetrating her with his tongue, then running it up to suck on her clit again. The pressure built unbearably, and she couldn't think. Pulling sharply at her nipples, she was panting, willing her body to go where it needed to—she was *so* close. He was sucking her now, continuously, in a rhythm, without stopping, probing his fingers into her, seeking out her sweet spot. He growled his encouragement as he felt her body suddenly wrench in pleasure.

Raine was caught off guard by the sharp release of pressure, the pulsing heat that exploded and spread out through her limbs. A cry escaped her lips and she bucked against him, seeking more, experiencing every last second of it.

Jack smiled when he felt her muscles gently clasping his fingers. He nuzzled her encouragingly, his groan vibrating against her skin, until he felt her relax.

He maneuvered himself up next to her, watching her face. Her eyes were closed, and there was a faint sheen on her skin that seemed to make her glow. He touched her face, and she opened her eyes, looking at him in wonder and shyness. He smiled, and kissed her.

"Heya."

"Jack God that,,,was…definitely not…the ordinary." She touched his face. "Thank you."

He chuckled. "Be careful, you'll inflate my ego…but I'm glad. I enjoyed that every bit as much as you did."

She frowned, reaching over to him. "You did?"

He laughed again, scooching down next to her, yanking up the blanket. "Oh, yeah. I, uh…when you came, it felt pretty good to me, too—but you'll have to change these sheets later, I'm afraid."

Raine smiled, exhausted in the best possible way, his admission making her feel womanly and wonderful.

"Stay."

"I don't have much choice, I think. We took your car."

But she was already asleep, and soon so was he.

RAINE WOKE FIRST, entangled in more ways than one.

Legs and arms were wound around each other, and the very handsome face of Jack Harris was facing her, close enough that she could feel his morning stubble on her cheek. He was beautiful—warm and lost in sleep. She stared at him, remembering. She found herself wanting to touch him, badly, but curled her hands into fists. As her mind cleared, she groaned, rubbing her face and wondering how she could have been so foolish.

Looking at him now, it was hard to imagine that the rude jerk in her office, a man she didn't even like, had just spent the night in her bed. Even worse, she had practically begged him for sex, and he had been the only man who had been able to…well…she remembered with a sigh, closed her eyes, and shook her head in a mix of regret and disbelief. She opened her eyes and looked at him again. He was Rider. Her Rider. But he was also Jack. Jack, who obviously couldn't stand her.

Panic caught her breath. Could this really be a huge coincidence? How could she trust him? He was an Internet expert—he could have set the whole thing up, right? What if he told the guys at the office? She would be a laughingstock. It was all too much to process. She needed to get out, to get away, but she didn't want to wake him. She couldn't handle that yet. She couldn't face him and see him gloat.

Quietly, little by little, she slid from the bed, hoping like anything that he didn't wake up until she could get dressed. She needed to be alone. She had made a very bad decision last night, and she was going to have to think about how to handle the consequences.

JACK WOKE TO HEAR the shower running, and was momentarily disoriented. Picking up the scent of perfume and sex from the sheets, he smiled, stretching like a big cat. Raine. Last night had been a shock, but not a disappointment. Well, to be completely honest, it had been a disappointment at first, but now it ranked as one of the best nights of his life.

He pushed up on the pillows, rubbed his face, and glanced at the clock. It was almost nine, but it was Sunday, so he was not in a rush to go anywhere. He wondered what Raine would want to do with the day. His smile was wicked as he considered what he would like to do with it, with her.

He swung his legs over the side of the bed, found his jeans and yanked them on. Nothing was as he thought it would be.

The house was small, a classic New England cottage. Raine had nice taste, he thought as he ran his hand over the solid wooden frame of the mission-style bed frame, the earthy tones of the unfinished wood blending beautifully with the rose-tinted walls, but the place was not exactly what he would have expected of the very wealthy. She had nice but not extravagant things. The rooms were comfortable, but hardly grand. Not at all what he would have imagined.

Flowers were peeking at him from wall vases she had installed in every room. Snow blew against the white three-over-three frames, making the place feel like a cocoon. Her bedroom dresser looked old, an antique no doubt, and the bedding was soft, good-quality cotton. He smiled, running a finger along the edge of a daisy on the pattern. It was all female, all soft and inviting. Like Raine.

So she was Nilla. His Nilla. Never in a million years would he have thought Raine Covington was even capable of the kind of charm that he found so attractive in Nilla, let alone the passion she had shared with him last night. It looked as if he was wrong.

Nothing he would have imagined about Raine Covington seemed right. She had been standoffish in high school, and she was sure as hell was not all that likable at work. How could he have been so wrong about her? Thinking of her in his arms, and how he had been able to help her experience passion she didn't even think she was capable of achieving, made his toes curl. He glanced toward the bathroom where the shower had just turned off, and thought about joining her.

RAINE STOOD in the shower, stalling, still not knowing how to handle the situation. How could she face Jack? She had clearly messed up. It just didn't pay to be impulsive; it never worked out for her. They had to work in the same office, and she would be lucky if he was just willing to forget about last night and keep his mouth shut.

She rubbed a towel almost violently over her hair and had a brutal moment of honesty as she looked at her scrubbed face in the mirror. What really bothered her, down deep, was that he didn't even like her—he wasn't even really with her last night—while they had been making love, he had thought of her as Nilla, called her Nilla, not Raine. He was just living out a fantasy.

She had been able to live one out as well, she admitted. It was fantastic with him. When he had seduced her that second, wonderful time, when he had shown her what real, satisfying sex could be like with a man, it had moved her deeply. But now, in the cold morning light, the experience felt hollow and wrong. She had opened herself to him completely, and he had only seen her as a fantasy, not as Raine Covington, but as some figment of his imagination come to life.

She put a hand to her face, sinking against the edge of the vanity as she realized how she had let him take her over, she had been so eager for what he could give her. He was likely motivated by a mix of male ego and pity, and while neither was a particularly great option, she would prefer the first to the second, thanks very much!

Her hands worked themselves furiously through her hair,

and she stopped, sighing in defeat, feeling tears sting behind her eyelids. It was just her lousy luck that the lover of her dreams was not the man of her dreams, nor she the woman of his. She spoke determinedly to her image, convincing herself of what she had to do.

"Remember, he wasn't making love to *you*. An idea of you, a version of you—yes—but not you. Keep that straight, and try to have a little dignity, in spite of the fact that you just made a tremendous fool of yourself. Try to keep it together, get him out the door quickly, and get through this. See it through."

Setting her shoulders back, she slipped on a mask of calm that hid the hurt. It was something she was practiced at—a skill she had honed to perfection in the lonely, painful years of her youth.

She pulled on a robe and walked out into the bedroom. The little bit of cool she had maintained nearly slipped away completely as she saw him standing by her bedroom window holding a cup of coffee and looking magnificent dressed only in his jeans. She licked her lips and blinked hard, reining herself in.

"Um. Good morning." She sounded like a frog.

He turned and smiled. "It is. I made coffee. Hope you don't mind."

She took another step awkwardly into the room. "No, no, that's good, fine. Thank you."

He set the coffee down on the table, and crossed the room, the sleepy, sexy smell of his body slamming into her and blowing away her rehearsed calm as his arms came around her and he pushed his face into her neck, inhaling, and making her head spin.

"I missed you there when I woke up. When I heard the

water running, I was going to come join you, but then you finished. Too bad…"

There was a warm suggestion in his voice that made Raine's knees weak, and she fought for control, keeping her body rigid, and put her hands lightly on his shoulders. Piling one mistake on top of another wasn't going to help, as much as her body was screaming for his. Using every ounce of strength she had, she applied gentle pressure, pushing him away.

Frowning, Jack loosened his arms, stepping back slightly, and looked into her face. She held herself stiffly near him, and didn't want to meet his eyes.

He thought, perhaps, that she was embarrassed. He had already figured that much of what he had assumed about her seemed not to be true, at least in what he'd experienced with her last night, and from what he could gather from her home. She probably wasn't used to taking a man home and, well, doing what they'd done.

He didn't know her, but he was willing to give it a try. Tilting her head up with his fingers, he made her face him and found her eyes dull and remote, the mouth that had been so hot under his was stretched tight. She wrenched her face away again and stepped back.

"Jack, this was obviously a mistake—we are just acting on ideas we got about each other on the Net. We don't even know each other."

His eyes narrowed, and he became cautious, hating the way the atmosphere in the small room had changed, had chilled. Confusion, hurt and anger rolled over him. He stepped forward and pressed her up against the wall with his body, holding her shoulders tightly, his gaze fierce, demanding something from her.

"I thought we had something starting here, Raine. What's going on?"

She shifted against him uncomfortably, a flush moving up her throat. She wasn't immune to him, that was for sure. She brought her chin up in that way that always set his teeth on edge, that imperious, arrogant tilt that drove him crazy, and she shook her head.

"Nothing is going on here, Jack. Nothing went on. This was just two strangers acting out a fantasy. It was a bad idea, especially since we have to work together. I would appreciate it if you would be, um, discreet."

Discreet? What the hell? She was lax under his hands, not resisting, not responding at all. She just looked him dead in the eye and told him to be discreet. It was somehow much more painful than if she had just told him to get the hell out.

"Well, what do you think, Raine? That I'm going to go post it on the Internet? Go tell all the guys at the office I had a hell of a night with Raine Covington and they should give you a call?"

She slapped him then, and though he knew he had it coming, it didn't matter. Her eyes were fiery and hurt, but he suspected it was a hurt that was reflected in his own.

"I don't know, Jack. I suppose that is possible. That's the problem. I don't know. I don't know you well enough to trust you, and that's why last night was a mistake."

All of the warmth he had felt toward her slid away on a greasy slick of anger and regret. He looked hard into her eyes, finding it difficult to believe what she'd just said. But it was real, and he had to leave before he said something he would really regret. He didn't look at her as he found the rest of his clothes, his tone reflecting the iciness he felt.

"Well, then, just let me get dressed now that you have made up your mind about me, and I'll be out of your way."

"Your car..."

"Don't worry about it.... I'll walk back."

His tone cut off any comment she would have made, and she turned and left the room, not breathing until she reached the kitchen, feeling unsure as she sat at the small white table. She heard the door click quietly shut out in the living room, the soft sound more wrenching than a slam, and fought back tears.

She told herself it was better this way.

6

THE DAY WAS SUNNY, and Gwen was just as bright, bouncing into Raine's office Monday morning. She poised herself on the edge of the desk, leaned over, and in a conspiratorial whisper asked, "So, how'd it go? I want to know everything!"

Raine didn't even look up, and tried to sound as if she had no idea what Gwen was talking about. "Busy, Gwen, not now." Her curt tone would have made most people cringe, but Gwen, as Raine had learned, was generally unrebuffable.

"That bad, huh? Was he a complete toad?"

Raine sat back and put her hands on her temples, sighing. Gwen would not let this rest, she knew. As her closest—and her only—real friend, she didn't want to hurt Gwen's feelings, but it was an annoying part of the girlfriend relationship that you were expected to tell all each Monday. She never could quite get used to it, and since typically she didn't have much to tell, she just listened to Gwen's tales.

But Gwen was relentless, and she felt herself cave. Maybe it would be good to vent. She opened her eyes, only to find Gwen regarding her patiently.

"I want to hear all about Rider, and your weekend, and then I'll tell you about mine, too. I met a new guy. He's dreamy."

"Don't you ever work?"

"Tons, but I manage my time so I can hear all about your

weekend on Monday mornings. I find this little storytelling session is good for motivating me to get out of bed on Mondays, it primes me for the day. So go ahead, prime me."

Raine had to smile. "I don't think you need any more priming, but okay. I'm not quite sure how to start. Let's just say this weekend was…unusual."

Gwen slid off the desk and into a chair in one lithe movement. "Ohhh…unusual is good! But details, I want details."

Raine sighed. "Okay. Well, good thing you are sitting down. Turns out Rider is someone I know. Someone we both know."

Gwen's eyes widened and she ticked off a few possible names. Raine shook her head. "No. Not even close. Rider is Jack Harris."

"Who?"

Raine rolled her eyes and leaned forward. "Jack Harris—the IT guy you thought looked like Superman the other day."

"Noooooo!" Gwen whooshed out the word on a breath of disbelief, and sat back in her chair, flabbergasted. "You've got to be kidding! What are the freakin' odds on that? Oh my God! Raine, I can't believe it. What happened? God, he's gorgeous."

Raine smiled faintly, absentmindedly arranging papers on her desk as she spoke. "Well, we were both pretty disappointed, to put it mildly. We argued a bit, then he…well, he—"

"Yeah? C'mon! What?"

"Well, he kissed me. Major-league kiss."

"Hold the phone. For whatever reason, you weren't happy to see each other, you argued, and he kissed you?"

"Yeah. I know. It doesn't seem to make sense, but it does, when you think about it. I guess we were both so worked up from the anticipation, the time online, we just had to find out. You know, what it would be like." She took a deep breath, blushing furiously. "It ended up being a little more than a kiss. We, um, ended up going back to my place."

Since Gwen looked as if she might fall out of the chair and let out a hoot, Raine jumped up to close the door.

"You slept with him?"

Raine nodded silently and Gwen grinned. "How was it?"

Too many reactions hit Raine at once. She started to speak, but stumbled, and felt her eyes burning. "It was great, but it was awful, you know? I mean, finally I meet someone who can...who could..." Just when she thought her cheeks wouldn't burn any hotter, they did.

Gwen smacked the table. "All right! It's about time, I was keeping my fingers crossed for you. But may I say that you don't look all that thrilled about it."

"Gwen, the guy I slept with Saturday night is not who I thought he would be—it was a fantasy. In real life he is a complete jerk with a horrible attitude who for some unknown reason can't stand me! And I can't stand him either. He's so...rude. And arrogant. And I went to bed with him! How could I have done that?"

She dropped her head to the desk for a moment, and then raised it to look at Gwen with miserable eyes. "When we were in bed, at a, um, critical moment, he called me Nilla instead of Raine, and I don't know—it was like he couldn't think about being with *me*. The real me. He just wanted the fantasy. He wanted Nilla. It was humiliating."

"Oh, Raine, honey, c'mon, people fantasize all the time in bed, and he knows you better as Nilla than Raine. I would think that was completely natural. It's only a name, for goodness' sake. I'm sure he knew exactly whom he was with. And you *are* Nilla, after all. It's not like he was thinking about a different woman."

Raine sucked in a breath and her voice became stiff and prim.

"Maybe so, but Nilla is a creation, she is many things that I am not at all. So, it just underlines the fact that he didn't want to think about who he was *really* with."

"Well, all right. What happened then?"

"He spent the night, and it was…nice. But then in the morning, I knew that it was all wrong, that we'd made a huge mistake. I feel like such a fool. I hate that I had such a lapse in judgment. I have never gotten so caught up in someone before, so swept away…"

Gwen offered only a satisfied smirk. "It's about time, if you ask me. That's what it's *supposed* to be like, Raine. You are supposed to get so caught up you don't care about anything or anyone else. We all wait to be swept away like that. Thank your lucky stars!"

"My lucky stars? Are you crazy? Not only did I sleep with a man who dislikes me, now I also have to think about dealing with him at work. Does it occur to you that this is a little weird?" She got up and paced the office.

"I have to see him here in the office and pretend nothing happened. I had phone sex with him, for God's sake, and was, well, pretty open with him online. It's so embarrassing! I'll thank my lucky stars if he isn't having a good laugh about it downstairs with the staff."

Crossing over to hug Raine, Gwen stroked her hair and cooed reassuringly. "Raine, this is not a bad thing. Maybe not ideal, but not bad. You guys just have to work it out."

"There is nothing to work out. He was very angry when he left…I guess I was a little, um, harsh. And that's just as well. Now we just have to get past a few awkward moments here, and as long as he doesn't go telling anyone else, it'll be fine."

Gwen sighed. Raine knew she thought she was too stubborn, and too afraid. But her voice was supportive.

"Hey, you took a chance, and you had a great night, right? So you had a tiff—those things can be smoothed out. Don't make up your mind so fast, just see what happens."

Raine nodded, though she did so only to placate Gwen. She had no doubts that she and Jack were definitely not a possibility. Gwen went on.

"I don't think he is the kiss-and-tell type, anyway. I wouldn't worry too much about that. He just didn't seem to be that way. More like tall, quiet and intense." She shifted gears quickly, sitting up and wiggling in the chair. "So, anyway, let me tell you about the new guy I met. I went down there, and…"

"Down where?"

"Downstairs. Remember we were joking about if there were more cute guys hiding downstairs where Jack works? Well, I decided to find out, and figured even if there weren't, maybe I would run into Jack—not that I would even have so much as a fantasy about him now that I know you two are having a thing—" Raine tried to interject that they were definitely *not* having a thing, but Gwen just rolled on with her story.

"Anyway, you should see it down there. I never knew. It's like something out of a movie. All these small offices circle around the edges of this one big room, and there are *thousands* of computers there. Well, maybe not thousands, but a lot. It's all kinda dimly lit, and romantic in a techno comic-book kind of way."

Raine raised her eyebrows, wondering at Gwen's description of the building basement, but listened as she continued.

"Anyway, I figured I would go down, and just see what or

who was there. So, I was poking around looking for Jack's office, and bumped into this guy." Her eyes took on that far-away look that Raine knew well.

"His name is Neal. Don't ya just love that name? It's so, I don't know, down-home." She smiled. "He's kinda cute, not as built as Jack, but cute in that nerdy I-work-on-my-computer-in-the-basement kind of way, you know? And he even had the thick, black-framed glasses."

Raine couldn't quite hold back her amusement when Gwen sighed, but motioned for her to continue. At least this was taking her mind off her own problems.

"Okay, so you met this guy Neal and…"

"He asked me why I was there, and I told him I was looking for Jack, and then we got talking and I asked him out."

"You don't waste time, Gwen."

"Life is short. Anyway, we had a very nice dinner Saturday night, talked a lot, you know, got to know each other a little bit, and then went back to his place and just made out for hours."

"Made out?"

Gwen sighed again. "Just kissing. Kissing and kissing and more kissing. I haven't done that since high school, and it was terrific. Hot, sweaty, got-my-panties-soaked kissing that went on for half the night and then we just said good night. We're going out again this Friday." Gwen smiled, and blushed a little, and Raine smiled back.

"Sounds nice. I'm glad for you." And she was. It was her turn to sigh, though, and she blocked out the images of what she had been doing for hours on Saturday night, and tried not to remember the feel of Jack's mouth on her skin.

"So, are you going to see him again?" Gwen's voice broke through the fog as she headed to the door.

"Hmm? Who?"

"Jack."

Raine screwed up her mouth and shook her head. "Gwen, I told you—"

Gwen put up her hand. "Okay, okay, just want you to be open to the possibilities. You know that's half the battle. If you are open to things happening in life, they tend to work out."

"Yeah, well, you have to be careful what you are open to." She'd been way too open lately, she thought, a wave of embarrassment washing over her.

Gwen made a face. "Pessimist. Focus on the positive, at least you got laid by a gorgeous guy, right?" She grinned. "I'm back to work. Maybe I can break something on my computer so Neal can come up and fix it. I'd like to watch him bending over to get down into all those wires under the desk."

Raine smiled. "In that case, may all your files crash today." Gwen giggled and waved as she left.

RAINE PARKED HER CAR in front of the castlelike building of the Witch Museum and walked across the street to the Salem Common, a large, open-area park where people came to walk their dogs, play and hang out.

It was a place where you could be by yourself but not alone. Exactly what she was looking for. It was too early to go home. She stared up at the looming statue of Salem's first settler, Roger Conant, and felt a shiver run down her spine. The statue always seemed so eerie to her. She turned her back on him and entered the park.

Some intrepid dog walkers were exercising their canine friends, and groups of children were having snowball fights, their shrieks of joy cutting through the crisp air. She started at the closest corner and followed the maze of walkways without paying much attention to which way she was moving. Snowmen in various stages of meltdown stood here and there along the walk, and she smiled as she walked past the form of a snow angel frozen into the snow. The snow lit up the night; she loved the way it looked like diamonds scattered all over the ground.

"Mind if I join you?"

She was startled to see Duane fall into step beside her.

"Um, sure."

"I usually walk through here on my way home, and saw you get out of your car over there. I live just over on Oliver. How about you? You live farther out, right?"

"Yeah, on Chestnut. I just felt like a walk. Long day."

He nodded and they turned the corner near the ornate structure known as the bandshell, a domed stage resembling a very large gazebo. It had stood there since Salem's early days.

"Listen, Raine, I was wondering how the column is going. I know I was a little hard on you about it before, and if you don't want to meet his guy, you don't have to. It was wrong of me to push you. We can work the article without the meeting."

Now she really didn't know what to say. She wasn't ready to let Duane know she had met Jack, and had no idea how to explain what had happened. She tried to sound unconcerned and professional.

"Thanks, Duane. I'll let you know how it works out."

They walked by a group of children in the playground and Duane bent, picked up a handful of snow and whipped a snowball into the group, smacking a young boy on the arm. Delighted yells followed, and before she knew it, they were running down the walk, being chased and pelted. Duane laughed, and she joined in.

"I forget," he said. "Never instigate a snowball fight when you are outnumbered."

Raine smiled. "I think that is the first one I have been in, so you're the expert."

He was looking at her differently, and she blinked when he raised his hand to brush some snow out of her hair.

"You have a pretty smile. I wish you would show it off more often."

The hairs on her neck stood up in awareness, and she took a step back from his hand. This was not boss-to-employee chat, at least not the kind she was interested in. He put his hands in his pockets, and bent his head down for a moment, and then looked at her, chagrined.

"Sorry, I guess that wasn't too smooth."

"Um, Duane, you know I like you, you're a good boss, but I don't think—" He held his hands up and interrupted her, laughing in a kind of embarrassed way that didn't make her feel any better.

"Listen, I'm sorry. I've just been trying to screw up the courage to ask you out for a while. I know you keep to yourself a lot, and I figured you wouldn't be someone who would get involved with anyone at the office, but I thought, hey, what the heck."

Raine held her breath, thinking of Jack, and felt her stomach sink a little more. Duane continued.

"And then, here I am forcing you to go meet some other guy, and I couldn't believe how stupid that was." He laughed again and kicked some snow, looking at her with intense, blue eyes.

Raine couldn't believe what she was hearing, and had no idea what to do with it.

"Duane, I just don't think going out with you is a good idea—"

He looked down again, and nodded, and she searched for something, anything, intelligent to say.

"I mean, we work together, you are my boss. And I like you, I do, but you know, things like this never work."

"Yeah, you're right. I knew that, but seeing you every day, and then thinking of you going to meet some stranger—well, I figured…hell, I don't know what I figured. But hey, I took my shot, and now we know." He tried to sound offhand, but Raine could hear the strain and felt terrible, though she wasn't quite sure why she should.

"I'm sorry, Duane." It was all she could think to say. She was freezing, her teeth were beginning to chatter, and she couldn't feel any more awkward.

"No, I know, it's okay. Listen, let me walk you back to your car. You're freezing."

She sighed and nodded. They walked across the park to her car in silence, and she was relieved to finally say good-night and watch him walk away. The situation was just surreal. She had never picked up one hint from Duane that he was interested in her—and she had never thought of him that way, not once. He could have his pick of just about any woman in the company, and he was asking her out?

Life was getting too strange.

She drove home with the radio blaring. She just didn't want to think about any of it anymore. She grabbed her mail, surprised to see so much of it, on her way in the door.

She put her coat on the hook, and looked through the stack.

Something wasn't right. These all came from the creditors she had just sent checks to. Opening the first envelope, she discovered a thank-you letter for her recent payment, but they had issued a refund check since her account was already paid in full. Another assumed she had overpaid and sent back the check. Raine blinked, and opened the other envelopes—all the same. Every one of the payments she had just made to credit cards, a parking ticket, and even her student loans, was sent back, and she was informed her accounts were paid in full.

How could this be? She slumped against the door. Just what she needed. Now she had to try to figure out this mess, resend all these payments and get this straightened out before her credit was completely destroyed. Just wonderful. She was already behind on her column, she had two men she had to avoid romantic entanglements with at work, and tomorrow she would have to spend half the day on the phone getting this mess fixed. What next?

JACK TOOK AIM at the multicolored dart board about twelve feet away. He rocketed his arm forward, and the red dart flew and just hit the board, barely sticking to the outside edge. He grunted in disgust as a couple of the guys he was out with cheered and slapped him on the back. They were happy because with that crappy shot, the next round was on him. He was off his game, to say the least, but he lost fair and square. Heading to the bar, he put in the order and went back to the table.

"So, Jack, where have you been lately?" Greg, a programmer with a high-profile company in Boston, tilted his head toward the dartboard. "It's been a while since I've seen you play that badly, not that I'm not grateful." Greg, an incorrigible flirt, eyed the waitress appreciatively as she placed a tray with several bottles of beer in the center of the table. Greg watched the young woman walk away, and sighed lustily.

"Now, if you had a pretty thing like that at home, we could understand why you might not come up for air for a while."

The other men laughed, and tipped their beers, and Jack just shook his head.

"Do you ever get your mind out of the gutter, Greg? No, don't answer, I already know. But if you got laid as much as you talked about it, we'd all be a lot happier."

A howl of laugher went up, and Greg took the jibe in good humor, shrugging and taking a swig of beer before sending one back Jack's way.

"Sounds like maybe I hit a nerve there. Did you get back together with Marley? Or did you meet another honey who dumped you out on your keister—again?"

Jack winced inwardly, Greg's comment hitting the target spot on, but he wasn't about to share that with these guys. And besides, tonight was not about women, past or present. He was happy to be out with his friends, having his evenings back, playing darts, drinking beer, talking trash.

"Yeah, well, part of why Marley dumped me, as you so eloquently put it, is because, as you know, she hated me spending one minute out with the guys—that would mean you."

They clinked bottles and talked about the usual things, which was good with him. But if he was dead honest with himself, he felt restless. He was missing Nilla—the nightly conversations, the sense of connection. And he was pissed at Raine. It messed him up to both want and miss and be furious with the one person at the same time. He took another swig of beer, and listened to the voices that surrounded him, trying to enjoy himself.

The nice thing about talking with the guys was that they didn't complicate anything. The conversation rolled over weather, politics, sports, women and work. He finished his beer, and joined in for a bit, but his heart wasn't in it. Standing up, he said his goodbyes, and headed home.

However, he didn't really feel like going home. It was early, and he was too jumpy to be banging around the house alone. Driving into the parking lot near the office, he decided to catch up on a little work. Neal had closed the gap in the security program. The kid had done a good job. But that morning, there were problems again. Jack just couldn't figure it.

He could shut down the computer, and then, when he rebooted, the problem would just show back up again. There appeared to be a simple glitch in the programming, but it wouldn't patch. The bug just kept reappearing. He supposed it was nothing earth-shattering, but it was annoying, and it gave him something to focus on instead of thinking about Raine.

Hours later, his head was aching, and his stomach finally would not be ignored. He had missed lunch, not really wanting to admit that if he went to the second-floor kitchen or to the cafeteria, he might run into Raine. He wasn't hiding, not exactly. He was avoiding. It was a different thing entirely. He grabbed his coat and headed out.

It was late. The building felt hollow as he walked through it to the exit. On his way past the offices on the first floor, he heard a noise over past the desks, and stopped for a moment to listen again. Someone working late? He heard something hit the floor in a solid clunk and decided to take a look.

Rounding the corner of the main desk, he was surprised to find a couple in a passionate clinch, and his eyes narrowed as he thought he recognized the profile of one of his men. It *was*

Neal. Wrapped around, as far as he could tell, the woman who had been in Raine's office the day he had been in there. And here he thought Neal was all work and no play.

Trying to retrace his steps and make a quiet exit, he misjudged his step and stumbled over a trash bin, cursing. Too late to be inconspicuous. The two lovebirds heard the clatter and were now looking at him in surprise, while he set the bin upright and tried to look apologetic.

Neal turned red up to his ears, and his friend—Raine's friend—seemed a little less concerned as she grinned, then laughed, tugging down her lacy, skintight shirt. Her voice was full of mischief, and Jack couldn't resist smiling a little.

"Oops, caught in the act, Neal, and by your boss."

Neal did not look as amused, from what Jack could tell, and he tried to put him at ease as much as possible.

"Sorry to interrupt, folks. Just heard a noise and didn't suspect, ah…"

"Sorry, sir, um, Jack." Neal seemed to relax a little when he realized he wasn't going to get chewed out. "I just bumped into Gwen on my way out, and we got talking, and…"

Jack held a hand up. "No need to explain to me, Neal. It's after hours. But you might want to take the party elsewhere."

Gwen grinned and threw her arms around Neal, smiling at Jack. "Thanks."

"Yeah, sure. Neal, find me in the morning, that bug is popping up again."

Neal just nodded as Jack waved and walked away. It wasn't hard to see that the woman, Gwen, would be a handful. Very pretty, and probably more than a little wild—definitely not a woman he would have pegged as Neal's type. But what the heck did he know?

Jack sighed, feeling a little old as he walked out of the building. It had been a long time since he had felt as carefree and crazy as Neal and Gwen. It seemed that as you got older, there were always more complications, and romance meant something else entirely than it did before. It all became more serious, and so...*adult.*

As he emerged outside, the cold slapped him, and he breathed it in. He liked the cold; it freshened him. Shaking off his mood, he headed down the street to a local café where he knew he could find something decent for dinner. He felt like being around people, even though he suspected that that would not ease the blues that were settling around him.

7

RAINE GOT an early start, plunging through the bitter cold to get to the office so that she could take care of the problem with her accounting and not get too far behind in her work. Her car didn't have time to heat up, and she still had to walk from the parking lot. She shivered all the way in and wondered why she hadn't requested a transfer to the Miami office.

A few hours later, discouraged and frustrated beyond reason, she hung up the phone from the last call. The story was the same across the board. As far as the records said—their records, not hers—her credit and loan accounts, and her parking ticket, were all paid up, and she was not required to send any more payments. Something was wrong, but no one would believe her. In fact, it was quite clear they all thought she was nuts.

She took pride in keeping her finances together on her own, not overspending and sticking to a budget that she planned. She did not take or ask for one cent of her father's money, and she liked looking after her own affairs. He wasn't really her father anyway, he was just the man who had adopted her. They certainly didn't have anything even resembling a relationship you could call familial.

She heard Gwen's laughter echoing down the hall, and looked up to see her friend in the doorway, attached to a tall, thin, dark-haired and serious-looking young man who blushed

furiously though his smile as Gwen squeezed his butt, not realizing Raine was able to see them through her partially open
door. Raine cleared her throat, and Gwen turned her head,
laughing.

"Oh, Raine, I'd hoped you weren't too busy. I wanted you
to meet Neal!" She stepped into the office, dragging Neal behind her. "Neal, this is my good friend Raine Covington, and
Raine, this is Neal Scott. Neal works downstairs in the IT
department."

Neal smiled at Gwen, and held out his hand to Raine, closing cool, dry fingers over hers.

"Nice to meet you, Ms. Covington."

Raine smiled. "Hi, Neal. Nice to finally meet you."

Gwen looked up at Neal brightly. "Isn't he just adorable,
Raine?"

Raine smiled as she watched the color deepen in poor
Neal's cheeks. He obviously was not used to being publicly
adored. He'd better get used to it fast if he wanted to be
with Gwen. So, this was the man who could kiss for hours
on end? The contrast between him and Gwen was a stark
one, but the opposites-attracted rule held fast. She smiled
at him.

"So what do you do, Neal?"

He shifted a little, and disengaged himself from Gwen. "I
mostly do C-Sharp application development and Solaris network administration. You know, troubleshooting."

Raine nodded as if she had some idea what he was talking
about, though she hadn't a clue.

"Sounds interesting." She smiled pleasantly and turned
her attention to Gwen. "Um, Gwen, I wondered if you had a
minute sometime today?"

Gwen nodded. "Sure. Neal has to get back down to the Bat-cave anyway—isn't that a riot, they call it that? So maybe you are Bruce Wayne, eh?"

Neal blushed again and smiled at Gwen, looking just slightly relieved to make his exit. "Uh, okay. I do have to go. Mr. Harris—Jack—has something he needs me to look at."

Raine smiled and nodded, feeling a slight twinge at the mention of Jack. "It was nice to meet you, Neal."

He nodded and left, offering Gwen a fleeting smile. Raine watched him leave, and frowned.

"You could break that boy if you handle him too roughly, Gwen."

Gwen just giggled and sat back. "You'd think so, but there's a lot more there than meets the eye. When he takes off those glasses he is just so yum. And he is very gentle, and shy, and then bam! He's hotter than hot. I mean, he was all over me last night…"

Raine held up her hand. "TMI, Gwen—too much information, that's okay. I'll take your word for it."

Gwen smiled widely. "Ha, no such thing. But, what did you need me for?"

Raine smiled, taking a moment to consider the beautiful and energetic woman sitting on the other side of the desk, before gathering up some papers. Gwen was a bundle of unpredictability. She could probably crook her finger and have any guy she wanted, but she chose Neal. Raine hoped he knew how lucky he was.

"I was hoping I could get some help on editing a few of these freelance articles. I am so behind, and I've just spent hours on the phone trying to straighten out a financial mess that I can't figure out, and now I am even more behind."

Gwen nodded. "Sure, I can do some edits. No problem. What's the financial thing? Do you need to borrow some cash?"

Gwen was just too sweet. Just like that, without so much as a blink, she would help. That made Raine feel more wealthy than her father's millions ever had. She smiled warmly.

"No, just the opposite." She told Gwen about the refunds, and sighed. "I just hope I can get someone to listen and figure out the problem."

"Well, if you can't, bank the money and thank your gift horse."

"It's not that easy, Gwen. There must be a computer glitch somewhere, and when they find it, I could get, well, screwed. I want them to find it now."

Gwen nodded. "Well, at least they didn't mess up in the opposite way. They could be telling you that you owe them millions or something."

Raine smiled and shook her head; leave it to Gwen to always find the upside. She glanced at her computer as it made the little sound that alerted her she had new mail. Looking at the screen, she didn't recognize the e-mail address, and there was no subject line. Opening it, it only said:

You're so beautiful.

And that was that. No signature. Raine spoke almost to herself. "Nice message—too bad the person it was for didn't get it."

"What's that?"

Raine gestured to the computer screen. "Oh someone just sent a nice note telling someone she's beautiful, but it isn't signed and there isn't an e-mail address I recognize, so it must have gotten misdirected."

"Well, you *are* beautiful."

Raine smiled. "Thanks, but compliments won't get you out of work. You can take care of these, and send them along later?" She pushed the pile of edits across the desk. Gwen took them and sharply tapped them on the desktop.

"No problem, I have time today. See ya later."

BY SEVEN, Raine's concentration was fading, though she had gotten an immense amount of work done. Her new column was all but done and ready to submit for the first round of edits. The Internet-relationships column had been a difficult one to handle. There were lots of issues to be dealt with: safety, honesty, and what to do when you meet someone whom you've only known on the Internet.

She thought she had kept her objective viewpoint fairly tightly in line. She had created a neat sidebar containing safety tips for romance on the Net, and emphasized that while her brief experience had not worked out, the fact remained that lots of people were finding happiness through online relationships. Regardless of her own experience, it was her job to report the facts for her readers, although now she could supplement them with a healthy bit of informed opinion.

In the current day and age, the Net was just one more place to meet, no more no less. That's how she pitched it. It didn't matter if you met someone on the Net, or at, say, the park. The same relationship issues existed.

Part of the problem, she wrote, was that people developed unrealistic expectations when they met online. Unrealistic expectations were a problem in many kinds of relationships, but the online universe seemed to multiply them. Or maybe relationships in general just never lived up to what we wanted them to be.

She needed to wrap it up, but for the most part, the article was done. It made her feel as if she could lock one more door on that chapter of her life. The chapter where Jack had played a part. She checked her e-mail once more before getting ready to go, and when she did, she was shocked. She had several more messages just like the one she had received earlier. At least fifty of them!

She read through them quickly. There wasn't anything lewd or threatening in them, but Raine felt a tiny shiver run up her spine. It was definitely weird. Maybe one of those funky Internet viruses or something.

She was being paranoid, and decided she should probably just e-mail the person back and let them know. So, she hit the reply button, and typed out a neat and impersonal message informing the sender that they had mistakenly sent several personal e-mails to the wrong address, and that they should probably check their address book.

"There, that should do it." She shut down her computer and stared out the window. It was snowing again. She crossed her arms over herself and hugged. She hated the cold, even more so when she felt so alone. This time of year, the days were getting shorter, but the winter seemed so long. And the nights lasted forever.

She had considered asking Gwen over for supper, but when she had popped back in to say good-night, she was clearly looking forward to seeing Neal at the end of the day. Raine wished it would go well for her. Gwen was exuberant and open, and dated all the time, but Raine couldn't remember the last time she had seen someone as steadily as she was seeing Neal.

Maybe it was because they were together in the same office, so it was easier to make plans, harder to avoid each other.

She frowned. Not that Jack had any problems with avoidance. She had not seen him in over a week, since Sunday morning when he left her. She knew he must come in to work, and she caught herself looking for him when she left her office to get coffee, or go to the bathroom. He was never there.

She wondered how it was she could still feel the touch of his hands on her skin, and the heat of his breath mingled with hers. Unconsciously, she squeezed her legs together remembering the pleasure he brought her, and a swirl of heat settled in her core that made her forget the cold outside.

The office was silent, most everyone had left an hour or so ago. Suddenly she felt strange, vulnerable, being there all alone. She stood quickly, grabbed her jacket and briefcase, and headed out. She'd put in a long day and felt edgy and unreasonably agitated. She needed food, a couple glasses of wine and a long soak in a hot bath. Feeling good about that plan, she turned the corner to the exit, and saw him.

Jack.

He had just gone through the door a moment before her, and was walking across the street to the parking lot. She moved closer to the door, placing her hand on the glass, and watched him. He was a graceful man, slow-moving and sexy. Sexy as all hell. Her knees wobbled a bit as she pushed through the door, unable to keep her eyes off him.

Even at a distance, she could see his hair being whipped around by the wind, and she curled her hand into a fist, her nails biting into her palm, as she remembered how it had felt to sink her fingers into those silky, burnished-copper waves.

Then he stopped, and turned, and she felt the heat rush into her face. Suddenly the cold dropped away. She should have turned and left, but it was too late, he saw her, his gaze locking in on her like a hawk on its prey. All the need and unanswered questions tumbled between them, and then he turned away.   .

She heard the door slam, the engine start. He drove out of the lot and disappeared down the road. Shaken for reasons she couldn't even imagine, she crossed over to the lot as well, finding her own car. She got in, and sat, seriously rattled.

God help her, she wanted him.

THE WINE AND THE BATH had been a very good idea, in theory. Except that as she sank into the relaxing effects of the merlot and hot water, she also sank helplessly into fantasies of Jack that tortured her until she had relied on her own hands, all the while thinking of his mouth on her, to find some release from the tension that was addling her brain.

It hadn't worked, but instead had brought all the memories of their night back to her full force, and she had gone to bed thinking she could detect his scent on the sheets, even though they had been washed days before. After a night of tossing and turning, trying to block erotic images from her mind, when she awoke she was in no mood to think about romance.

But romance was exactly what was blooming all over her desk when she walked into her office. The bouquet of roses was so large that the spray of flowers practically obscured the top of her desk, their crimson petals eerily resembling blood on snow in the stark winter sunlight shining through the window. Raine stopped in her doorway for several minutes, staring at them until Gwen came up behind.

"Looks like you and Jack made up—or at least he wants

to! Good for you—oh, aren't they *amazing*—they must have cost a fortune!" She wiggled past Raine, who was still caught in the doorway staring. Gwen fussed over the roses and inhaled deeply.

"Ohhhh. My allergies are going to act up for the rest of the day, but it's worth it, they smell as good as they look. You know, that's how you can tell the quality of flowers, especially roses, they smell so *wonderful*—some of the inexpensive ones, like the ones you see at the grocery store, they don't smell at all, or they have some weird kind of chemical smell, probably from the preservatives, I mean, who knows where they came from, but these are certainly not like that. These are amazing!" She turned to Raine, eyes sparkling, out of breath. "Have you looked at the card yet?"

Raine stepped forward, amazed that Gwen could make it through that entire speech on one breath. She set her coat down on the chair and took the little white card out of the holder. Opening it slowly, she inhaled sharply as she read the simple, male script.

"You're so beautiful." She whispered the words written on the card. There was no other signature, no hint as to the sender, and her heart pounded as she looked at the flowers again, frozen.

Gwen wrinkled her forehead, and took the card, shrugging as she looked at it. "That's kinda weird. Same as that e-mail you got yesterday, huh?"

Raine nodded. It was hard to believe that these were sent to the wrong person—her name was clearly written on the card's envelope. She looked at Gwen. "I have no idea why anyone would be sending me these."

"Well, looks like maybe someone is trying to get on your good side. Maybe it *is* Jack, and he's just trying to soften you up a little before he talks to you in person. I suppose it could be Jerry. Have you been seeing anyone else?"

Raine shook her head. "No, not in months, not really—just that one date with Jerry, and I haven't heard from him since. Nothing so serious that they would be sending me *these*." She thought of Duane, and closed her eyes. He wouldn't. Would he?

"Except for Jack."

Raine nodded. She hadn't told Gwen about Duane, and didn't intend to. But this was not Jack's style. Intuitively, she knew he would not try to get around her this way. But if not him, who? She had seen Duane daily since their talk in the park, and after he apologized profusely one more time, it was back to business as usual.

She and Jack *had* seen each other last night—he had been too far away for her to make out his expression. Maybe he was trying to reconnect with her. Then why had he driven away? She shook her head and paced the office, no, that didn't make sense. She didn't know him very well, but she sensed that he would be more direct.

But no one else had any reason to send her flowers. There simply was no one else. She looked at Gwen.

"Well, I guess there is only one way to know for sure."

Gwen's eyes widened. "You're going down there? To see him?"

"Yes. I need to get this settled. This doesn't seem like Jack, but if it is, I want to know why. If not him, I want to know who."

Gwen nodded and smiled. "Well, you are going down to see him. Maybe that is the whole point. Very romantic."

Raine pursed her lips. "More like very creepy. I prefer to know who is sending me e-mails and flowers."

Gwen shook her head on her way to the door. "Raine, you

are the only woman I can think of who would think that getting a dozen of these long-stemmed beauties was at all creepy." She sighed dramatically. "Anyway, good luck! I want to know all about it later!"

Raine summoned up the calm she needed to go deal with Jack and this problem. If the person responsible for sending the e-mails and flowers was him, though her instincts told her it wasn't, she wasn't exactly sure how she felt about it.

Still, she needed to know, for her peace of mind, one way or the other. Raine crossed to her desk, looking up his extension, and dialed the numbers, her fingers tightening on the receiver as his phone rang.

"Jack Harris."

The sound of his voice on the phone threatened another avalanche of erotic memories of the last time she had spoken with him on the phone, and she squelched them ruthlessly, keeping her voice neutral.

"Hi, Jack. It's Raine, I'm in my office, upstairs, and need you to come up when you get a moment." Of course he knew where her office was! God, just hearing his voice had turned her into a babbling idiot.

"Are you having a computer problem again? If you can tell me what the trouble is, I can send someone up to fix it."

His voice was impersonal, as if he was talking to a stranger. She nearly hung up, there was no way Jack had sent these notes and flowers. But she had to make sure before checking out other possibilities.

"Um, no, I just need to ask you about something. It won't take long."

She heard him sigh, and he said he would be up in a few minutes. Foolishly, she nodded, and hated how breathless her voice sounded when she said goodbye. Trying to get a grip, she took a deep breath, and looked at the work stacked on her desk, trying for normalcy while she waited.

JACK HEADED UP the stairs, hating the feeling that he was being "summoned." He had been avoiding her for days, and now was going to have to be in close quarters with her in the office; he would just settle whatever problem she had, and get out as quickly as possible.

Last night, seeing her standing there like a statue in the doorway, he had almost let go of his pride and gone to her. He found himself hungry to have her in his arms again in a way he had never experienced before, not with any other woman. He wanted to crush her to him, and make her want him, regardless of their differences. At this point he wasn't sure he cared about her past or her attitude or what she thought about him; he wanted her body naked and hot underneath his.

He wanted to make her beg for him and for what he could do to her. He had replayed making her come over and over in his mind, and wanted to do it again. He sighed in disgust at the direction of his thoughts. It had been like this ever since he left her, and he didn't like it. Most times he got past bad experiences with women easily.

Opening the door to the main floor, he walked down the hall to her office, his stride more controlled than usual. Rapping a knuckle on her door, he pushed it open a bit, and felt his mouth go dry.

How was a mortal man supposed to deal with this? She was so damn hot, her blond hair spilling over the shoulders of a royal-blue sweater that hugged her breasts in a way that made him ache. She looked a little pale, and there were smudgy shadows under her eyes, which, perversely, only made him want to touch her more. She brought out his protective instincts; he wanted to comfort her. Maybe because doing so brought comfort to him, as well, among other things. Stuffing his hands in his pockets, he spoke first.

"Okay, I'm here. What's the problem?" His voice was gruff and unfriendly, he knew. Good.

She shifted in her seat a little, and motioned him to a chair, which he rejected. "I only have a minute."

She nodded vaguely. "Um, okay. Well, I feel foolish even asking this, but I needed to make sure. Are these from you?"

He stared at her blankly and she pointed to the flowers; he saw them and his eyebrows lifted. Then he felt something twist in his gut—someone had sent her these? Although he had no right to feel one way or the other about the situation, it angered him.

"You think I sent these to you?"

She felt a slight color tinge her cheeks. Was she destined to be humiliated by this man?

"Um, well, I figured it wasn't you, but there was no name on the card, and I couldn't think of anyone else…I haven't seen anyone for a long time. Except you."

He was at a momentary loss for words, and walked to the roses, which must have cost a mint. They would have put him back a good percentage of his paycheck if he had bought them. He looked at the card, and read it aloud, making her color even more deeply, hearing the words in his voice. He dropped the card carelessly back on the shelf.

"No, it wasn't me. Is that it? Is this all you needed me for?" He raised his eyebrows as she nodded. "Looks like you have a secret admirer, Raine. But it's not me." *How ironic,* he thought.

Her forehead wrinkled and she nodded again. "I didn't really think it was you, but the message on the card matched the one on the e-mail, so—"

"What e-mail?"

"I got a bunch of messages yesterday from the same person, and one of them had the same message as the card. Seeing as you and I met online, I thought, maybe…"

"But you know my e-mail address—we didn't use work addresses, but you would have known what was from me."

"Yes…I know. I didn't think it really was you who sent the notes, but, well, I don't know! This is all so confusing. The last few days all kinds of things have been going crazy. I didn't know what to think of it. I'm sorry I bothered you."

"Do you still have those e-mails?" She nodded, and he crossed to her desk. "May I see them?"

"Sure…they're all right here." She shifted in her chair, trying to ignore how close he was to her, leaning over her shoulder. She could feel the heat of his skin, and moistened her lips unconsciously, remembering his taste. Hoping her hands didn't tremble, she opened her inbox, the list of messages displayed. And one more. A new one.

She clicked on it, and caught her breath. This message did not seem harmless. It was not overtly threatening, but starkly sexual. The comments about admiring her beauty were still there, but this time the sender was describing, in great detail, what he would like to do with her—what he liked to do for himself while he watched her.

"Watching me?" Her voice had tightened to a harsh whisper, as fear made it hard to breathe. Jack was leaning over her, focused on the screen, his eyes intense.

"Let me sit." She did, rising to pace the office, rubbing her arms with her hands as he took her chair and tapped away madly at the keyboard. She stopped and stared at the roses, unable to tear her eyes away, and startled when Jack's curse cut across the room.

"Bastard! He's using a dummy e-mail account, but it's been bounced around so many locations it will take forever to dig through to the source, and even then, we might not be sure it's real."

He looked up to see Raine standing in the middle of the office, pale and shaken, and was consumed with anger for the jerk who was messing with her. He was still angry with her, but he didn't want to see her harassed and afraid. He tried to reassure her as best he could.

"I won't say you shouldn't worry about this, but chances are that this is just a lot of empty words. This could be international, or whoever is doing it could be far away from here. You are a published personality, after all—anyone could contact you and send things here."

Raine just nodded. He stood, and crossed to where she stood, trying to keep his tone and behavior professional and not take her in his arms, as every voice in his head was screaming at him to do.

"I'll grab those messages and work on trying to trace them downstairs. If I can track down the sender and find the source, we can have his accounts closed, and that should solve the problem." Raine nodded again. He moved to the door, thinking back for a moment, reconsidering. "Raine, what did you mean, things have been crazy all week?"

She took a steadying breath, and told him about the bills, the refunded checks, and felt a knot form in her gut as his eyes darkened, and he came back into the room.

"Sit down before you fall over. You need to calm down and think clearly here—make sure you have given me all the details. Are you sure you didn't make a mistake in your checkbook and double pay your accounts? It happens."

She looked at him, snapping out of her fugue for the first time since he had come into the office. "Of course I checked. I didn't double pay anything. There was just an accounting error, and I have to get someone to pay attention and fix it, but I don't see how—"

"Raine, you said it was credit cards, student loans, and what, a parking ticket?"

She nodded.

"How do you suppose the same error happened with all those different creditors? How could the same thing happen at the same time with all of them?"

Raine hadn't considered that—she had been so caught up in trying to straighten out the mess that that simple fact had not occurred to her. Now that he'd pointed it out, she felt so stupid. She looked at him. "What are you thinking, Jack?"

His mouth was set in a grim line. "It means someone probably messed with your accounts." His eyes flashed to the roses and back to her again. "I guess you do have a secret admirer. Someone who knows how to hack into banks, too, by the looks of it. I guess he thought that might have been a nice gesture. And those flowers. He's really trying to impress you, whoever he is."

A chill ran over her skin, and she wrapped her arms tightly around herself. "Someone is doing these things on purpose? Why? What do I do? How do we find him?"

"Well, we should tell the police, and since he has found you at the magazine, you should let Duane know."

She paled, and he gave in. Closing the distance between them, he pulled her a little roughly into his arms and held her close. She smelled so good, felt so right. He knew there were other things they should be doing right now, but the minute she relaxed into his arms, his body went on full-scale alert.

He released her gently, moving back just a bit before she could detect the evidence of his arousal. *Focus, Jack, focus.* But she looked up at him with those passionate green eyes, and he was lost. She wanted him, too, he could see it. She trembled under his hands, and he lowered his mouth to hers, kissing her hungrily. There was no gentleness in it. He wrapped her tightly against him again, releasing all of the pent-up desire he had been holding back.

Then, in a flash of sanity, he pushed away from her, angry with himself that he would take advantage of her at such a time. She was afraid, confused, and he had pounced on her like a wild man. He walked to the other side of the office, his chest heaving as he fought for control. When he had his voice back, he spoke.

"I'm sorry, Raine. I know this isn't exactly the time."

"Let's not talk about it, okay?" Her voice was not much more than a whisper, and he felt even worse.

It wasn't okay, but he nodded. "I'll tell you now, the police probably aren't going to do much about it—this is small stuff to them, and the New England chapter of the hi-tech crime investigation unit is in Boston. They might be interested because he got into your bank accounts. Has anything happened at your home? Any phone calls or strange people hanging around?"

A chill settled at the base of his spine; he knew she could be in real danger.

Raine shook her head. "No. Not since the bills. And he didn't send them, technically."

"So, we'll tell Duane first, and get his take, then let the authorities know."

"We?"

Jack nodded, feeling a little something inside twist as she looked up at him, a slight edge of fear, and then—something else—gratitude?—shining in her eyes. "Yeah, since I'm the security administrator, he'll want my take on the situation."

She nodded, and the light dimmed a little. "Okay."

THE CONVERSATION WITH Duane was tense, and by the end of it, she had a raging headache. He ordered Jack to make sure all the magazine's systems were secure, and while he was concerned about Raine, he was obviously more concerned about a security breach bringing down the magazine's computers. It appeared he was over his little crush.

Raine took the thought back as soon as she thought it— Duane was just doing his job. By protecting the magazine's computers, he was protecting her, too. And it wasn't as though he wasn't concerned about her, there just wasn't much he could do.

They called the police from his office, on conference call, and the detective responded just as Jack said the police would—unless things got more serious, their hands were tied. She could go down to the station and file a report to formally document the incident, just for the sake of having it on record. They could send it on to Boston. She didn't even know whom she was complaining about—she had an e-mail address and that was about it.

Jack insisted on driving her to the police station, though

she didn't know why. He just seemed unwilling to leave her alone, which she thought was odd. He was brusque and businesslike, but she admitted to herself that his presence did help. She didn't allow herself to think about the kiss in the office, and what it could have meant. But for one lovely moment she hadn't been cold and afraid.

8

JACK RETURNED to Raine's office after clearing up some matters before they could leave for the police station, and stood in the door for a second watching her, fighting off the coil of protective feelings that he'd been struggling with all morning. She was sitting at her desk, her head in her hands. She didn't move, she didn't even look as if she was breathing. Her skin was porcelain, and he remembered its taste. He shook himself and tapped on the open door. She didn't jump, but just looked at him, expressionless.

"Okay, I'm ready." Her voice was quiet, smooth and calm. He wanted to hold her. But he didn't.

"Let's get some food first, you look like you could use something."

"I'm fine, I just want to get this over with."

"You're white as a sheet, and you need to eat. We'll just stop for something quick." His tone of voice told her he had already decided for them both. She grabbed her coat and realized she wasn't going to win this one, and besides, she was a little hungry.

When she picked up the flowers as she left the office, she got a curious look from him.

"I don't want them," she said, "so we can stop by the hospital on the way and leave them at the desk. They can keep them or give them to someone who will enjoy them."

That annoying feeling itched at him again, the one that made him think maybe he was wrong about her. Or maybe it was a convenient rationalization so that he could be more comfortable with the fact that he wanted her in his bed. Again. Soon. But it still stung how she had turned on him the last time. No guy in his right mind set himself up for something like that twice.

As they drove off, her scent and the fragrance from the roses combined in the most erotic way possible, and he felt himself harden unexpectedly. Shifting in his seat, he adjusted his coat so that she wouldn't notice. She wasn't saying anything, and he felt the need to break the silence.

"Do you like Italian? There is a good little café-deli place down the block."

"Anything is fine."

More silence. He shifted in his seat again, staving off the image of her sprawled naked on a bed covered with rose petals. Hell, forget the rose petals.

"Are you okay?"

The rough concern in his voice made her look at him, and she was able, for the first time, to really appreciate what a gorgeous man he truly was. His profile was sharp, straight nose, full lips. Those intense eyes that seemed to pierce through everything were focused intently ahead on the road. For a moment, she forgot he had just spoken to her.

"Yes, I'm just a little…freaked out, I guess. I've never had anything like this happen."

They pulled up next to the deli and parked. As they entered, Raine felt a shock of pleasure at the flood of warm colors and the spicy smells that had her lifting her hand to her stomach.

"Oh, I am hungry."

"Let's order and sit then. They are pretty quick here. Great soups."

After ordering sandwiches and soup at the counter, they found a small booth in the back, and waited for their food with steaming cups of coffee. She wanted to talk about anything but work, so she tried her hand at small talk.

"Have you always lived in Salem?"

He shook his head. "No, I grew up in Connecticut."

"Huh. Me, too. Where?"

He wanted to avoid this question for now—it would just open a can of worms when things were wormy enough. Instead, he sort of slid around it a little.

"My family owns an inn there. It was just my mom and dad and me."

"No brothers or sisters?"

"Nope. They wanted to have more kids, but I think there were some problems, and they couldn't. Didn't matter, I never felt alone, I had people around me all the time, the guests at the inn, some of the part-time staff."

"Didn't you hate not having a regular home?"

He blinked, as if surprised by her question.

"I never really thought about it as not being a regular home. It was where I lived, it was comfortable, homey. My mom cooked all the food for guests, and there were never more than six or eight at a time. They seemed more like relatives, several people we came to know very well, since they came back each year. There was always work to do, but it was fun."

"Where are your parents now?"

"Still there. I go home for holidays, talk to them all the time. I miss them, even though they are not too far away. They close the inn for half the year now and travel themselves. They're good people."

Stirring her coffee, she smiled slightly. "That sounds wonderful."

"It is." He phrased his next inquiry carefully. "Raine, speaking of families, do you think that this harassment could have something to do with your family?"

She glanced up sharply. "What do you mean?"

"Well, children of wealthy families are often targets for crimes like extortion and kidnapping."

A chill set over the table.

"How would you know about my family's money?"

Jack silently cursed his slip. He should come clean about knowing her when they were younger, but he couldn't. Not yet.

"Someone at the magazine mentioned it. Your father is pretty well known around New England. Lance Covington Industries seems to own half of Massachusetts and New Hampshire."

She pushed her coffee to the side, and met his eyes squarely. "I am more or less estranged from my family—if you can call it that. It's really only my father, and I haven't seen him for years, since I left for college. I have never really thought of myself as attracting any negative attention because he's wealthy. Most people probably don't even know I exist."

Jack watched her, saying nothing, and thought about that interesting little detail—she had said that her father was wealthy, but had not included herself in that definition. Yet surely she was heiress to her father's fortune? She was the only child, after all. She must have money of her own, a trust fund, or something of that sort. He pushed a little more.

"I'm sure your father would want to know if you were being threatened. He might want to set up some security for you."

At this she laughed out loud, though not happily. It was the first time he had ever seen any kind of hardness about her, though it changed quickly to a deep sense of sadness he could see reflected in her eyes and the tightness around her mouth.

"Hardly. If I was kidnapped, I am not sure he would see it as a smart investment to pay the ransom."

Their food came, and as he dived into his, he watched her play with hers. He wanted to draw her out, to find out more.

"Did you have a falling-out?"

She bit her sandwich, and chewed slowly, waiting to answer, unsure about opening up to him but feeling irrationally compelled to do so. Somehow, she wanted him to know something about her, about who she was. Not Nilla, not the Raine he knew at work, but just her. Her voice was not much more than an edgy whisper.

"No, never that. Nothing as emotional as that. Though he was disappointed that I didn't want to make more out of myself. We didn't argue about it because he wasn't paying for my education. I was on scholarship. So I did what I wanted. He didn't see journalism and sociology as leading to much of anything. He would probably have approved if I owned the magazine rather than just writing for it."

She sipped her soup. It was delicious, but her appetite had gone.

"I don't want to give the wrong impression," she said. "He's not a tyrant or anything. He never hurt me or left me wanting for anything. He made sure I had all the things I needed, clothes, food, education."

"Love?" It escaped his lips before he could stop himself, and he regretted it as soon as the word passed between them. She looked away, staring at her food.

"No. But a home. People to take care of me. A place to be, the things I needed. More than a lot of people have."

"Children need more than things, Raine." He thought of his own home and parents, the happiness they had together and had shared with him. They weren't wealthy, but they had had what they needed materially, and more. He'd never been unhappy, or lonely, even though he had no brothers or sisters. The inn was busy most of the year, and there were always people around, but his mother and father always made him feel loved and valued. He couldn't imagine what she must have grown up with. How could a child deal with that kind of coldness? He quieted his own thoughts, and focused on what she was saying to him.

"Well, it doesn't always work out perfectly for everyone. But I shouldn't complain. He was good to me, in his way. Better than he had to be.

She continued in a matter-of-fact voice, "I mean, after all, I was adopted. So it's not like I am his blood. I never got the whole story, he didn't like to talk about it. But the staff talked, and every now and then I would pick up bits of information. Enough to know my situation. Apparently he and my mother couldn't have children, and she insisted on having a family and they ended up adopting me."

He nodded, sipping his soup, and let his silence encourage her to continue, at the same time he was kicking himself. He had terribly misjudged her.

"She left when I was about two. I don't remember anything specific. He never said anything about her, why she did what she did. There were no pictures around."

Jack was quiet, unsure of what to say. He was very uneasy about how he had treated her in the past. He realized he didn't know her at all. But he wanted to.

Meeting her as Nilla had offered him some small glimmers into who Raine really was, and it had been enough to capture his interest, until his latent adolescent fantasies had gotten him off track. They were silent for several minutes, then Raine smiled, a little too brightly.

"So, that's me. The poor little rich girl."

"Don't." He reached out a hand to grasp hers, and was immediately shocked at the heat the simple touch produced, but he held on and kept his gaze on hers. "Don't make light of it. That was a horrible way to grow up."

She relaxed, and nodded at him. Pushing her food aside, she sounded resigned. "Yes. You're right. But don't feel sorry for me. I like my life."

Her voice was stronger now, and she sighed. "Anyway, I wouldn't ask my father for money for protection or for anything else. I make a nice living at the magazine, but not enough to afford something like personal security. I'll just have to deal with the situation the way most people would, through the police, or on my own."

Jack squeezed her hand again.

"Thanks for telling me, Raine."

She just shrugged. After a moment, they stood and gathered their plates, setting them back on the counter, and headed back out into the cold. To the police station. Jack hoped that the stalking situation wouldn't get worse; she had been through enough already. But whatever happened, he planned on being there.

DURING THE AFTERNOON, Jack got to know a very different side of Raine. At the hospital, she dropped off the roses and suggested that the nurses save a few for themselves at the nurses' station, and split up the bouquet to bring a rose to patients who needed the lift. She had taken an ugly gesture and had turned it into a giving one. To say he was impressed seemed shallow; he was deeply moved.

On the way up the stairs of the police station, he found himself reaching to clasp her hand, enjoying the way it felt small but strong in his, and noted that she didn't pull away. Anyone looking at them would have thought they had been together for years.

He glanced at her as they walked down the hallway, and she looked like a woman with a purpose, her stride strong, her eyes direct. She didn't look frightened, and he added admiration to the list of new feelings he seemed to be quickly accumulating for this woman. At the main desk they asked for the detective they'd talked to on the phone, then took a seat, waiting for him to come down.

Raine looked around, feeling very much out of her element, but intrigued all the same. She had never been in a police station before. It looked pretty much like any office building, but had a different sense about it. There was something in the air; the weighty presence of authority, the stale smell of coffee, and a weird sort of tension.

Normally at this time of day she would be working on an article, wrapping up a meeting or tracking down research. But her life continued to veer far away from normal. She felt a draft of cold air wash by her, and watched two policewomen walk through the doors she and Jack had just entered.

They were average-looking women, but they had an aura of power around them. One was slight, with brown hair and ebony skin, and the other thin and muscular, with long, auburn hair pulled back tightly under a cop's hat. The auburn-haired one glanced at Jack as they passed by, and Raine detected her glint of appreciation before they continued on and disappeared down the other end of the hallway on the other side of the desk.

The smaller woman had been wearing a wedding ring—married—would she have children? Raine made a mental note—this was her next article pitch. She wanted to know about these women, their personal and professional lives and relationships, how they made it all work. She wanted her readers to think about women who put themselves at risk daily to help others. Her mind turned to the nurses at the hospital—maybe she would broaden it out to writing about women in emergency services….

Her line of thought was cut short by a booming voice saying a hearty hello to yet another cop that was passing by, and she looked up to see a man walking toward them.

Raine felt a smile tilt up as he walked over and extended his hand. There was no way you could not smile at him. He was at least six feet tall, probably in his late forties, she thought absently. And he was like a huge…leprechaun. Not fat, but muscular and wide. His green eyes twinkled at hers, under a thick shock of hair that was a riotous mass of salt-and-pepper curls surrounding a full, friendly face. He was a handsome man and he sure filled up the room.

She eyed his gun and holster and felt as if she was in a movie. His huge hand wrapped around hers, squeezing in a friendly way; then he shook Jack's hand as well, a little more firmly.

"Hello, hello…just follow me right back here where we can talk. I'm Detective Delaney. I'm glad you found time to come down. Like I told you on the phone, there isn't much

The Harlequin Reader Service® — Here's how it works:

If offer card is missing write to: Harlequin Reader Service, 3010 Walden Ave., P.O. Box 1867, Buffalo NY 14240-1867

NO POSTAGE
NECESSARY
IF MAILED
IN THE
UNITED STATES

BUSINESS REPLY MAIL

FIRST-CLASS MAIL   PERMIT NO. 717-003   BUFFALO, NY

POSTAGE WILL BE PAID BY ADDRESSEE

HARLEQUIN READER SERVICE
3010 WALDEN AVE
PO BOX 1867
BUFFALO NY 14240-9952

Get FREE BOOKS and a FREE GIFT when you play the...

LAS VEGAS
GAME

Just scratch off the gold box with a coin. Then check below to see the gifts you get!

YES! I have scratched off the gold Box. Please send me my **2 FREE BOOKS** and **gift for which I qualify.** I understand that I am under no obligation to purchase any books as explained on the back of this card.

350 HDL DZ94   150 HDL D2AK

FIRST NAME	LAST NAME

ADDRESS

APT.#	CITY

STATE/PROV.	ZIP/POSTAL CODE

(H-B-07/04)

7	7	7	Worth TWO FREE BOOKS plus a BONUS Mystery Gift!
🍒	🍒	🍒	Worth TWO FREE BOOKS!
🔔	🔔	♣	TRY AGAIN!

www.eHarlequin.com

Offer limited to one per household and not valid to current Harlequin® Blaze™ subscribers. All orders subject to approval.

we can do except take a statement, but if things heat up, that could come in handy down the line. It's wise to have everything documented."

The thought brought her back to the moment, and she felt the weight of why they were there return. Following the detective down the hallway and into a small office, Raine sat in the one chair he pulled out from under a pile of papers and boxes, while Jack stood beside her.

Jack met the detective's eyes briefly. He knew he was being sized up. Crazy boyfriend? Jack knew his posture clearly declared: "Mine." Detective Delaney nodded, more to himself than to Jack, smiled and turned to Raine, his voice professional and friendly.

"So, Ms. Covington, it appears you have a bit of a situation at work?"

She nodded and reached into her briefcase, pulling out a sheaf of papers, and handed them to the detective. "These are all the e-mails—the last one is the worst—and the card from the flowers."

He took them, and looked them over, not showing any reaction until he read the most recent e-mail, his mouth turning down disapprovingly.

"And you said you suspect the person who sent you these has also intruded into your bank accounts?"

Raine explained about the returned checks, again. She was tiring of the story, but went over it detail by detail, and had written down the dates, and creditors, handing him that piece of paper too. He sighed and looked at Jack.

"Do you have any proof these things are related, the flowers, and the bank accounts—any sort of computer evidence you could find?"

Jack shook his head. "Nothing from the e-mails—it's a dummy account, impossible to trace back to the original source. But it's the same guy."

Delaney sighed and nodded. "Well, that would seem logical, though we need proof for us to take any action. We'll get your statement down formally, have you sign it, and keep the papers you gave us here. Then it will just be a matter of wait and see."

Raine sat forward, placing her hands on the edge of the desk. "What can I do? I need to do something. I can't just sit around waiting to see what happens next."

Delaney sat back and gave her a serious look. "Well, waiting isn't really a choice—the ball's in his court. But you might consider living somewhere else for a while, changing your e-mail accounts, notifying your creditors and banks. Basically, you have to make it difficult for him to get at you, if he tries again."

Jack knew that made sense, but he couldn't stand watching how pale she got as the detective spoke. "Why don't you just do your best to scare the life out of her, Detective?"

The cop's eyes narrowed, and he nodded.

"Sometimes these folks get bored and move on, sometimes not. Fear can be your best friend now—makes you pay attention to things. Warn your workplace to be very cautious about deliveries of any sort. Don't work alone late at night, walk to your car with someone, check it before you get in. It pays to be careful."

At their silence, he continued. "So, let's put this down in a formal statement, and then you can get out of here and go enjoy the rest of your day, or what's left of it."

Raine answered his questions, and it didn't take too long

to finish the report. They needed copies of all her bills, and then she just had to wait. Relief flooded over her when it was done. They all shook hands again, and parted ways.

It was dark outside now, and a burst of frigid wind met them when they opened the door. She disengaged her arm from Jack's hand, not liking how he was pushing her along. He let his hand fall without comment, but slowed his stride slightly.

His jaw was set, and she had no idea why he was in a mood. Maybe he was just tired of dealing with her problems. She didn't blame him, she was sick of it, too. But a little thread of hurt wrapped itself around her heart at his sudden coolness, though she tried to school her face and voice not to show it.

"If you want to take me back to the office, there is some work I have to do. Nothing got done today, obviously."

"Fine."

In the car, he didn't say a word. He was afraid for her and the only way he knew how to handle it was to get angry as hell. He knew he shouldn't be taking this out on her, and tried to get a grip. He took a deep breath, willing his mind to calm.

"I have some things I want to check," he said. "I can bring my laptop up and work from your office."

"That's not necessary."

"It is—don't argue. As the good detective pointed out, you shouldn't work alone at night. So you're not going to."

Raine raised her eyebrows at the peremptory tone of his voice, and while she knew he was right, she didn't like anyone bossing her around. She was tired, and just wanted to get to the end of this very long day. She didn't have the energy to put up with Jack's domineering attitude tonight. Her voice was clipped.

"Listen, I appreciate you going through all this with me, and I know it has cut into your day as well. I can wait to catch up on work tomorrow, so you can just drop me at my car and we can both get home early tonight."

He pulled to the side of the street, and put the car in park, gripping the wheel tightly, trying not to be so incredibly pissed at the woman sitting beside him. That queen-bee attitude just pushed him over the edge he was trying to hang on to.

When he looked at her, she drew back, shocked by the sharpness of his eyes.

"No—*you* listen." He leaned in. "I don't like someone breaking into my networks, I don't like them harassing you or anyone else, I don't like that the cops can't do crap about it, I don't like the way that cop looked at you, and I don't like that prissy little tone you always use when you think you are calling all the shots."

Unsure of how to respond to his litany of complaints, she tried to control the fact that she felt a little breathless, and went for the easy one.

"I do not have a prissy tone."

He narrowed his eyes. "Oh yes, you do, princess. And you use it whenever someone steps on your pretty little toes, or gets closer than you want them to. Like now. Like the morning we woke up together. Remember that, Raine? Remember how we made love, how hot it was? Do you remember how I felt inside you, how I made you come?" He gripped the steering wheel a little harder. "God knows I think about it every day. Every night."

He watched her lips part as she caught a breath and simply stared at him. He liked reminding her of what they had shared, didn't want it leaving her thoughts any more than it had left his. She wasn't so cool and prissy now, he thought.

He turned and reached out, cupped her cheek in his palm, rubbing his thumb over her silky skin. She flushed and went hot under his hands. He saw the flash of desire in her eyes, and knew that she remembered every detail, just as he did. He smiled, satisfied, and gentled his tone.

"We'll go back and work together for a while, okay? I want to help, Raine. Let me."

She nodded, and turned her face into his palm, rubbing her mouth against his skin. When he drew his hand away, she could see that it wasn't steady, and she smiled.

9

SPICY SCENTS OF GARLIC and ginger filled the office, and little white Chinese food containers were scattered everywhere. Raine had not had Chinese food in a very long time; they'd practically bought half the take-out menu, and had been quietly working and eating for the last several hours. Stopping her research for a moment, she picked up a container and scraped out the last of the lo mein noodles at the bottom, feeling sated and relaxed for the first time in over twelve hours.

It was almost nine-thirty at night. Time to leave, she supposed. She watched Jack, lost in deep concentration as he tapped away on the keyboard of his laptop, occasionally grunting or cursing to himself. She hated to interrupt him, to break the easiness they had fallen into. She enjoyed the happy hum of work that had settled over the office.

She never really worked with anyone around and had thought she would find it distracting, but they were enveloped in a companionable silence that was not the least inhibiting. In fact, there was something about working together that helped her get into a better groove. She wondered if it would be that way with anyone, or if it was just that way with Jack.

Jack heard Raine shove away from the desk, and out of the corner of his eye could see her beginning to pack up. He had mostly been puttering, contacting some friends about his quandaries about the network break-in and cleaning up some bugs in a program he was testing. After checking over the entire network, he couldn't find anything wrong—not even the little oddity he had been struggling with before.

"Here, let me help with that." He got up and helped her fit all the small containers into one larger bag for disposal. Raising an eyebrow, he surveyed the desktop. "Wow. We actually ate all that? No leftovers. Damn."

"Why? Are you still hungry?"

"God no, I just like Chinese leftovers—good snack at three in the morning."

"Or for breakfast."

He nodded, grinning at her. "Oh well, maybe next time."

Raine felt a little squeeze in her chest—did he mean next time *they* ordered Chinese? Next time *he* ordered Chinese? Or next time they had midnight snacks or breakfast together? Although technically they had never had snacks or breakfast. She took a breath and stopped the whirl of overthinking—bad habit, analyzing everything. It had probably just been a meaningless comment. She was a little overwrought.

Out in the parking lot, Jack chucked the garbage into a Dumpster and then walked to his car, reaching in to start it, before closing the door and turning back to her, snowbrush in hand. A light layer of snow had fallen, and everything around them sparkled.

"I'll follow you."

"Hmm?" She had been too busy watching his lazy, sexy walk to pay attention to what he was saying.

"Home. I'll follow you home. We can check your place, make sure everything is okay, and then I'll head home."

Raine started to protest, then realized she wasn't really

completely comfortable going back to her dark house alone, and felt relieved he'd offered. She took a deep breath, hating the situation. She had never been afraid to go home. Her little house was her sanctuary, and now she had to be paranoid about walking in the door. Hopefully, it would be over soon.

"Okay. So you remember where it is, in case we get separated?"

"Yes. But we won't."

She looked at him from underneath soft lashes, her eyes a mix of emotions. "Thanks, Jack—you are being way beyond nice to me. But I am thankful. It would be hard to go back there alone at this time of night."

Jack nodded, considering.

"Maybe you should take Delaney's advice and move out for a while."

She shook her head definitively. "No, it may be a little creepy to think I have to watch my every step for a while, or be careful about things I take for granted, but I am not being driven out of my house by some lunatic who may or may not even be around here."

She wrapped her arms around herself, looking around them into the cold, stark night. "Besides, where would I go?"

"You are friends with Gwen, right? Good enough friends to stay with her?"

"Oh yes—Gwen is one in a million. She would probably sleep on the floor and give me the bed. But she has a small apartment, just one bedroom. And she is, you know, involved right now."

"Yeah, I saw that, with Neal Scott." He smiled at her surprise that he knew. "I caught them in a, um, clinch in the office a few nights ago."

Raine smiled. "Yeah, Gwen is crazy about him. Though I never would have thought of them as each other's type. Considering the circumstances, my staying there would be a painful inconvenience for her, and I don't think the situation really merits it."

His eyes turned very serious. "Raine, until we know exactly what the situation is, you should just be extremely careful. I'm sure if Gwen and Neal want to fool around, they can go to his place. They didn't seem to care about using the office floor the other night." He smiled, but saw she wasn't going to bite.

Her voice brooked no argument. "No, I want to be home. In my home. I am not going to let this situation get to me any more than I already have. It's already disrupted my work life, and I am not going to let it make a shambles of my home life."

Jack grimaced, but understood and admired her resolve. Still, he wished she wouldn't be quite so independent at the moment.

"Then I guess you will have to get used to me dogging you home every night. And if I can't, I'll make sure someone can."

Raine observed the stubborn set of his chin, the glint in his eyes that was just short of begging her to argue with him, but she decided to take a different route this time.

"Okay. I think I can handle that—if you will let me make dinner for you one night when you—how did you put it?— dog me home." She grinned, feeling absurdly happy, given the discussion and the situation.

Jack felt everything inside him melt as she looked up at him with a smile that he couldn't have imagined in his dreams— she was like pure sunshine, and, for that moment, standing here in the bitter cold, he was warmed.

As she looked up at him, her features softened and her eyes

became pools of clear green. He didn't know if she leaned into him, or if he pulled her close, he only knew he couldn't wait another minute for her. He leaned forward, offering a soft kiss, licking the spicy taste of dinner from her lips. Then he covered her lips more fully with his, gently at first, but when she sighed into his mouth, he plunged as deeply as he could. He'd forgotten how passionate she was—no, not forgotten, heaven knew—but his memory had not quite served the reality justice.

When she dragged the tip of her tongue along his lower lip, he pressed her closer, and she felt him, hard and ready, rubbing against her hip. Her body responded, and she felt her lower abdomen tighten and ache. They stood in a fog of heat and car exhaust that was piping out into the cold air, oblivious to everything but each other.

She buried her hands in his hair, forgetting reasons and reasonableness, wanting only to lose herself in him. The man had a mouth like none she had ever known, and he knew how to use it. She felt her knees quiver when he nipped her lightly.

He burrowed into her neck, biting a tender spot, then moving on to another. Raine swallowed, her breathing ragged. She knew she wanted him, but she didn't know what else she wanted from him.

She wanted to be safe—and right now, Jack was safe. She wasn't sure how much of one was combined with the other. He had been so good to her all day, so helpful, and she was, when she thought about it too much, frightened. It was easy to misunderstand one need for another under these circumstances.

"Jack, we shouldn't—"

He inhaled the scent of her hair and perfume and knew he wasn't backing off—not this time. He wanted her in his bed, and maybe in his life. The unbidden thought shook him, but he pushed it aside. For now, bed would suffice—or the back seat of his car, as luck would have it.

"Raine, just be quiet."

He didn't wait for a response but kissed her again and wound her arms tightly around his neck as he reached to the side and opened up the back door. To be honest, he felt a little thrill but also a little apprehension—it had been many, many years since he had had a woman in the back seat of his car. He hoped he was up to the challenge.

He disengaged from her slightly, and met her bemused stare as he began to unbutton her coat. Her eyes widened. He finished unbuttoning the coat, unwound her scarf and pushed them both from her shoulders.

"Get in before you get cold."

Shivering once, she slid into the car, but eyed him warily. "Jack, seriously…"

His own coat was off and thrown down on the seat, and he was glad to find the car toasty warm. They were alone in the parking lot, and the windows were nicely fogged. Perfect.

"No, Raine…absolutely no seriousness. Let loose a little—remember online you told me you have never had sex in the back seat of a car before, and wondered what it would be like? Let me show you."

"But…"

He somehow slid his hands under her butt and pulled her up next to him, then shifted and settled her over his lap, where she could feel the hard ridge of his cock pressing against some very sensitive places. She wriggled a little to get comfortable, and he moaned and lifted his hips up.

His kiss was so hot she started to break into a slight sweat.

He murmured against her lips, words no one had ever said to her before. Things he had only written on the screen of a computer were now coming to passionate life.

"I'm so ready for you, Raine. I've missed this so much… how hot you are…"

She replied with a vague sort of "me, too," but he didn't seem to care much what was coming out of her mouth, he was too busy doing other things.

Her head swam, and she lost track of exactly what it was she was going to say. As she tried to remember, his hand was slithering up inside her sweater, and closed over the warm skin of her breast, kneading and pinching until she couldn't think at all.

Sighing in pleasure, she gave in and slid her hands up inside his sweater as well, hungry fingers remembering the shape of his body. She put her hand over his heart, and felt it pumping madly.

"That's better, baby—just let go."

His voice was rough with need, and she joined him in frantic touching, kissing and biting. They laughed as they fumbled in the confined space, pushing her skirt up, his jeans lower, until his hot, velvet shaft sprung free and jutted against her.

He closed his mouth tightly over her nipple, drawing hard as he worked one hand between them, rubbing and stroking her sex quickly with his able fingers, applying just the right pressure, knowing just where her most sensitive spots were, hardly letting her take a breath as she rocked into his touch and she shuddered against him with one of the fastest, sweetest orgasms she had ever known. He continued to stroke, his hand hot and wet next to her skin, probing and stretching her tender nether lips.

She felt his hand move away, and looked down to see him closing it over his huge erection, rubbing her glistening juices over himself. She felt her insides liquefy as he touched himself, and she licked her lips, meeting his hungry, dark eyes with hers.

"Raine, I need you, I can't wait..."

She didn't want to wait, either, but couldn't form the words. Straddling him, she moved up close, steadying her hands on the back seat, and took him inside in one smooth move. He groaned, lifting up underneath her sharply until he was buried to the hilt, and she dug her fingers into the material of the back seat as her body found a seductive rhythm of its own. His hands gripped her ass firmly, squeezing and guiding her as she rode him hard and fast.

His head was thrown back on the seat as he gave himself over to her, and she felt a swift rush of power she had not experienced before. She was still sensitive and shivering from her own climax as he slid in and out. She wanted to give him as much as he had given her, and focused on how she could make this as good for him as he had made it for her. He was panting, his head was thrown to the side, and she smiled, loving how it felt to have this hot, needy man underneath her.

She ran her hands over him lightly, teasing, and took his mouth in a wide-open, wet kiss as she thrust against him, taking him whole each time, squeezing tight. Suddenly he cried out her name and his entire body stiffened underneath her. She didn't let up, but adjusted to his body's movements, sliding her body along his as he trembled with release. He stroked her back, emptying himself utterly, until he simply sighed and let his head fall forward, his face buried in the hollow of her neck.

His voice was muffled when he spoke.

"Okay, you killed me. Call nine one one."

She smiled again and kissed his temple, and he lifted his face to see her looking at him with satisfied, happy eyes. It was a look he could get used to. He felt himself go flaccid, leaving the warmth of her body, and hugged her close.

"They would have to bring two stretchers. One for each of us. I'm not sure I can move—they could find us here in the morning."

He smiled and laughed lightly, not wanting to let the moment pass, not knowing what to expect when it did. Would she just dismiss him, the way she did before? Would he be even more addicted to her now, had he gotten himself in too deep? As if he had a choice. She was all he could think about—all he had been able to think about for months. She was everything he wanted—fantasy and reality all rolled up into one. Now all he had to do was convince her of that. His heart sank a little, as she was the one to disengage first, her voice light.

"I guess I'll have a hard time explaining this skirt to the dry cleaners."

She was tugging her clothes back into place, smoothing her hair, making a light joke. He did the same, pulling up his jeans, searching the front seat for his jacket. She smiled at him, looking shy. He touched her face, and kissed her, not saying anything. Maybe things were best left unsaid for the moment. This was better, he knew, than last time, when she had kicked him out—but still, it was less than he wanted—not that he could define what that was.

"You stay here, let me get your car warmed up, then I'll follow you home." It was on the edge of his tongue to ask if he could stay when they got there, but he bit down. Too much too soon, and he wasn't even sure how she was going to react to this once it set in.

Heading out into the cold, his body was still so hot from their lovemaking that he barely needed his coat. It was snowing harder now, and it took him a few minutes, but he found her car and started it. When he opened the driver's door, she was there, waiting.

"You're all set."

She nodded, and stepped forward, seeming awkward and unsure. He marveled—this woman who had just ridden him with such confidence and intention that he had almost spontaneously combusted underneath her was now uncertain about what to do next? He met her halfway, and slipped his arms around her, pulling her close, and sighed a deep breath of relief when hers went around him as well. They stood like that for a quiet moment, and then she pulled away gently, and gave him a warm look before getting into her car. He went to his, and followed her out of the lot.

Neither of them noticed that by the corner of the magazine's office building, a figure in a long dark coat stood watching, deftly sliding into the shadows as they drove by.

THE NEXT MORNING, any hopes Raine might have had about the stalker going away were leveled. There was a message on her desk to come down to Duane's office immediately, and without so much as turning on her own computer, she headed straight there.

The news was not great. She had not been able to deal with her reader correspondence for more than a week, due to the chaos in her life, and had been planning on taking care of it that very day. But apparently the stalker decided to take care of it for her. Raine sat in shocked silence as Duane explained.

"Somehow, he got into your e-mail, and got hold of all your reader notes—and responded to them. The responses were insulting or sarcastic. He used every offensive word in the book, Raine. I've had phone calls and e-mails flooding in nonstop complaints, demands to cancel subscriptions, and we've been explaining that there's a problem and giving the readers an extra year for free to convince them not to cancel."

He looked down, shook his head.

"We can't afford this, we are still a relatively new publication, you know that. I think readers would believe it wasn't you who wrote the replies, and we plan on printing an immediate explanation and apology on the Web site and in the next issue. But this is a real mess, Raine. I know it's not your fault, but it's not good."

Raine nodded, barely containing her fury that someone had interfered with her work this way, and had tried to tarnish her reputation with her readers.

"I know, Duane. I don't know how he could have gotten in. Jack told me that he had sealed up the network, and there was no way he could have gotten in again."

She unwrapped her fingers that had been gripping the chair arm like a vise, stood, and squared her shoulders. "I'll send personal thanks and apologies to each of the readers affected. Can you tell me their names?"

Duane looked stressed, and paced around to the back of his desk, staring out the window for a moment, and then looking back at Raine. She felt the hairs on the back of her neck stand up, not knowing what that look meant, but she knew she wasn't going to like it. He sighed, and looked her in the eye, clearly ill at ease.

"Sure, you can do that, I will get you the names. It will probably help. But until this thing is over, the publisher wants you to take a break."

He held up a hand, staying her immediate objection.

"Raine, listen—I went to bat for you, and you know I want you here. But right now, they feel you are indirectly making the magazine a potential target, and if this guy would go this far, then he may be willing to do a lot more damage, and we can't risk it. Neither can you. A few weeks off—paid—is not so bad, right? Maybe he will lose interest, maybe he'll do something stupid and the police will catch him. Either way, you can still work independently."

Raine sat again, miserable. "How are you supposed to explain that I'm not here? Why I'm not at meetings?" she said, her voice reflecting the numbness she was feeling.

Duane nodded. "Well, if anyone asks, you are taking part of your vacation, sick, working from home, whatever. It's just until this thing blows over, Raine—then you are back here, no problem."

She raised her eyes to his. "What if it doesn't blow over? What am I supposed to do? The police said they can't help, the magazine wants me out…" Her voice started hitting a hysterical pitch, though she hated it, she couldn't control it. Duane was around the desk, his hands firm on her shoulders.

"No, we don't want you out—you aren't losing your job, okay?—I promise. Get it out of your head that you are in trouble here. But try to see the situation from our perspective, Raine. This may ultimately be safer for you, too—it's obviously too easy for him to get at you here. Just take a few weeks to let it settle down. Then if it continues when you come back, we will have to find some way to get the authorities more aggressively involved."

"But right now you don't see the point in doing that? I know, the publisher doesn't want the bad press. You know, he may come looking for me even if I am not here." She chilled at the thought.

Duane sighed, and nodded. "I will talk to the police again, and see if we can get them to move on anything. Until then, maybe you should take a real vacation, get away from here, visit home or something. Go to the beach somewhere warm. Get out of the target zone. Don't worry about the next issue. We can expand Gwen's section to fill the space for one month."

Raine didn't—couldn't—respond. Now he was cutting her articles? She wouldn't be in the next issue. Her heart sunk. Her readers would probably think she was fired.

She would be damned if she would go on a *vacation* when her life was falling apart. She was going to find out who— and why—starting with how someone could have accessed her computer after Jack had said it was safe. Anger flowed through her veins, replacing numbness, and she stood, and left his office without a word, heading straight for the basement.

10

"JACK." RAINE STOOD in the doorway of the small, softly lit office. She was surprised, it was nothing like she would have expected. The way Gwen had described the basement made it seem like something out of a sci-fi thriller, but while there were many, many computers humming, it was basically just another floor of offices.

Jack's office was particularly nice. Twice the size of her own. He had eschewed the fluorescent lights for lamps that sat on the desk and a wooden bookcase, and several plants appeared to be thriving in spite of the artificial light.

He was bent over his desk, angled away from the door, set back in a corner. Not the typical power-position office design. This office design stated: "Don't bug me if it's not important."

Well, this was important, and he apparently hadn't heard her the first time. She stepped into the room—something smelled very nice—and walked up directly behind him. "Jack."

He looked up calmly. He had been so focused she had expected him to jump, or at least startle, or scowl. Instead, he smiled. It was a warm—no, hot—smile that made awareness skitter over her skin as time stopped for a second and she remembered every moment of the night before. God, she had been so riled by the meeting with Duane, she had forgotten when she'd stepped into his office that just a little more than twelve hours before, they'd had wild sex in the back seat of his car. She was completely knocked back. Wow. That was one killer smile. And it was for her.

"What?" he said.

"Hmm?"

He raised an eyebrow at her. "Um, you said, 'Jack'— twice—and I said, 'What?'"

She frowned. "If you heard me the first time why didn't you answer?"

"I'm sorry, I was just finishing a thought on this report. Someone fried my mind last night—more than my mind, actually—and I am having a little trouble concentrating today."

"Oh." There was that smile again. He got up and walked to her, standing so close she just wanted to fall against him and forget it all.

"So, what can I do for you?"

Raine raised an eyebrow now, not sure if she'd heard a suggestive inflection in this simple question. Her anger was dissolved by the smile and the comforting atmosphere of the office, and she walked over and slumped into a chair, closed her eyes, raising her hands to her head.

"He got into my e-mail."

"Tell me."

All jokes aside now, he turned his full attention to her. She relayed the details of the break-in, and what the stalker had done to her readers. Jack's eyes went to ice, then fire, as he listened.

"Jack, I guess these things aren't infallible, but how could he have done this, and not have left a trace? I thought you said it was impossible. That things were locked up."

Jack nodded. "They are. I scanned the network this morning for any intrusions in the last twenty-four hours, and there were none. I changed your e-mail login last week. But there are a lot of ways still that he could have gotten your address book—a single-purpose virus, or a trojan attached to one of those earlier e-mails—not all of this stuff is easily detectable, or detectable at all—it depends on how good this guy is, and how determined. But I'm sorry, Raine. What did Duane say?"

Raine tried to follow the explanation. Trojans? What the heck? She shook her head, and made a note to ask what those things were—insofar as computers were concerned—later.

"He said the publisher wants me to take a 'vacation.'" She spat the word out derisively. "They think I am indirectly making the magazine a target, and that if I go away for a while, the problem will, too."

She looked up, and was shocked. Jack was at the boiling point. She had never seen him so angry, not even with her. But his voice was calm—in the way a frozen lake was calm.

"I'll talk to him. You shouldn't be punished for this. The publisher is an ass." He started to leave the office, and she stood quickly, catching his elbow. "Jack, please don't. I mean, thanks, but it's not Duane's fault. He did what he could. He says if the guy is still out there when I come back, they will try to get the police to do something more aggressive."

Jack glowered. "Well, that's just dandy. How noble of them to be willing to put you out there to take bullets for the magazine."

When she paled, he shook his head, and put his hand over hers and squeezed.

"Not literally, Raine, I'm sorry—bad phrasing. But it's much safer for you to be here all day with all these people around, than home, or anywhere else, alone. They are just worried about their precious bottom line instead of thinking about your safety first. Their attitude is inexcusable, and I intend to talk with Duane about it."

She nodded, seeing he was committed to the cause. And it wouldn't hurt, having someone in her corner. In fact, it felt pretty damn good.

"How did you find out about this? Was there anything in your e-mail today?"

Raine blinked. "Duane left a note on my desk that he had to talk to me—that's how I found out. I haven't even checked my e-mail, I completely forgot."

Jack nodded, and guided her to the seat. "Do it now, let's see if there are any more nasty little surprises there."

Raine nodded, sitting at the laptop and tapping in her login information. She swallowed hard when she saw the long list of e-mails pop up, all from a strange-looking account, all with the same subject heading:

Whore!

The word streamed down the screen in an endless parade of slurs, hundreds of lines all the same, filling screen after screen after screen.

She heard Jack swear, and he leaned over her shoulder, opening one of the e-mails, and found no message. Tapping away at the keys, and cursing mightily, he finally slammed the laptop shut.

"There's no trace. At least at this level. I'm going to have to dig deeper. This slime won't keep breaking in, I can guarantee you that."

"Well, it doesn't really matter anymore, does it?" Her voice was hushed, as she felt the crushing wave of blues set in. "I won't be here. And I am not going to send one single e-mail from home. I am not even going to hook up at all. No more Internet for me."

Jack rubbed her shoulders, digging his fingers into her neck, where the muscles were so tense they were hard as a rock. He wanted to comfort—he wanted to *do* something—this whole situation was making him feel ineffectual, and now he couldn't even make sure she was okay here at work. With him. He inhaled the scent of her hair, and continued massaging until he felt her loosen up.

"Feel better?"

"My neck does. Thanks. You probably just helped me avoid a killer headache."

Although his hands on her had inspired aches in other regions of her body, which surprised her, given the circumstances. Suddenly the softly lit office seemed close and intimate, and she realized his hands hadn't left her shoulders, but rested there, rubbing the hollows of her shoulder blades. Funny, she had never before thought of that as such an erotic spot. But it was now.

"Raine."

"Hmm?" His hands were melting her stress into a light buzz.

"Why do you think the sudden change in attitude? This guy seemed to want to impress you, sent you expensive roses, cleared up your bills—he wants you to know how skillful he is, how much control he has, how much he likes you—but he seemed to be trying to do good things for you, perverse as they were. But now, well, now he sounds pissed off."

Raine nodded slowly. "Well, it's not exactly a stable person who does this kind of thing in the first place. Maybe he is angry that I haven't acknowledged his gifts, or that you changed my e-mail login."

Jack nodded. Possible. There was another possibility, too. That he had seen them. Perhaps last night, in the parking lot. Perhaps earlier in the day, holding hands at the police station, when Jack had followed her home, or when they had been talking in the café. This guy could be watching. He could be jealous. Jack didn't want to let Raine know that—she had enough to deal with; he didn't want to scare her with suppositions, but he had a bad feeling.

The stalker had somehow figured out that she had a man— him—in her life. He was angry. That made him dangerous. And for Jack, it made it even more personal. He couldn't share this with anyone, not when it was just speculation, and not when he had to send her home, alone. He felt anger rise again, bitter in his mouth; oh, he would be talking to Duane about this. The magazine wasn't just going to abandon her. And neither was he.

Raine wasn't looking at him but felt his hands go still on her shoulders, and she could almost feel him thinking. She wondered about what.

"Raine. I want you to move out of your house, and maybe move in with Gwen."

"I already told you, Jack, I am not going to do that…."

"Listen, I don't think sex with Neal is so all-consuming to her that she would put you at risk. It's nice of you to be thoughtful, but you need to consider the idea more carefully."

"No. I'm not letting this maniac drive me out of my home or endanger my friends."

"Then move in with me."

He said it so calmly, so matter-of-factly, that she almost thought she'd imagined it.

She stood, facing him. "I can't do that, Jack. I am not leaving my house. It's bad enough I'm being booted out of here."

Jack's eyes sparked, and he realized hers did, too, her jaw set as stubbornly as his own.

"Then we'll talk to Duane and have the magazine pick up the expense of some sort of protection. The cheap bastards are going to do something."

Raine nodded, not opposed to that idea, and feeling a little disconcerted that she had won that argument so easily. And a little disappointed—did this mean that Jack was opting out?

She had gotten used to the idea of him being her self-appointed protector, but she guessed she couldn't just expect him to go on being her bodyguard. He had work to do, and he had been spending a lot of time watching over her. Without really thinking too much about it, she had let herself get a bit dependent on him, and that wasn't like her at all. Usually she just depended on herself. But he had insinuated himself into her life. He was her…well, her lover. Or maybe it was just those two times? She felt a sinking sense of loss, and the issue added even more confusion to everything she was already feeling.

Jack watched the emotions play over her face. She didn't realize what an open book those green eyes were. Surprise, fear, anger, sadness, and something else—despair? Loss?

He was struggling with his own demons. This situation allowed him to see her differently, to look a little deeper than he had before. He was losing emotional ground, and fast. While he didn't want her in this dangerous position, he had to admit a certain male pull of satisfaction at being her protector.

There was the beginning of something between them. He had felt it with her online, as Rider and Nilla, and at her house that one passionate night, and last night. God, though they hadn't spoken of it, last night she'd blown him away. He didn't know what was next.

He needed to know she was safe, and now he wouldn't be able to have any control over that. He was sure he could push the magazine into anteing up for some protection. After all, all he had to do was mention a lawsuit if something happened to her and they would be held responsible. But even if they got the best protection in the country, he wouldn't sleep easy with it. Not unless it was him. Because he was starting to care. And that meant he had more investment in protecting her than some stranger being paid a high fee.

But he wasn't exactly in a position to do too much for her now. He eyed the computer; perhaps the best way he could really be of help would be to track down this psycho. Then they could just forget it. Having focused on this purpose, he felt more steady.

Raine had been lost in her own thoughts, and as if someone flipped a switch, they both came back to the present, and found they had been staring wordlessly at each other. Fire caught in her cheeks, and she looked away. She must be losing it, she had never behaved this way with any man; Jack was definitely a different experience for her. And he had been great, there was no denying it. But now she was on her own. She sucked up a breath.

"Well, I have some stuff to do here, and I guess I will head home. On my *vacation*." She drew out the word, ended on a sigh, and Jack reached out to touch her hair lightly with his fingers.

"Hey, not a bad deal if you can get it, having extra time off and getting paid for it. Make good use of the time."

She shrugged. "I suppose. I can get ahead on some story ideas and work for when I get back, get ahead of the game."

"Relax a little, Raine. This has been a tough week." He kept his hand in her hair. "Would you mind if I dropped by?"

Her heart skipped a little and she smiled. "That would be great. I don't think I have all that much on my calendar."

He smiled at the light comment, and felt his own tension ease as he backed away and nodded.

"Good, then don't be surprised to see me on your doorstep. Probably in a few hours."

She nodded, and turned to leave, stopping by the door for a moment to turn and look at him again. He wanted to go with her, to hold her, to make things easier, but instead his eyes sent her a silent promise that she wouldn't be facing this alone.

RAINE SAT IN HER CAR out in front of her home. In the back seat she had a briefcase full of work and a box of papers she had brought from her file cabinet. A few people had wondered why she was clearing out, and she had managed to smile blithely and keep her voice normal as she chatted briefly about taking a working vacation, and listened to comments about her luck and how they wished they could have it.

Yeah, right.

She couldn't seem to get out of the car. She should feel free, right? Unfettered. All this spare time, paid leave, she could get work done, sleep, exercise, read, and clean her house. She had plenty to do, and now she was free to do it. But she didn't feel free. She felt…exposed. Abandoned.

She grabbed the handle and opened the door, forcing herself to move and haul her work up the walk and into the house, finally getting it all inside and put away where she wanted it.

She had to keep moving, to keep busy, and not let herself mope or dwell on the situation. Hopefully, Duane was right and whoever was bothering her would just go away. Maybe he would figure she had been fired from the magazine and be satisfied after his mischief with the reader e-mails. Maybe it was someone trying to get back at her for something, though she couldn't imagine what.

She sat down at her desk and spent a few hours writing out personal letters to each reader who had been affected, letting them know that there had been a problem on the computer network, and that she had not sent the e-mails they had received. She dearly hoped they would accept her apologies and continue to read the magazine and her column.

When she was finished, she decided to walk to the mailbox to stretch her stiff legs. The sun was still up. It had been a bright winter day, and there was no biting cold at the moment—a perfect time for a walk. Closing the door behind her, she felt more cheerful, and set out down the steps.

HE COULDN'T CONCENTRATE. He wondered what Raine was doing, if she was okay. He had hacked open those e-mails that were sent to her as far as he could, and he couldn't trace anything. Everything led back to dummy accounts piled on to more dummy accounts, and finally he realized it was just useless.

They weren't going to find this guy electronically. He was either going to disappear, or they would find him when he tried something more aggressive. He hoped it was the former, but something in his gut told him it wouldn't go away that easily. He looked at the clock. He could still get some work done, but his heart wasn't in it.

He wanted to see her; it was as simple as that.

He couldn't remember any other time he had missed a woman after just a few hours, or anyone he had worried about as much, except for his own family. But he would let her be for now, let her settle in, get used to the situation before he went knocking at her door. After all, it had only been a few hours. For now, he would go home, and try to relax and get Raine off his mind for a little while. Good luck, he thought as he grabbed his jacket and left for home.

RAINE HAD RELAXED considerably by the end of the day. The walk had been pleasant, and she had come back and made herself a delicious salad and pasta, taking her time and making herself the kind of dinner she rarely had the chance to enjoy during the week. She called Gwen and filled her in on the recent happenings, and then spent a half hour convincing her friend that she was okay on her own, for now. It was nice to know that Gwen wanted her to come stay, but she didn't intend to lead danger—if there was any real danger—to her friend's door.

Now she was stretched out on the sofa with a blanket, a glass of wine and a novel. The novel may not have been the best choice—a hot romance, the kind she secretly read and had boxfuls of in her attic.

Ever since she was young, she'd loved escaping into romances for hours at a time, losing herself in the world of emotions and experiences she never had. She enjoyed seeing the heroines and heroes grow over the years as she herself had grown, the story lines became more daring, the women more independent, the men more sexy and complex.

How was it that the men in these novels were so amazingly clued in to the needs and feelings of the heroines? She smiled to herself—because women created them, of course. But maybe there were one or two out there who really were like that in real life. Or maybe just one.

She averted her thoughts, took a sip of wine, her eyes glued back to the page as the hero seduced the heroine for the first time, and she felt her own blood heat as the two lovers experienced the ultimate pleasure together. She smiled, squirming a little on the sofa, feeling a tickle down low.

For once in her life, she could relate—she knew what a man could do for a woman—thanks to Jack. It seemed like aeons ago that they had made love, even though it was just last night, but her body remembered every single sensation vividly.

She felt heat move up her face; she was incredibly warm from the book, the wine and the blanket. Fanning her face with the book, she decided it was time for a break, or sleep would not come easy tonight. Apparently, she couldn't keep Jack out of her head for more than five minutes, though she had to admit that her reading material wasn't helping matters.

She looked at the phone. It was late, but he would be home. She could call. But what would she say? Their relationship was changing, but maybe not so much that she could feel comfortable calling him at this time of the evening. She had no idea how to handle these things.

She wished she was brazen enough to call him as she had done that first time, to hear his voice on the phone, to seduce him with her words.

But that was Nilla—it wasn't really her. Was it? Her body was humming, she missed him, and she felt very alone in the house. It was late, but it wasn't *that* late. Maybe she could just call to let him know she was okay, and they could talk, and that was all.

Jack's number. Where had she left it? Yes—the night-stand—she'd put it there. Running to the bedroom, she let out a small cry of dismay when she didn't see the paper on the table, and got down on her hands and knees to find it. There it was! It had gotten knocked down under the bed. Thank God she hadn't sucked it up in the vacuum, though in her mood, she might have gone digging through the dusty bag to find it.

She reached for the phone, her hands trembling slightly. It was just a phone call, for goodness' sake. She shook herself mentally, and grabbed the receiver, lifting it to her ear, and heard nothing. She dialed the number, there was no sound. Her phone was dead.

She clicked the hook a few times, held the phone back to her ear, and nothing happened. But she'd paid her bill…she set the receiver back down in the cradle, and fear seeped through her, chilling her to the bone.

Had someone messed with her phone? She felt panic skitter down her spine, and she tried to control her breathing. It was late, and she was afraid. She had her cell phone…. Frantically, she ran to her desk and dug through her bag, finding the small phone she only used for work. She had almost forgotten that she had it.

Hands shaking, she dialed the number. She only got his office message. Dammit! Damn! She felt tears squeeze against the back of her eyes; this was his cellphone number, too, not his home number. She sat on the floor, wedged tightly to the wall, and tried to calm down.

She called back, and left a message. Hopefully he would check. She willed herself to think. She could call the police, but if her phone was just dead and her lines not actually cut, she would look like a fool. What if this was another billing mess-up?

She needed to take control. Running into her bedroom, she pulled on jeans and a sweater, put on her jacket and headed for the kitchen door. She grabbed a flashlight, keys and a sharp nail file. She would go see if her lines were cut herself, and if they were, she would call the police from the safety of her car—she wouldn't go back in the house, just in case. All the women in the movies always went back in the house; it was always a mistake.

Armed with her plan, she went out the back door, and kept the flashlight off until she got to the side where she knew the phone hookup was. She kept close to the house, looking all around her. The snow made it almost as light as day outside, and she took comfort from the fact that she could see clearly that no one was there but her. Her neighbor's windows, only a few yards away, were lit. There was help nearby if she called out.

She turned the flashlight on and searched the side of the house, and saw the phone connection—the wire was indeed cut. Swallowing down her fear, she forced herself to follow her plan—she walked quickly to the front of the house, her breath coming raggedly. In a wave of panic she realized that she had left her cell phone on the bed. *Stupid!*

Now she would have to go back in. She turned around and headed for the door, when she felt a hand grab her from behind. She screamed, reaching for the nail file in her pocket and spinning around, struggling away from whoever had hold of her arm, flailing the file in front of her.

"Raine! Stop it! It's me, Jack—you're okay…*stop!*"

Jack managed to get hold of both wrists, and held them tight, as her eyes, wide and blank with fear, finally focused in on him. Her face was deathly white, and he saw recognition dawn; she let the nail file fall from her fingers. It glittered in the light as it fell to the ground.

Her teeth were chattering, and she stood, frozen, staring at him wordlessly. He released her wrists from his tight grip and pulled her close, walking her to the door. "It's okay. I was on my way home and got your message. I tried to call back, but no one answered. Scared the hell out of me, Raine. Where's your cell?"

She tried to talk through great gulps of panic and shivering. "The…phone l-line…is cut…I checked…I left my… c-cell in the bedroom…I f-forgot…"

Inside the door, he spun her around to face him. "You did what?"

"I…I…l-left my…phone on the b-bed…." She was shaking from head to toe now, and he pulled her to the couch, warming her hands between his.

"Raine, you went out to check if the phone line was cut? Are you nuts? Someone could have been out there."

She shook her head.

"I looked around, it was bright…I h-had the file…I couldn't ca-call the cops if the phone was just dead…and I didn't know where you were…."

Tears were starting to flood her eyes now, and he took her shoulders. "Okay, I'm sorry, baby. Hold it together, just for a while, okay? It's okay. We're getting you out of here."

She nodded faintly.

"You get clothes together, I'll call the cops. Go pack what you need. Don't pack light—we don't know how long this will be for."

She nodded and stood on trembling legs, unsure of exactly where he thought she would be going, but she knew she couldn't stay home alone and feel safe. She went to pack, hearing him in the distance, calling the police.

It didn't seem like very long before she heard voices in the living room, and she came out. Jack was talking with two uniformed officers, and they were taking notes. She joined them, feeling steadier but no less afraid.

"Evening, ma'am. Mr. Harris reported that you had some trouble here?"

She nodded. "Someone cut my phone line."

"The phone is dead?"

"Yes. Someone cut the line into the house—I checked."

The officer raised his eyebrow, but didn't say a word for a moment. "Okay, we're going to go out and check the premises. Just sit tight for a few minutes."

Jack thanked the officers and took in Raine's face. She was still ghostly pale, but the trembling seemed to have stopped, and she was calmer.

"All packed?"

"Yes. I just need to get some work together. I suppose that I could see if the inn down the street is open, but it's late…"

She felt the sharpness in his voice cut through her fog. "Inn? You aren't going to a damn inn, Raine—what the hell are you thinking? You are going home with me. You can stay at my place."

She blinked at him. "Your place? I can't stay with you."

He stared at her. "Yes, you can, and you are. You said yourself you don't want to go to Gwen's, and this way, you have built-in security—me."

"But—"

"Listen, I have enough room, and two beds, if that is what's worrying you."

She felt heat invade her face, and her throat tightened. "No, that's very kind of you, I don't want to intrude. This isn't your problem."

His voice was cooler now, his eyes glittering as they bored into hers.

"Don't do that, Raine. Don't do it, not now. Not this time."

She just nodded, went quiet under his hard stare. He relaxed, and backed off as the officers came to the door, looking serious.

"Yep, the phone line is cut. We can look for prints but I don't imagine we'll find anything. There are a lot of footsteps in the snow, but some of those will be yours, from what you've said. You're going to have to have your car taken care of. All four tires were cut. Maybe you scared off whoever did it when you went outside, but it isn't safe for you to stay here alone."

Jack's arm came around her shoulders, holding her fast. She couldn't say anything, but she heard Jack tell them that they had already filed one complaint with Detective Delaney about a stalker, and that this was probably connected to that incident. The uniformed officers nodded, and looked at Raine.

"The detective may want to talk with you again, ma'am. Do you know a place you can stay for the night?"

Raine looked at them mutely, and Jack stepped in, giving them his address and number. Grabbing her bags, and shutting off the lights, they left the premises with the police officers, and went to Jack's car.

Raine looked at her car sitting lopsidedly in the driveway, and felt the panic surge up again. Who would want to do this to her? She had never hurt anyone. She kept to herself. She hardly even *knew* anyone.

She felt Jack guide her into the passenger's seat, and she let her head fall back against the headrest, closing her eyes, feeling a massive headache coming on. The car rolled forward, and everything dimmed to gray.

11

THE NEXT THING she knew, she was being shaken gently, and she startled upright, not exactly sure where she was. It was dark, there were comforting smells of spice and—Jack. They were in his car, he was leaning over, his hand on her shoulder; she must have fallen asleep. His voice was quiet, gentle.

"There you are—I didn't realize why you were so quiet for a while, you had me worried. I was talking to you and there was only silence. I didn't realize you had fallen asleep, but I'm glad you got some rest." He was smiling at her, but his eyes looked tired.

She yawned, still groggy with sleep. "I'm kind of surprised, too. I guess it was just being in the car, warm, and I relaxed a little." With you, she added silently.

He nodded. "Well, we're here. My place. If you want to go in, I can get your things." He held his keys out.

She blinked hard.

"No, I can help."

She opened the door before he could argue, and felt the cold blast of air hit her in the face, waking her. She stepped out, and looked at the beach cottage in front of her. It was dark, but she could see the house was not a new construction, not one of the parade of characterless condos that had sprung up along the shoreline, but an old, square, two-story stone house, with a cobbled chimney.

Brambly beach-plum hedges poked gnarly branches up from underneath a light layer of icy snow and little wooden tents stood duty under the windows, protecting the bushes from the weather. The place, glistening and shadowed under the moon, looked magical. It was set far back from the shoreline, but she could still hear the waves crashing behind the house, and salt hung in the air.

The winds were frigid, and she shivered, turning to the car. Jack had already pulled her bags out from the trunk, and she grabbed one of the heavier ones and walked toward the charming wooden, cathedral door with a heavy brass knocker. The single, wide step was a large stone slab, and she felt the crunching under her boots where Jack had salted the slippery walk. A bright porch light in the shape of a lantern helped her see clearly as Jack slid the key in the lock and pushed open the door.

As she walked in, she was enveloped in the scent that she had come to associate with the man himself, a heady aroma of wood, cloves and sea. She set her bags down and looked around the small entry that was simply decorated with some antique naval items on the walls and a straight-backed Shaker bench where she sat to remove her boots. The floors were all hardwood and gleaming, and colorful Persian rugs were scattered everywhere. Everything about the house seemed sturdy and square, but it was inviting as well. *Cozy,* she supposed, was a weak word.

Secure. Solid. *Safe.*

Jack's voice interrupted her observations.

"It's a little chilly in here. It gets that way if I let the fire go out for a long time. Let me get it going, and I'll show you your room. You can look around wherever you want." He pointed down a narrow hallway. "The bathroom is down that hall, up the stairs to the left, if you need it."

She nodded, and stood up, feeling strange. The whole evening had been surreal, and here she stood now, in Jack's house, feeling both incredibly at home and yet like a complete stranger. She just stood in that spot, and he walked up to her, placing his hands on her shoulders.

"Raine, I want you to feel comfortable here. You're safe. No one except my closest friends and family have this address, and it's not even listed in my name. I have lived here for a long time, but it is actually my grandparents' property. I use a post-office box in town. No one can trace us here. No one could possibly know you are here."

She nodded and felt the warmth from his hands on her shoulders move across her skin, and she thought she might be safe from the stalker and even from Jack, but she wasn't too sure about herself. Some of her thoughts must have shown in her eyes, since his eyes snapped in recognition as passion ignited between them.

But he let his hands drop to his sides, smiling slightly as he turned and walked into another room. Raine went to find the bathroom, pleased but not surprised to find it very modern, offering every convenience including a large set-in tub with massage jets that made her purr with anticipation of a hot bath. She ran her hand along the edge of the cool, granite-textured porcelain. Tension had made her ache from head to toe, and she felt like a piece of raw meat.

Pursing her lips, she walked back down the hall, where she was treated to a very nice view of Jack's backside as he bent over, stoking a fire. The central room with the fireplace was as beautiful as the rest of the house, but she wasn't really paying attention to the details at that very moment.

"Um, Jack?"

"Yeah?" He looked over his shoulder and smiled. "Almost done, this will warm the place up fast."

"Oh, it's fine, I love it. I was just wondering, I know it's very late, but…"

He stood and looked at her, and she was mesmerized, watching him. He almost seemed to glow as the flames started to leap up in the background, and she licked her lips.

"I am feeling pretty achy, and was wondering…"

He shot her a huge grin.

"Ah, the bath. Absolutely. No one ever resists that for long once they've seen it. Help yourself. I'm serious, Raine, that I want you to treat this place as you would your own home. You want something, you don't need to ask."

She nodded, still staring at him standing in the firelight, and felt her insides melt, and she wasn't thinking about the tub now.

"But you may want to get in there now, before you get too tired. I'll show you your room so you can just hit the sheets if you want. You've had a tough night."

She nodded, then followed him into the foyer again and grabbed her bags, walking behind him up the stairs and past the magnificent bathroom to a room at the end of the hall. He opened the door, and turned on the light.

"I'm afraid it is the smaller of the two bedrooms, but I hope it will be comfortable. It has a nice view in the daylight."

Raine caught her breath. The room was smaller than hers at home, but the high four-poster bed covered in white and blue linens looked like something out of a dream.

Jack walked to the window and gazed out.

"Actually, the moon is so full tonight you still have a nice view—the snow makes it so bright."

She joined him by the six-over-six, square-paned window that looked out over wind-bent trees and dunes. The corners were edged with snow, like something out of a postcard. The room had the same homey feel as the rest of the house.

Someone cared very much about this old place. A lovely old waterfall-style dresser and full-length mirror filled one corner of the room by a closet and a quilt stand. The walls were a pale green, and ink drawings of seabirds and flowers were on every wall. She sighed, turning back to the room.

"You may never get me to leave."

He smiled, wondering why that thought caused his breath to come up short for a moment, and walked back to the doorway.

"It's yours for as long as you want it, Rainey. I'll be downstairs. Enjoy your bath."

And he was gone. Raine sat on the bed, which she practically needed a stepstool to crawl up onto, and tested its mattress. It was just right. Of course. She gathered up her bath necessities and headed back to the bathroom, her thoughts on the tub and her aching muscles.

JACK SAT BY THE FIRE, exhausted but unable to sleep. He had been badly shaken when he had received that message, Raine's voice, tight and panicked, telling him her phone was dead and pleading with him to please call back on her cell. He ran a hand over his face, reminding himself that he had her here now, with him, safe and sound. He wouldn't let his imagination torture him with what ifs.

He barely remembered the mad drive from the highway

back to her house. He was glad he was still so close by. After leaving work, he was too restless to go home alone, and had stopped for some food, then for a few drinks. A pretty brunette had flirted with him at the bar; she had received his polite but clear "not interested" message quickly and left him alone.

His mind was consumed with thoughts of a particular blonde. Who was upstairs naked in his tub right now. Who would be sleeping just yards away from him tonight. He felt his body react to the thought and tried to stem his desire. That wasn't what Raine needed right now. She'd had a nasty day followed by a nastier night, and though his mind swam with images of what could happen between them here in his house for an undetermined length of time, he primarily wanted to make sure she was safe and taken care of.

But he also knew that he had not mistaken the flash of desire in her eyes when she had looked at him in the entry hall. That had spoken to him loud and clear. He stared at the fire for a long while, sipping a cognac and sinking into his dreams.

RAINE PADDED DOWN the stairs; the house was amazingly silent. She had sat in the bath until the water had turned tepid and she was in danger of drowning by falling asleep. But then when she had gone and crawled into the huge, soft bed, she'd laid there wide maddeningly awake. So she went in search of some reading material to try to take her mind off things.

When she went into the den, she was surprised to find Jack stretched out on the huge burgundy sofa, slumped down in a half sitting position that didn't look very comfortable, but he was sleeping deeply nonetheless. She sat carefully on the opposite edge, in front of the fire, watching him sleep.

He was an incredibly beautiful man, something she hadn't

fully appreciated before. His face was softened by sleep, and she longed to reach out and touch him. Instead, she curled her feet up underneath herself, and opened the book she'd chosen from the bookcase against the far wall.

Jack was awakened by the familiar scent of citrus and flowers filling the room. He opened his eyes slightly, looking around, and saw Raine sitting on the sofa, legs curled beneath her, staring at a book. The flickering light played off her face, and he took in her long hair, damp and curling, pulled up on the back of her head, exposing the graceful length of her neck.

She was dressed in flannels—green, blue and white check, and white, fuzzy socks. Baggy pants and a button top, cinched modestly. It should have been more cute than sexy, but he remembered her telling him about her flannels once before, and he felt himself go hard.

"Raine." His voice was barely a whisper.

She lowered the book and looked at him, her face freshly scrubbed, glowing in the firelight, eyes sleepy.

"Oh, I'm sorry, I didn't want to wake you, but I just didn't…well, I couldn't sleep. I came downstairs and saw you sitting here, and thought I would just sit with you, and…"

She was babbling and couldn't stop. He was looking at her, sleepy, relaxed, and with undisguised desire in his eyes.

"Come here."

His command was simple, and quietly spoken, and she never in a million years would have thought of not following it. Sliding over, she placed the book on the table, and sat on the edge of the sofa, in front of him, snuggled between the heat of the fire and the heat of his body. He reached up and slid his hand over her cheek, traced a finger down her neck, and she shivered, but not with cold.

He drew her to him, sliding his mouth gently over hers. Then, he drew back, muttered something into her mouth, and kissed her again. Heaving himself fully up onto the long, lush sofa, he settled back against the pillows. His look invited her to join him. She did so, bringing her legs up and stretching out along the length of him, nestling her head in the crook of his shoulder.

A wave of heat washed over her skin when she felt the hardness of him against her hip. He kissed her hair, and made soft comforting sounds, drawing her more intimately against him.

She worked her arms around him as well, and nestled in closer. Slowly, she heard his breathing even, and felt her own eyelids fall. She fell into dreamless sleep, more safe and secure than she ever remembered feeling in her entire life.

THE FIRE HAD DIED DOWN a bit and the room was cool but not uncomfortable. She had no idea what time it was. Feeling relaxed for the first time in ages, she didn't care. She could feel Jack's breath stirring against her cheek, and smiled. He slept like a rock. That bit of knowledge felt...intimate. She saw springy chest hair curling in the V where he'd loosened the buttons of his shirt; he was still fully dressed.

Sliding her fingers out from under his arm, she touched the spot tentatively. She was curious about his tastes and textures, wanted to memorize the geography of his body, learn what he liked, what he wanted.

She was surprised at her thoughts, but he was sleeping, they were alone. Her thoughts and desires were hers, and she wanted to indulge in them.

Tilting her head backward she memorized the sinewy muscles of his neck, the angle of his jaw, and marveled at his skin.

It was manly, a bit tanned even in winter, and just rough enough. He had the beginning of a beard that had miraculously appeared overnight. Running a finger over the stubble lightly, she wanted to know how it would feel scraping over her skin.

Her finger continued its journey along the shallows of his throat. She pushed herself up slightly, and holding her breath, turned her face into his neck, and let the tip of her tongue just touch him, ever so lightly, delighting in his salty, manly flavor.

Jack was having a difficult time keeping his eyes shut and body still. He had buoyed quickly into consciousness when she'd been touching his chest, and every part of him was becoming fully aware and awake more quickly than he had control over.

Finally, he gave up the pretense of sleep when she nipped the sensitive skin beneath his ear. He released a long groan, gathering her more fully against him and burying his face in her fragrant hair, which had somehow come loose in the night. His voice was gruff, and he felt surprise in her body as she realized he was awake.

"Morning—don't stop on my account."

Raine pulled back a little. He was wide-awake now, and ready to go, from what she could feel as he rubbed an impressive morning erection against her leg. He turned his face to slide his tongue along her ear. She caught her breath, feeling the zing from the subtle kiss travel straight down and land deep in her belly, the sharp bite of pleasure soaking her panties. She wished he would promise to never stop tracing his tongue over her skin—oh yes….just like that.

Moving her legs apart, she rubbed the crux of her sex along

his hard-on and moaned with need, seeking and finding his mouth with hers. She licked his lips into a wet kiss, wanting to lose herself in it. He slid his hands down and grabbed her derriere firmly, settling her against him, smiling into her mouth when she whimpered and strained, bunching her fingers in his shirt.

"We're both overdressed for this." She nodded and slowly, reluctantly, pushed away, standing by the side of the couch. Smiling at him, feeling free and bold, she slowly unbuttoned her top, and dropped it to the floor. She felt a blush steal up her cheeks when she saw him swallow deeply and clench his hands at his sides.

Sliding her hands down over her full breasts, across small, rosy nipples, and down her stomach, she eased her thumbs under the waistband of her pajama bottoms, lowering them slowly, until she stood before him wearing only a pair of scant, pink silk panties. He reached out, but she backed away, out of his reach, her voice coy.

"Uh-uh…your turn."

Though he appreciated her show, he was impatient, and lost his own clothing quickly, tossing them on the floor behind the couch. He stood up next to her, drawing her against him, taking her mouth in a bruising kiss. Slipping his hands down her back, knotting his hands in the scrap of silk she wore, he pulled the crotch up tight, evoking a cry from her as he tugged the soaked fabric tight—and released—then did it again.

Biting his bottom lip, Raine absorbed the growl of his response, and pressed her thighs together tightly around his steel-hard erection, loving the feel of him rubbing against her skin. She dropped her head back and bent into him like a bow when he cupped both breasts in his hands.

He squeezed her aroused nipples sharply, but when he shifted, prodding against the barrier of thin silk, seeking entry, she made a sound of slight protest, and put her hands on his stomach, pushing lightly. He blinked, unsure of what she was doing.

He smiled, reaching his hand up to touch her face tenderly but still with a quizzical look in his eyes. She slid her hands from his stomach to chest to shoulders, and pressed him back to the couch, shushing his questions with her lips.

Her eyes were hazy with desire, but clear with purpose. His heart missed a beat when she smiled against his lips and whispered, "This time, for you."

Then she was trailing kisses down his body, licking her hot little tongue across his stomach, and creating a ball of need so tight in his groin that he thought he would explode without her even touching him. When she bit the inside of his thigh, he had to protest, loudly; he was going to lose it before she went much further. She just smiled, and leaned back for a moment.

"Jack?"

"Hmm?"

"Move up on the sofa a little. I want you to watch."

His limbs went so weak he didn't think he would be able to lift himself, but somehow, he did. His chest was heaving with effort and anticipation as she tormented him by trailing her fingers lightly up his leg, and she made sure he had a clear view as she drew her luscious, pink tongue up the rock-hard length of him, and then back down again. She cupped his balls in her hand, stroking gently, her fingers finding the spot down between his legs that she knew would push him to near the edge. His head dropped back in ecstasy, and she scolded gently.

"No, Jack, look at me…look at me."

God help him, he watched her descend again, wrapping her lips tightly around him and taking him to the hilt. Her eyes never left his. His head spun with pleasure, and he couldn't have controlled the noises he was making if he'd tried. She sucked and nipped at him, lolling her tongue around him until he was crazed. Just as he reached the edge, she drew back, always making sure his eyes were on her. Sucking the pulsing head of his throbbing cock hard and sharp, she watched him lose control, his eyes blind with passion, but glued to hers. His breath heaved, he arched up under her, and he choked out a single plea that taught her a new kind of pleasure.

She sighed, taking him deep, gladly giving him what he needed. Sucking him hard, she gloried in his harsh cries of release but didn't see the pleasure contort his face, focused on draining the last drop of pleasure from him as she tasted the hot, salty evidence of his ejaculation at the back of her throat.

He called out to her, but she kept him inside her until he softened, and lapped him clean, nestling her face into his stomach when she was done. Sliding up his body, and wrapping herself against him, she buried her face in his throat. She was very aroused, but also oddly satisfied.

His breathing calmed and he kissed her hair, holding her. He didn't remember ever having such a wildly strong orgasm in his life; every muscle in his body felt like jelly. He wasn't sure his arms worked, but he wanted to touch her. He could feel the heat coming off her body, and stroked her back.

"Rainey…you are, well…nothing I can say…"

She smiled and rubbed her cheek against him like a cat. "I liked it, too. I never…um, did that before, with anyone. I wanted to with you."

His eyes became soft and dark; he was deeply touched that she wanted to give to him so deeply, and he stroked her hair. She kissed him lightly, trying to calm her own arousal. This had been perfect. She had gotten more from pleasuring him than she ever would have expected, and it was enough.

He shifted himself a little more solidly beneath her, bringing her fully on top of him, and buried his face in her neck, light kisses sending flares of desire racing across her skin. His hands stroked her back, moved down over the gentle curves of her bottom, pressing her against his thigh, and then moved back up over and over until she felt her heart pounding.

"Jack, it's okay...I'm okay..." Her breath hitched as he wrapped his hands over the tender flesh of her rib cage, under her arms, and stroked the sides of her breasts. She raised her head to look at him. He was smiling, his eyes glinting with something like mischief, and she gazed at him warily. "What are you doing?"

His grin split wider.

"You know what I'm doing...you don't like it?"

He licked a hot trail from her collarbone to her mouth. She pressed against him, her body leaving her brain behind and acting of its own accord. He pushed his knee up, positioning her on his hard thigh, urging her to ride him.

She shook her head. "No..." Her voice squeaked a little as she panicked.

"*Yes.*" He pressed her down, whispering lovely hot things as he felt her melt over him, and bit her ear. She relaxed and pressed against him shyly, reluctantly, and made those soft kittenish sounds he loved. After a few minutes he felt her starting to lose control, grinding herself against him without his help, her breasts pressing hotly against his chest as she moved.

"There you go…yeah…that's it…let it go, sweetheart… take what you need." He planted wet kisses on her ear as her thighs squeezed him and she cried out, her fingers digging into his shoulders. He felt the release of tension in her body as the orgasm rippled through her, smiled when he felt the flood of warmth on his leg. Slowly, he lowered her, holding her close. He stroked her back and felt her body shaking slightly.

He reached up and slid his fingers under her chin, lifting her face, worrying he would find tears, and instead saw her eyes alight with laughter, her neck and face flushed with pleasure. She shook her head, burying it in his neck once more. She spoke, her voice muffled.

"I can't believe you made me do that."

"What? Come? I *like* making you do that."

She laughed, and sounded shy; it made him smile. Her voice squeaked, "Like that though—I mean…geez…Jack."

"Hey, it's about whatever works, *Rainey*. We have all these parts, it's a shame not to experiment with them, wouldn't you say?"

She nodded against his chest, and sighed deeply.

They stayed there for a while, lost in the warmth of each other, and Jack felt that he could stay in this position, wrapped around her naked body for a long, long time. He felt good. What they had shared had been even more intense than the last time, and he wouldn't have thought that was possible.

But even though it had been damn near perfect, he missed being inside her, and was already wanting her again. He couldn't escape the unceasing, and somewhat annoying, urge to connect with this woman in every way possible, and he needed time to think about that. He wanted more. He wanted it all. He sighed and rubbed her back, enjoying the feeling of her nestled against him, but forced his thoughts back to the day.

"It's got to be halfway through the morning. The troops are going to wonder where I am."

"Hmm?" She lifted her head, looking at him.

"Work. Some people may be on extended vacation, but we poor working stiffs still have to go out and earn a dollar."

He tweaked her chin, and smiled, shifting them both up and feeling the cool air of the room sneak in between them when she lifted herself.

She was looking around for her pajamas, standing there completely naked in his den, her hair in complete, gorgeous disarray, skin rosy, nipples hard from the coolness of the air. He felt himself go semi-erect again, and was abashed enough to feel a little heat rise in his face as she stared at his erection, and then smiled up into his face, her eyes playful.

"You must really like your job."

He snorted, swatting her on the butt as she reached for her pajamas on the floor.

"I do, but I like your job better." She turned a rosy shade of pink, and he chuckled. Standing, pulling his pants on loosely as she dressed, he smiled and reached out, bringing her back to him for a moment.

"I like it when you look like that—satisfied and happy. We haven't had too much of that together, really, have we?"

She felt unsure of how to respond, unable to handle the intimacy he obviously wanted to share with her.

"I, um…" She just squeezed him back and stepped away, brushing off the front of her pajamas absently and turning around. "Oh, look, it is almost ten. Are you going in?"

Jack stared at her, more curious than upset about her obvious discomfort. He pursed his lips. "No, I can telecommute today."

Then he crossed his arms over his chest and leveled her a serious look.

"Raine, why are you doing this?"

Pulling on a sock, she looked at him. "My feet get cold."

He sat back down on the sofa, still warm from their bodies, and reached up and tugged at her elbow for her to sit down with him. She looked away but sat, putting her hands in her lap when she couldn't figure out what to do with them. He moved closer, took them in his and held them steady.

"No, not that. Why, after we have sex, do you withdraw emotionally? The first time we were together, you did it—you backed off so fast I could feel the ice forming. I didn't even think there would be a next time. In the car, you did the same thing, and now again. But it's especially confusing at this moment, Raine, because we share more now, we knew this was going to happen between us. I figured we both wanted it."

Raine grimaced, looked out the window and then back at Jack. Unable to sit, she got up, paced, and looked back at him.

"I'm sorry. I didn't realize I was being so...rude." When his eyes narrowed to annoyed slits, she realized her mistake, made a frustrated sound and came back to the couch, faced him, tried to speak normally.

"Jack, I don't know how to make you understand. I didn't have family, didn't have many friends. I don't know how to handle these moments that seem to come so easily to everyone else. I'm not always sure what to say. I didn't have boyfriends until college, but that was nothing like this, that's for sure. Nothing has ever been like this."

He liked hearing her admit that, and saw more in her eyes

than he thought she probably knew showed there. He nodded, took her fidgety hands back in his as she went on.

"And then there is the fact that we really don't know each other, not really. I don't know much about you, really, except your job, the bits and pieces I picked up online, and what you have told me since I've been here, which really hasn't been much."

He frowned at that; she was right. They hadn't spent much time talking about their lives, they were too busy reacting to circumstances. They hadn't really dated, there was nothing traditional about their relationship. Her voice lowered, but she continued.

"And I…I do want you. I have never felt like this before—physically—with anyone. But I don't know what else we have, and if it is just the circumstances, you know…"

He angled his head, prompting her to continue, and she took a deep breath, plunging forth.

"Just our situation. I mean, it's human—you're human. You have been so good to help me, but it's like we are in a movie—this isn't real, an evil stalker and a handsome hero who saves the damsel in distress—it's like playing a game."

He shook his head adamantly.

"I'm not playing games with you, Raine—not now—and what we just shared was very, very real. It's all been real."

"Well, yes, in one sense…"

"No, in *every* sense. I agree with you that we met under odd circumstances, and that we haven't had time to get to know each other like couples usually do. But that doesn't mean that what we have isn't real. It's real, Rainey. Trust me."

She stood up again, her uncertainty wrapping around her like an old robe. It was familiar, and kept her safe. It kept her from risking too much.

"I do trust you, in a way—but how can I know what will happen next, if you will still feel this way once the danger and drama are over with? Or how can you know that anything you feel is more than that? You may just feel sorry for me...now that you know about my background, and my problems in bed." The color in her face burned and she looked away, trying to hide from the heavy burden of self-consciousness that she carried. He stood, crossing the distance between them quickly, turning her to him.

"Are you crazy? You turn me inside out with a touch, with a look—how can you think you are bad in bed? We just finished with each other and I could pull you back down on that couch right now and do it all over again." He took a deep breath.

"As for the orgasm issue, Raine, you just need to explore what works and what doesn't—that doesn't make it boring, hell, it's the exact opposite! I get worked up just thinking about ways to make you come. And I've been thinking about it a lot. I like it. You're incredible in bed."

She shook her head, started to interrupt, but he wasn't finished yet.

"As for the rest, I'd like to think at this point of my life I'm grounded enough not to just get caught up in circumstances, though I'll admit that I do feel protective toward you, and the situation has emphasized that. I'll even admit to using it a bit to get you here with me."

She gave him a shocked look, and he smiled, touching her face.

"I wanted you here with me so I knew you were safe, yes, but selfishly I wanted to have more time with you."

He stepped in, pulled her closer, the heat from his still-bare chest burning through the flannel of her top.

"As for feeling sorry for you, I hate it that you were unhappy, but that's the past. I do feel sorry for the child you were. I hate even thinking about how you grew up. But you aren't a child anymore. There isn't much room for pity in what I feel for you. Desire, interest, admiration…hope. But not pity."

He stroked her back in that way he knew she liked and felt her ease against him. Her face on his shoulder, Raine sighed. He had neatly dissolved each one of her doubts as if they were snowflakes melting on his tongue. Though she believed the things he said, she still had reservations, she just couldn't help it.

He made it all sound so logical, so easy, but it wasn't as easy for her. He rubbed his cheek against her hair.

"Just one promise?"

"Hmm?"

"You'll stop withdrawing from me emotionally and be open to seeing what we have here."

She smiled slightly. "That's two promises." But she nodded, and he smiled.

"Okay, I'm going to grab a shower—you can join me if you like." The wicked grin drew one from her in return.

"My stomach is growling." She made the excuse, but didn't tell him what his offer caused other parts of her anatomy to do. "But thanks for the offer."

"Anytime. Like I said, feel free to help yourself to anything you want."

With that suggestive offer, he left her there, staring after him. She shook her head, feeling as if her life was being turned upside down in more ways than one. But some of it wasn't so bad.

12

THE NEW ENGLAND BLUES and whites of the small kitchen made it appear bright and charming. She particularly admired an impressive collection of yellow-ware bowls displayed on an antique walnut stand. Like the rest of the house, the kitchen was compact and old-fashioned, but well equipped. Except for the refrigerator. She found one egg, a near-empty quart of milk long past the expiration date and some English muffins that had seen better days.

She found supplies for coffee and grabbed a banana from the counter. She would go shopping. She could feel useful and thank Jack for his generosity by stocking the kitchen and making dinner. She looked out the window, toward the shore, and felt an itch to take a long walk by the sea, which she rarely did in the winter months.

She liked being here in the cozy house with Jack—maybe too much—but this wasn't a permanent arrangement. The sooner she could get back in her own house, with her life back on track, the better. As for where that would leave her and Jack, she was willing to wait and see, and maybe hope a little. It was all she could manage at the moment.

She heard the shower running and decided to go get dressed. Walking by the bathroom, she inhaled the scent of musky soap that drifting into the hallway. She stood outside the door for a moment, contemplating, and then shook her head, and walked down to her room, firmly shutting the door.

Quickly brushing her hair and tying it back in a long, thick braid, she put on a well-worn pair of low-rider jeans and a boxy dark blue sweatshirt, the edge of which just skimmed the top of her jeans. She heard the shower stop, and she grabbed her small cosmetics kit. Opening her door, she stepped gingerly out into the hall and almost collided with Jack in the narrow hallway.

His hair was wet and tousled and water gleamed off his skin; he wore only a white towel, and even that, loosely. His stomach was muscular and lean, the five-o'clock shadow was gone, and the eyes she met as she finished her long survey of his body were laughing. He reached out, tugging on the braid that lay over one shoulder.

"Hey there, Heidi. Wanna come out to play?"

She raised an eyebrow, resisted grinning, and stuck her nose primly in the air. "That's Swiss Miss to you."

He stepped to the left to let her pass, and she did so, but didn't take her eyes off him, not trusting the glint in his eye. She had just made it to the bathroom door when…*thwack!* She felt the sharp sting on her butt and jumped, hollering in surprise.

She spun around, and could only stare with her eyes wide. Words stuck in her throat as she watched him saunter down the hall away from her, his fabulous bare buttocks in full view as he twirled the damp white towel victoriously in circles at his side. She could have sworn he chuckled as he disappeared into his room.

SHE SIPPED COFFEE and looked out the window, then back to the pad of paper on the counter, jotting down some things on her list.

"What'd'ya got there?" She hadn't even heard him come in, and glanced up with a start; he was all dry now, and she noted how his amber hair curled where it was still damp, just around the edges, and settled in waves across his forehead. He picked up the steaming cup of black coffee and repeated his question.

"Oh, sorry. Shopping list. You have no food."

He grimaced. "Yeah, I eat out a lot."

"No problem. I'll go to the store. I want to make you dinner, and it will give me something to do."

"I'd like that a lot—haven't had anything made at home in a while."

"Great! I won't be too long."

She went to grab her coat and make her escape. She needed to get out for a while, to think. Or to not think. As she passed by, he snagged her elbow and yanked her up against him, sealing a kiss to her mouth, then abruptly letting her go.

She lifted her hand to her mouth, her eyes dazed. When she looked up at him he had a lazy kind of self-satisfied look on his face that made her blink, and before she thought about it too much, she flung her forearm around the back of his neck and pulled him down to her, kissing him back and running her tongue sensuously over his bottom lip for good measure. Now *he* was dazed. She smiled, and headed out.

RAINE LOVED the town of Gloucester. She had been here a few times in summer, but it was glorious in winter. She wandered around for a long while, visiting the Fisherman's Memorial, which always tugged at her heart. In the stark cold it seemed an even more brutal reminder of what had happened to those that had "gone down to the sea in ships." How many of them had loved and been lost—or worse, had not loved at all before sailing out to their deaths? Running her gloved fingers over some of the names, she sighed and turned away.

She wandered the streets a little more, gazing out over the harbor, before eventually strolling into a small specialty-food store. Grabbing a basket, she went up and down the aisles, making choices carefully, and thinking about what Jack had said.

She did want to thank him for being so good to her, and cooking was one way she could do that, but she didn't mean it in a distant, formal way. In fact, this would be the only time she had ever shopped and cooked for a man in his own house. It was an interesting feeling.

It wasn't long before the basket was full. She had even decided to try to make some bread. How hard could it be? She read the recipe on the back of a bag of flour, and thought it looked fairly straightforward. Why not?

Happily, she unloaded her goods on the single counter by the cashier—they must not get too much of a rush around here, she thought, smiling. Her groceries rung up and bagged, the young girl turned to her, obviously uncomfortable.

"Um, miss, your card didn't go through."

Raine stared at her. "What? There must be a mistake."

The girl shook her head. "I'll try it again, but the machine says it was refused."

The cashier slid her card through again, and her face was tense as she turned back to Raine. "I'm sorry…."

"No, that can't be right! There isn't even a balance on this card."

"Would you like to try another one?"

Raine nodded, and slid the only other credit card she had with her across the counter. A heavy weight sat in her gut and she knew something was wrong. A few moments later, the same story; that card didn't work, either.

"Do you have an ATM?"

The cashier nodded and pointed to the machine by the door, and Raine went to it, slid her card in and paled, feeling her knees go wobbly when not only did the screen tell her that she had a zero balance, but it wouldn't return her card. The cashier was calling her, someone else was in line waiting.

"Miss? Miss? Are you taking these groceries?"

Raine stared at her and shook her head, turned abruptly and fled out the door, making her way on shaking legs back to the car. She drove back to the house caught somewhere between fear and rage, trying to concentrate on driving down the winter highway, dealing with the winding road and the thoughts jamming in her head. By the time she parked, she was numb with anger.

As she went up the walk, she saw the door open, and Jack appeared on the step, handsome and smiling.

"Need help? What—" He stopped, looked at her once and raced down the walk. "Raine…what is it? What happened?"

She was so angry—she had never been this angry—she could barely form thoughts. He put his hands on her shoulders, looked into her stormy eyes filling with tears, and he noticed she was shaking. He put his arm around her and guided her inside.

"Tell me."

She told him what happened at the store and felt his hand tighten on hers, his eyes darkening with fury and concern. She fell back against the sofa.

"So, I have no money, I have no credit, and I have no food. I don't know what to do. I can't go to my house, I can't go to work, I can't use my car. He is stripping my life away bit by bit. It has to stop. We have to do something, if no one else will. I can't just sit around taking this. I won't."

Jack was glad that she wanted to fight back. He had been thinking along similar lines while she was gone, but didn't know if she would feel inclined to try to trap her harasser.

"Yeah, he's ticked—he knows you have moved by now, but he doesn't know where. He's probably checked the magazine somehow, noted no use of your e-mail. He may be trying to flush you out."

He took her hand in his and played with her fingers. "He won't give up and go away, Rainey, so maybe the next best thing is to lure him in. Let him find us."

She nodded, feeling scared, exhilarated, and without a clue as to exactly how they were supposed to do that.

"Yes, I want to do that—but how?" She paced around the coffee table. "I have to call the police—this should be reported, anyway, not that they can do anything."

Jack nodded. "Do that now. I might have a plan. We'll talk about it after you get off the phone."

She nodded, went to the phone and called Detective Delaney. Luckily, he was in.

When she got off the phone, her mouth was set in a grim line, and she wondered what Jack's plan was—they weren't going to wait for this guy to slip up—they would *make* him slip up. She wanted her life back.

Jack came to sit with her on the sofa and she told him about the phone call.

"What did Delaney say?"

"Still not much he could do personally, but he was going to contact someone in Boston at their computer crime unity to come down and talk to me, said he would let me know when."

"Good, at least he's doing something."

She rubbed her hands over her eyes. Someone must have a voodoo doll and they were jabbing a pin right between her eyes that very moment, because that's what her head felt like. He peeled her hands down, and pulled her up off the couch.

"C'mon."

"Where?"

"We're going to run by your house, get your credit card statements so tomorrow we can make some calls, try to do some damage control. Then I'll tell you my plan."

13

LATER THAT EVENING they sat in the corner of an out-of-the-way seafood restaurant, munching on fried clams and spicy French fries, and drinking glasses of a fairly decent chardonnay. Raine hadn't realized how hungry she was—her stomach was in such knots from stress that she'd forgotten she'd only eaten a banana all day, and Jack had not even had that much.

They went to her house, which felt strange—it was her home, and yet it felt unsafe to be there. She found her recent statements, took a few more things she needed and called a truck to come take her car to a local garage. Having it sitting in the driveway with its wheels all flat was a depressing sight. The garage said it would be a few days until they could get to it, but she felt lifted by the idea of having one normal thing accomplished.

She looked out the window into the darkness. "So, you said you had thought of a plan?"

He nodded. "Yeah, well, I have some information." He paused as her eyes went wide and focused on him intently. "I was messing with those e-mails that were sent to you before, and seeing if I couldn't trace something more in them, and I did manage to trace some of them."

"And?"

Jack sighed. "Well, I don't have an ID, but I have narrowed down the field. I think it's someone at the magazine."

Her voice dropped to a whisper, and he could see she went pale even in the warm light of the restaurant.

"How do you know?"

"The e-mail was traced back to the office. Whoever sent it sent it from inside. That's why I couldn't find any break-ins. I've been working on this for a few days, and wanted to be sure before I said anything, and even then, it's a little vague—I know where the e-mails came from but not from whom."

"How do you know?" Her voice and eyes burned into him insistently.

"After the first bunch of e-mails, I placed a monitor behind the firewall—we call it a sniffer—no one would see it if they didn't know to look, or where to look. It tells me about all the Internet traffic going in and out of the magazine. The weird thing is, the bunch of e-mails sent to you first—the ones before the roses—came from outside, and were anonymous. The second ones, the reader responses, were also anonymous, but they came from inside—no traffic left the network. A little more work, and I could tell that some of them—the ones that went to subscribers—came from your own machine. He sent them directly from your office, Rainey. Sat in your chair and answered your e-mail for you. Ballsy bastard."

"So what now?" She felt slightly queasy and pushed her food away—the person who did this worked at the magazine. She could have stood by him at the coffeemaker, passed by him in the hallway? He had been in her office—at her desk. Her stomach turned, but then the anger kicked back in. The idea that someone she possibly knew, even slightly, had done this was reprehensible.

"Whatever it is, I want to do it. I don't care what—anything is preferable to sitting and waiting."

"Okay, but we have to move fast, capitalize on the credit card thing that happened today. I figure you can send him an e-mail and tell him that we know this much, and soon will know more. You can say you don't want more trouble, but you will make it if he doesn't come to meet you."

Raine frowned. "He might know that's a trap. Kind of obvious, don't you think?"

"Yeah. I thought of that, but I also figure he's running out of options. He's lost the ability to contact you, he's done everything he can do for the moment, and may just be cornered enough to bite. And we can add the pressure that we are going to the cops and the magazine with what we know if he doesn't show. Then we can just see who shows up."

Raine nodded. "That's good—it might work, but I am going with you. I'm not just sitting home and waiting while you go save the world. Let's do it. We'll send the e-mail when we get home tonight. I want this done with."

Jack grinned and stroked her fingers where her hand lay on the table. "Wow, you're sexy when you're tough."

Raine grinned back. Their dinner plates were empty, and though she was full, she was actually considering dessert. Her appetite surged back; she figured trapping a bad guy took a lot of energy.

"Share a dessert with me?"

Jack lowered his voice. "Maybe we can take one home and find some…*creative* use for it."

Raine raised her eyebrows and remembered getting that same offer from Jerry, which seemed as if it had happened a million years ago. But then it hadn't been nearly as appealing as Jack made it sound now.

Jack watched the movements of her eyes and wondered

what she was thinking. He imagined licking hot fudge off her breasts, and shifted in his seat, suddenly a little uncomfortable.

"We should have bought some goodies when we were at the store."

Her voice was husky and sexy as hell, and he definitely couldn't stand up now without embarrassing himself completely. He cleared his throat, and smiled.

"I think I could manage a piece of pie, if we share. And as for the goodies, we'll definitely add them to the next grocery list. I'm thinking hot fudge."

Raine felt her heart pound a little harder at the thought of it, drifting away until the voice of the waitress shook her from her erotic reverie. She glanced at the pretty young girl, but forgot what she wanted to say—what was she supposed to be doing right now? She flushed as Jack's fingers squeezed hers, and he smiled at her knowingly as he ordered them a piece of cherry pie and coffees. Raine licked her lips.

"You are full of surprises, Jack. I don't think I have ever been so distracted by thinking about a trip to the grocery store."

"I don't think it was the grocery shopping that had you distracted." He laughed in a low, sexy way that made her skin tingle, then he became more serious. "So, we are going through with this?"

She nodded. "Yes—let's do it."

ON THE WAY HOME, Raine thought she already felt lighter just because she was finally taking some action, doing something rather than just sitting around waiting for the situation to resolve itself. It felt good.

She had a gut feeling this plan would work, that she could get her life back, and the thought gave her new energy and focus.

Jack responded to the change in her, perhaps feeling better himself. They bantered and chatted all the way back to the house, enjoying the ride and each other's company.

Jack grabbed the few bags of things they had picked up at the town grocery, and headed to the door. His hands full, he dropped the keys into Raine's hand and asked if she could get the door and the mail. She did, checking the box, and picked up a small package wrapped in brown paper. They got through the door, hands full and anxious to get their plan started.

Jack took the bags directly into the kitchen, and Raine set the stack of envelopes and the package on the table, noting that several of the pieces of mail had come in cheerfully colored red or green envelopes with snowman stamps. She had almost forgotten. Christmas was only a few weeks away.

She hadn't intended to look at Jack's mail, but her eyes slid across the address on a large sticker attached to the package, and she frowned when she took a closer look. The return address was from the town she had grown up in—in fact, she knew the street quite well, as she had gone to piano lessons there—and the name on the return was Harris. She was standing, staring at the package when Jack called to her.

"Hey, what was that package—can you bring it in here?"

She glanced toward the kitchen guiltily. Hanging her coat on the rack, she picked up the package and brought it into the kitchen. She set it on the table and looked at him. He cocked his head, curious about what had put that odd look on her face. Then, crossing, he looked at the package, and it hit him— she'd noticed the return address. Oh boy. Okay.

"Ah, a Christmas package from my parents."

"Your parents? They live in Essex?"

"Um, yeah."

"I lived in Essex."

He hesitated. "I know."

Jack pursed his lips, choosing his words carefully. It was best to deal with this before they got deeper into their relationship. He was already more than half in love with her, and before he fell the rest of the way, she had to know the whole story. He braced himself for how she would react.

"We lived in the same town. Growing up."

She looked up at him, her forehead creased.

"What do you mean?"

They stopped and faced each other, and Raine stared at him.... He was making her a little nervous now, as he looked at his feet, then out over the water, then, finally at her.

"You and I grow up near each other. We lived in the same town, Essex. Went to the same school, Eaton Marsh. I recognized you immediately when I saw you at the magazine."

She looked at him quizzically. "That can't be. Maybe you just thought you knew me, it may have been someone else...."

He bristled. "No, Raine—I'm not mistaking you for someone else. Is it so hard to believe I went to Eaton? I may not have been one of the upper crust, but my parents worked hard to send me to that school. They own the Arbor Inn—perhaps you know it?" He saw the recognition dawn, and continued. "I was there with you, whether you find that believable or not."

Raine blinked. She had offended him, and hadn't meant to. She just found this so hard to process, and wondered why he had kept such a thing to himself.

"But why didn't you say something? When I thought I recognized you in the office, you said we had never met before...."

"We never did. Not really." He looked her in the eye now,

and felt more than a little uncomfortable. He grimaced, and kicked at the rug with his toe.

"I had a crush on you, but you were way out of my reach. I tried to talk to you once, but you didn't say anything back. I figured you thought I was not exactly your type."

"And what did you think my type was?" she whispered. She hadn't had a type back then. She hadn't had anything.

"Someone with a lot more money and position than me. It was intimidating as hell."

Raine stood back, still shocked. He had known her? He had known her all this time, and had never said anything? And he had *liked* her? Had a crush? On her? Had been intimidated by *her*? That was ridiculous! She thought he must be joking, and it showed in her face. As she fought to come up with words, he read meaning into her silence that wasn't there. She stared at him, and started to speak, but he interrupted, sounding defensive and even a little hurt.

"I should have said something about it sooner, I know. But obviously you don't remember me at all. No problem. I knew that. Why would you have? Even at the office, for months, you would look at me and it was like I wasn't even there. Let's just chalk it up."

He went back to finish putting the groceries away, and she stood for a moment, sorting it all out, then strode over to him, taking his elbow and tugging him back around to face her.

"Jack, I'm just surprised, that's all. You have always seemed a little familiar to me, so that's why."

She stepped in front of him, looking up into his face. The lights played softly in his russet hair, but his jaw was tense. She discovered that she didn't like it, the loss of connection with him, and she wanted to get it back. She lifted her hand to his cheek, stroked him with the back of her fingers, and spoke gently.

"I wish I remembered. I'm sorry. I was so alone and screwed up back then…I knew the other students didn't like me, that they thought I was strange—and I didn't know how to make them like me. It was hard, I didn't fit in anywhere. I didn't belong at home, I certainly didn't belong at Eaton. If you spoke to me, I wouldn't have even known how to respond. If I didn't see you, it wasn't because of who you were, it was because of who I was."

She smiled slightly. "As for the office, I was so busy thinking of Rider, I wasn't paying attention to any other men. No one seemed to be able to measure up to him—and you were so pissy all the time, I figured you found me annoying."

He smiled a little. "I did."

She stared at him, and laughed. "You had a crush on me? An actual crush?"

He absorbed her words—he hadn't been seriously offended, just slightly peeved, and quickly melted when her hand touched his face. He turned his mouth into her palm, covered her hand with his and pressed her soft skin to his lips.

When he smiled at her, she felt everything lighten.

"Yeah, I couldn't sleep for thinking about you. You were so untouchably beautiful. You *are* beautiful…even more now than then. I guess I still have a crush on you."

She smiled, and loved how the world zoomed down to the two of them. It all made her feel daring, and so she spoke her heart.

"Yeah? Show me." She moved closer to him, looked into his eyes fearlessly. "I can see you pretty clearly now. I like what I see."

His eyes sparkled with heat. She lost her breath in one whoosh when he grabbed her and pulled her flush against him. His mouth came down on hers in a branding kiss, a meeting of the lips meant to claim her and be claimed by her.

He wound his hands in her hair, tugging her head back and urging her to open for him even more as he tenderly explored every sweet curve and crevice of her mouth. She strained against him, moaning into his mouth, dragging her tongue across his teeth, tickling the roof of his mouth. He didn't take his lips completely away from hers when he spoke, his voice guttural and full of undisguised need.

"Come to bed with me, Rainey."

Her breath came in short gasps and she could only nod, letting him lead her from the kitchen, but they stopped in the hallway. Unable to wait, he pushed her up against the wall, finding her mouth again. Tearing at each other's clothes, then underwear, they stood naked in the entry hall, hands and mouths all over each other. Raine caught their reflection in the hallway mirror on the wall across from them and laughed breathlessly.

"We're never going to make it up to the bedroom, are we?"

Effortlessly, he lifted her, thrilling in the feel of her skin against his, and started up the stairs. She lifted her head from his shoulder and looked at him, snaking her arms around his neck as they climbed the narrow stairwell.

He smiled, and squeezed her to him, walking down the hallway past her room to his. Nudging the door open with his foot, he carried her in, and stood for a moment, holding her by the bed. The room was lit by a small lamp on the dresser, but even in the low light she could see the emotion in his face, and it overwhelmed her. He spoke, nuzzling her cheek, his face close to hers.

"This time is special, Rainey. I want you in my bed. I want to be able to roll over at night and touch you, to catch your scent off the pillow, hear you breathing. I want to make love to you in every way I possibly can."

He set her gently down on the huge bed, and stood looking at her, risking more of his heart than she could imagine.

"I need to know you want that, too. That you want to be with me like that, as well. And not just for tonight." He could barely keep his feelings for her from spilling over; it was time to risk it all. She extended her hand to him, her answer in her eyes. He smiled, relief and lust coursing through his body, chased along by something deeper. Lowering himself to the bed, he took her in his arms and held her—just held her—for a moment, as if she were the most precious thing on earth.

Raine listened to the drum of his heartbeat under her cheek, her body tense with anticipation, but easing as he held her, his breath fanning her cheek, his foot moving slowly up and down her calf. She was stunned to notice how even those parts of them, the curve of his instep along her leg, fit so perfectly. She'd never been held before, not like this—so close and so long that it was a source of pleasure unto itself. She slipped her arms around him, too, reveling in the sensation of closeness she had had so little of in her life. It was addictive.

Their bodies warmed, and his hands stroked the curve of her back and hip, his fingers moving lightly down her thigh, then back again. She answered his call, raining small kisses along his collarbone and fluttering her hand lightly over his back. With every touch he cherished her, and she basked in it. Once again, she felt what it was like to truly connect with someone, and the emotion made her giddy with desire. The fingers that lightly teased her skin began leaving trails of fire behind, and her nipples beaded against his chest in response.

Still on his side, holding her close, he reached down, lifting her leg up over his hip, opening her to a fuller exploration. When his hand found its way between her legs, seeking her through the damp, hot folds of skin, she moaned, and brought her mouth to his, sighing as she surrendered to his touches.

She let her body follow his lead, let herself be carried away on a wave of sensation that peaked when he slid a finger into her, and flicked her to a quick, soft climax that only increased her need for something more intense. Eyes dazed with passion, she looked up into his. He stared at her with such need, and such emotion, she thought she wouldn't be able to breathe.

Moving a finger across his lips, she teased her fingers across his chest, experimentally pinching a nipple, heard him gasp, and was encouraged to continue. His fingers played with her sex absently, stroking her and creating wonderful sensations that urged her on.

Snaking her hands lower, she wrapped her fingers around his velvety, hard penis and stroked lightly, down to the base, then back. When she reached down a little farther, running her nails lightly over his balls, he groaned and removed his hand from her, pushing her back onto the mattress, and slid down her body, burying his face between her legs. She writhed on the bed as he brought her to the edge and left her there, tortured with wanting him.

"Jack…make me come…please…"

With a growl, and a promise to himself that he would stay in control for as long as he needed to, regardless of the fact that his body was taut as a wire, he brought himself up over her and slid the entire hard length of himself into her. Leaning down close to her, he kissed her deeply, rubbing his cheek, slick from her sex, over her face, and then licked it from her cheek with hungry kisses. His voice was hot and commanding next to her ear.

"Oh, you will come, Rainey. Hard and long…and with me inside you…."

She squeezed her eyes shut, feeling the panic and doubt starting to rise. The expectation chilled her. "I…I can't… you know…"

He brought his hands up to her breasts, kneaded them, pinching the nipples sharply, causing just enough pain to draw her attention away from her negative thoughts.

"Look at me, Raine."

She opened her eyes and he kissed her, staring into her eyes, hypnotizing her. He weighted her down almost flat to the mattress, his legs spread out flat as he lay between hers, and moved up, pushing himself into her in such a way that his hard pelvic bone pushed insistently against her swollen sex. His voice was rough, the effort of holding himself back warring with the powerful urge to let go and drive himself to completion.

"Focus on how it feels, Raine…feel me, every bit of me filling every bit of you…."

Opening her legs wide, letting them fall to each side, almost flush to the mattress, she rocked back against him and moaned, learning quickly how to maneuver in this position that touched all the parts of her she needed touched at once.

He said sweet, hot things to her, his voice becoming her world. He didn't allow her thoughts to slip even for a second to any other subject but the two of them bound together. She kissed him deeply, her eyes never moving away from his as he cradled her head in his hands, thrusting into her in deep, sure movements that maintained the pressure in all the right spots.

She began to feel a sweet pressure that she wanted to let build, yet wanted to release as well, and she moaned, begging him to help her.

His breath was ragged, and she felt him swelling even larger inside her, knowing he was close to climaxing, and the knowledge pushed her even higher. He was beyond words now, murmuring unintelligible sounds. He buried his face in her neck, his hands wound in her hair so tight it should have hurt, but it didn't. Tensing, he rocked into her harder, faster. She cried out when the burst of heat exploded from her loins and spread down her legs, curling up her back and twisting through her with the most wonderful sense of pleasure she had ever known. She pushed back against him fast and hard, seeking every last drop of it.

Jack moaned when he felt her contracting around him, felt her hot, wet muscles shudder and clench, and he buried himself in her as deep as he could, letting her climax take him the rest of the way. He came furiously, chanting her name, his body unable to stop thrusting even after the orgasm passed, he laid on her, quivering with the sheer intensity of it.

She was slack and panting beneath him, and he waited a few moments before rolling to the side, knowing he must be heavy, but smiling when she whimpered an objection as his softening cock slipped from her body.

He gathered her close to him, kissing her hair and yanking the blankets up to fend off the chill of the room on their hot skin. It was dark now, and the room was quiet except for the sounds of their gradually calming breathing. Kissing her hair, and feeling her curled up close against him, Jack took the reckless leap into love.

14

LIFE WAS GETTING more complex, but she didn't have too much time to sit around and think about it. After making love, they'd gotten back up, dressed quietly, touching and murmuring as lovers do as they walked back down to the kitchen. They got some wine and went to the office. It wasn't the most romantic follow-up to an evening of passion, but it had to be done. The trap had to be set.

Raine's hands were cold as she sat in front of the laptop trying to ignore the words on the screen. She hit the reply button and sat staring, then looked at Jack.

After a few moments she focused on the screen and typed experimentally:

We know you work at the magazine. It's only a matter of time before we find out exactly who you are. If you agree to meet me, and tell me why you have done what you did, and make things right, I might not report you to the police. If you don't meet me, I will absolutely report you as soon as we track your identity. This is not a bluff—we have proof that some of your e-mails were sent from computers in the magazine's offices. At the very least, we will inform the magazine of recent activities, and advise them to launch an inside investigation. Make it easy on yourself, and meet me at the Main Street Coffee Shop at one, tomorrow. RC

Jack nodded—that should get his shorts in a twist—but looking at the words on the screen, he felt a sudden flash of trepidation and wondered if this was such a smart idea. She hit the send button before he could say anything else, and heaved a sigh.

"Well, I guess now we just wait and see what happens to-morrow. Maybe he isn't even checking e-mail."

Jack rubbed her shoulders through the soft material of her sweatshirt.

"Let's hope he takes the bait."

She nodded and looked at him. "I want to wait for him—alone."

"No." He squeezed her shoulders once and walked to the other side of the office. She spun the chair around, aggravated at the tone of his voice, and her own cooled.

"Listen, he may be watching before he comes in. He may sense it's a trap. If he sees me there, he will be more inclined to think it's not a setup. And you can still follow him, get a picture, proof—"

"Raine, the plan stays the way it is. This guy is plainly dangerous. You don't want to meet him face-to-face. Anything could happen, too quickly for anyone to help."

"It's a busy coffee shop. There are lots of people there all the time, nothing can happen—"

"No, I can't let you do it."

She frosted over and looked at him, arching one eyebrow in a way that had him shaking his head and muttering to himself as he crossed the room toward her.

"It's too dangerous. We should keep it simple. I can sit at the counter and see who comes in that we know, and then follow him out, and everyone is safe."

"What if it is someone we don't know?" She closed her eyes.

"Jack, it could be anyone—a janitor, a secretary. Do you honestly think you can recognize everyone? Remember, over two-hundred employees work for the magazine. I don't know half the people in my department, and you rarely come out of the basement."

He swore. She had a point. He scowled, and paced the office behind her.

"I don't want you in there, at least not separate from me. We don't know what he might do, especially since you threatened him."

Raine shivered a little, but pressed on.

"True—but I won't lift my butt out of that chair to so much as go to the ladies' room, and you will be there, along with dozens of other people. I'm sure if things get out of hand, the cops would be there before we knew it. And that is if he even shows up—though I hope he does. I want my life back. I want this nightmare over with. A little risk seems like a small price to pay."

Jack watched her, and felt love and fear and admiration well up together in his chest. He wanted to take care of this for her, he wanted to keep her protected, but he saw strength in her eyes that he had never seen until just this moment, and he couldn't deny that she had a right to be involved.

"Okay. Okay. But you will not go anywhere alone, where I can't see you, no matter what happens. And if anything hits you wrong, you make noise, and lots of it."

She nodded and smiled.

"Thanks. For understanding that I need to be part of this. I need to get the control back."

He nodded, and drew her next to him, wrapping his arms around her and resting his cheek against hers. She moved her hands soothingly up and down his strong back and smiled. This was nice. For a moment, she believed everything was going to be okay.

THE NEXT DAY SHE didn't feel so sure of the plan as they drove into Salem. Nerves skittered along under her skin, giving her goose bumps and making her hands freezing cold, even under her wool sweater and jacket. She looked at the holly and garland on the lampposts, the colorful lights on the houses and businesses, the Santas ringing bells collecting coins in black pots. The world was a very odd place indeed.

So many happy and sad things always going on at once, you only had to look in one direction or the other to see someone sad or happy, ugly or beautiful, and if you were wondering if things would change, all you had to do was wait a minute. Here she was, herself, going to meet a criminal who had been terrorizing her life, while simultaneously thinking that she needed to look for a Christmas present for Gwen.

She had almost completely forgotten about the holiday. It had never meant much to her, as she'd never had anyone to celebrate it with. With Gwen, she had celebrated her first holidays, and had bought—and received—her first real Christmas gifts. She looked forward to it, but this year she almost had completely forgotten.

And Jack—should she be thinking of something for him, too? What was to become of them once this was finished? He had told her the night before that he wanted her in his bed, in his life, for more than one night. She wasn't completely sure what that meant.

Jack drove into a parking space quite a distance away from the coffee shop so that they could split up and go ahead separately. They had about a half hour, and he hated to admit that he was edgy enough to turn the car around and head back to the house. He looked over at Raine. She seemed cool enough, gazing out the window at Christmas decorations, lost in her own thoughts. He hoped that he was included in them.

"Okay—you have the tape recorder in your purse? It will only pick up forty-five minutes, so hopefully it won't take more than that—hit it before anyone comes in." He turned in the seat, grabbed her hand and pulled her over to him. "I'll be nearby, and I won't take my eyes off you."

He pressed his lips to her cheek, letting them drift to her mouth, where he kissed her with such tenderness it eased the anxiety that had taken hold of her. She sighed against his mouth, kissing him back then set her forehead against his.

"It's going to be just fine. I'll be fine."

He nodded. "Okay, let's go get this over with."

She moved away from him, then checked the recorder in her purse. Stepping out of the car, she started down the walk by herself, confident that Jack was not too far behind her. She saw the coffee shop and felt her stomach tie into a knot, but she kept walking, across the street, in the door, to a table in the back that, thankfully, was free. She sat, shrugging off her coat, and looked around. The door chimed again, and she looked up, saw Jack come in, and he looked away, heading for the counter directly across from her but facing her direction. His back was to the door.

Raine took a deep breath. It was shortly before one, so she

turned on her recorder, and left her bag lying half-open on the table.

A waitress came over to her table, took her order for a coffee, black, and Raine sat back and waited, pretending to be involved in reading the local newspaper. Minutes ticked by slowly, and she looked up at Jack; his gaze burnt into hers for a moment, and then he lowered his eyes.

He isn't coming. Raine felt a sense of despair drift over her—she had so hoped this plan would work. But fifteen minutes passed and all she had on her tape recorder was the sound of her drinking coffee and rustling a newspaper she'd already looked over three times. Her head popped up when the door chimed, and her eyes went wide.

Jack saw, and pivoted swiftly to see what had caused her alarm, and groaned inwardly—*great—just freakin' great*. He saw Raine's friend Gwen, on the arm of his employee Neal, hustling in the door, laughing and talking, their heads close together, until Gwen saw Jack and squealed in delight.

"Jack! Neal—it's Jack!"

Raine got up from the table and headed to the counter, and when Gwen saw her, another shout went up. Raine tried to smile, but was frustrated beyond reason when Gwen's arms came around her in a big hug.

Even so, how could she be mad when Gwen was telling her how worried she had been and how much she missed her? Dammit! They were busted. Even if the stalker did come in now, there was nothing they could do. Worse, he might think she was trying to set him up by having her friends there. Terrific. She caught Jack's eye, and knew he shared her thoughts. "Hi, Gwen. Neal."

Gwen slid right over the tension in the air, not even appearing to notice it. "Raine—I hate being at work without you—it's so *boring* there. Except for Neal, of course. But I miss coming by your office for girl talk. I called you at home and no one was there. What's up? You had me worried sick! Ask Neal, it's all I could talk about yesterday."

Neal smiled in agreement, then sent a knowing look at Jack. "She did. She is very worried about you, Ms. Covington. Jack, you are working from home?"

Jack nodded, but Gwen jumped in before he could say anything else. "Raine, where have you been? You called me the other day when you left the office, but I haven't heard from you since then. I was worried—I called your house and there was no answer, and your car was gone."

Raine felt color edge up in her cheeks, and she stumbled a minute, but Jack interrupted this time.

"She's staying with me, Gwen, at my place up near Gloucester."

Gwen's eyes widened; she stared at Jack, then at Raine, when a huge smile overcame her face and she nodded at both of them in a very knowing way. "Oh, that's terrific! I knew you two had something going on. I knew it!"

Raine tried to interject, wanting badly to change the subject, but Gwen pressed on.

"We're on lunch—do you guys want to get something to eat with us?"

Raine shook her head. "Oh, I don't think so, but—"

"But why don't you both join us for dinner tonight. You can come out to the house." Jack's invitation was smooth and quick, and he ignored Raine staring at him, her eyes slits.

"I know Raine has missed you too, Gwen, and it's been kind of a crazy few days, so we can catch up. Neal, we can talk shop." He grabbed a napkin from the counter, took a pencil the waitress had left there, and scratched out directions. "Here—how about seven?"

Gwen hugged him and accepted for them both. Saying some quick see ya laters, Raine and Jack headed back to the car. The plan had failed, they hadn't accomplished anything. He had dearly hoped that by this time today they would have something solid, something to help wrap this mess up. He bent his head to Raine's ear, his voice low and sympathetic.

"I know. It's too late for us to do anything now. We'll have to send another message maybe, since this got blown out of the water. Could be that he never even got the e-mail—or chose to ignore it."

Nodding, she got into the car, feeling bad tempered and frustrated.

"He won't come back. He could have been there and seen the whole thing. If he knew we were trying to set him up this time, he'll be especially cautious, and probably livid—God knows what he'll try to do this time. Maybe burn my house down."

Jack glared at her. "Don't even joke, Raine. We just have to play the hand we've got. Anyway, we can keep working on it—I know this came from inside. I want you to tell me about anyone you have had a hard time with, anyone who was passed up for a promotion that you got, someone you refused a date with—anything. We'll start there, and I am going to get into the files and find whatever leads I can, and we'll still keep trying to flush him out."

She felt a little less disgruntled at the idea. At least they could keep working at it.

"But how are you going to get into people's files?"

"You don't want to know."

His eyes had taken on the glimmer of the hunt, and Raine felt heat curl through her body, responding unexpectedly to the bad-boy appeal he emitted. She was coursing with emotion from the afternoon, switching back and forth between anxiety, despair, and excitement so quickly she was on overload. She felt as if she had just downed about ten coffees. Though she'd barely finished one.

Raine reached over and laid her hand on Jack's thigh, felt him tense. He looked over at her, his eyes hot, and she squeezed, sliding her hand up a little higher, and felt powerful when she heard him catch his breath. He sent her a sidelong glance.

"If a little illegal hacking gets you all worked up, I'll willingly turn to a life of crime, Rainey."

She laughed, and leaned over, stretching the seat belt as far as she could, and traced the tip of her tongue along his ear, then dipped it inside and felt him shudder. Fortunately, they were close to the house, and he managed to concentrate on the road as her hands explored other, more interesting places and her mouth worked magic on his skin.

By the time they parked in the driveway, he seriously considered tumbling her into the back seat again and just taking her there, fast and hard. Turning off the ignition, he hauled her across the middle and into his arms, covering her mouth with his in an insistent kiss, but his hands were frustrated by the thick material of her jacket, and he growled.

But his jacket was unzipped, and the next thing he knew, she shifted over and was unbuttoning his jeans; he grabbed her hand, protesting. Then he looked into her eyes, saw the fire there and let his hand fall away from hers.

She reached down, fitting her hand around him beneath the

material of his jeans. Her lips and tongue were all over his face, in his mouth, down the side of his neck, while her soft, delicate fingers massaged and caressed him. He gave himself over to her, dropping his head back as she stroked him and feeling the quick throb of pleasure take him over right there in the driver's seat, in his own driveway.

Raine felt wild and female and daring. It was one of the best feelings she had ever had, seducing him right there on the spot, knowing that he would let her have him, however she wanted, when she wanted. She fondled him, whispered to him gently, covered his mouth with hers, the kiss tender but rife with female satisfaction. She slid her hand up and grabbed a tissue from the dash while he blew out a breath and buttoned up his pants. He looked at her, she at him, and they both smiled. The windows were fogged, and his eyes were deep and soft.

"I'm loving this car thing. You can count on getting yours later."

She wiggled her eyebrows at him and popped the door open. "I hope so."

LATER, THE FOUR OF THEM sat over plates of spaghetti and meatballs that Jack and Raine had made together. It was both entirely natural and totally weird to be entertaining friends as if this were her home; they had cooked together, showered together, and now sat with good friends eating and chatting as though this was an old habit. While the sauce was simmering, Jack had made good on his earlier promise to "give her hers"—right on the kitchen floor. Raine smiled to herself, having acquired a new appreciation for hard surfaces.

She watched Gwen leaning into Neal, who had been

quiet most of the evening. He did, however, seem to complement her friend's effervescent personality. Gwen was really, really happy. She was going on now about something that had happened at her Reiki session, and both men listened with rapt attention, though Raine felt Jack's foot on hers, his toes scratching at her ankle, and she smiled at him openly now.

"And you guys can stop playing footsie under the table for a minute and listen to my new idea."

Surprised, Raine looked at Gwen, and her friend laughed. "Well, I'd like to say I knew that psychically, but you can always tell when people are fooling around under the table, can't you, Neal?" Suddenly Neal jumped a little in his seat, and his face went quite red. Gwen laughed, leaning over to plant a kiss on his cheek.

"So anyway, I was thinking when I finish my Reiki lessons maybe I can volunteer at the local animal shelters and do some healing for the animals there—if they are more peaceful and happy maybe people will adopt them faster. Or I can at least help them feel happier and like someone cares about them."

Raine frowned when she thought she saw Neal almost roll his eyes, but then saw him squeeze Gwen's hand. Jack, stacking more pasta onto his plate, appeared completely serious and interested, and Raine could have kissed him for that alone.

"So what is this you do, exactly, Gwen?" Jack asked.

Gwen smiled, and leaned toward him.

"Reiki is an ancient form of healing. It works with the natural energy forces that flows through our bodies and spirits, and helps us to manage them. Reiki can help us to figure out where energy is being channeled incorrectly, or where problems are, and can bring a more peaceful, balanced kind of energy to a person through specialized touch. I think it can work for animals, too. Poor babies, after being given up, or even abused, they need lots of good touching."

Jack nodded, and Raine just looked on.

"My mother used to massage our dog. The dog had arthritis, but also Mom thought if you touched in a very particular way, it helped the dog relax and feel happier. It always seemed to work."

Raine smiled. "Like sex."

The entire table was dead quiet for a moment, and she felt the heat move up into her cheeks as she realized she had spoken out loud. Then everyone roared with laughter, which would have been mortifying, but Jack pulled her over and kissed her, looking delighted, so she smiled, too, and shook her head. Gwen, still bubbling over, nodded.

"It's true—there are lots of ways it can work. Usually touching, the right kind of touching, is key. When people go without being touched, or are touched in bad ways, it can really mess your energy up—and making love is a great way to touch." She sent a particularly glowing look Neal's way, then turned her gaze back to Raine and Jack.

"There are lots of studies connecting touching and sex with emotional and physical health. Reiki just adds a spiritual dimension."

After dinner, Gwen and Raine sat chatting on the sofa, while Neal and Jack got involved in some technical issue in Jack's office.

"So you and Neal look like you are doing well."

"Oh yeah—we haven't, you know, said anything too much yet, he's very quiet, and I think he would be very careful about telling someone he loved them, but…"

"You love him?" Raine whispered, holding her hand to her heart as she gazed at her friend.

Gwen's doubts were evident in her eyes.

"I'm not sure. God knows, when we have sex, it's like heaven, and he is so sweet—he is so, I dunno—attentive, I guess. Not in front of people, then he is shy, but when we are alone, he's completely different, and well, I know I like him—a lot. But sometimes I think I don't know him, like there are layers there, things I don't know. I have tried to see in the cards, but they don't seem right."

"Gwen, do you really think you should be looking at your tarot cards for relationship advice?"

"Well, it's not like hard-and-fast advice. The cards are good reflective tools. They help me see things I may not otherwise, just by making me think about it."

"And so what are you thinking?"

"That I want to wait and see, but that this could definitely be going somewhere."

Raine smiled. "Then I hope it goes well."

Gwen grinned back. "Yeah, and who would've thought you'd be living here with Jack?"

Raine winced. "We're not living together—we weren't even dating—but all these things happened at once and coming here seemed to be the best thing. But yeah, it's good. Really good."

Gwen bounced up and down on the sofa cushion, and Raine continued. "But we are not living together. This is a temporary arrangement just until this stalker mess is figured out."

Gwen sobered. "Yeah—what's the word on that? I didn't want to bring it up at dinner. Buzz kill."

"Not much. We thought we had a plan to move things

along, but it didn't pan out." She didn't go into detail, not wanting Gwen to feel responsible for messing up their trap. "But Jack has a plan, he is tracking down a lead, and so maybe we can find something there."

"It completely sucks that the police can't help. What the heck are they there for?"

"There is an Internet crime expert Jack has been talking with in Boston, but no word yet." Raine sighed.

"The guy was at your house, for pete's sake."

Raine nodded, feeling as if that took place a million years ago, when it had only been less than a week. "Yeah, but he didn't leave any traces behind. Hopefully something will shake loose soon."

She thought of the list of names that Jack had started working on earlier. As soon as Neal and Gwen left, he would be back at the computer, she knew, trying to pry out whatever information he could on magazine employees, which she found kind of exciting, in an illicit way.

On that thought, the guys came back in the room, and Raine smiled when Jack squeezed down on the couch beside her and planted a kiss on her lips. Raine caught Gwen's knowing look and blushed, but Gwen's eyes just danced as she leaned back against Neal, who was sitting on the opposite arm. It was late, and the fire was burning low. Neal stood up, yawning.

"This was great—thanks for inviting us—but I think we should leave."

Jack stood as well. "You're welcome to stay if you want— we have an extra room."

Neal shook his head. "No, thanks. I have to get in early. Ready, Gwen?"

She nodded, and crossed over to hug Raine, and then Jack. "I missed you—I hope this mess is straightened out soon."

Jack nodded, placing his hand possessively back on Raine's shoulder. "We do, too. He'll make a mistake at some point. And we'll be ready."

Gwen nodded, and Neal made the move to end the evening, shaking Jack's hand, then Raine's, and guided Gwen out the door. As they stepped out into the night, Jack shook his head.

"I still have a hard time seeing those two together. She is like a ball of fire, and it's like pulling teeth to get Neal to say anything unless it is about computers."

Raine shrugged. "Well, she says he is different in private. She's nuts about him—I hope he knows it's—kinda hard to tell."

Jack smiled, linking his arms loosely around her waist. "Do you think people notice that I am crazy about you?"

She smiled, and felt herself melt a little. "You are a lot more obvious about it than Neal."

"Is that bad? Does it bother you?"

Raine considered, then shook her head. "No. I like it."

He smiled, grateful for her answer, and pressed a kiss to her forehead. "Good. Because I want to yell it from the rooftops."

Raine hugged him back, and buried her face in his neck. She knew she was feeling something for him—definitely more than friendship—certainly more than simple lust. But she didn't completely understand it yet, and didn't trust how things would be when life went back to normal. She had led a pretty normal, even boring life. Would that be as interesting to Jack as playing hero to her damsel in distress?

"I want to go do more work on those names—see what I can find. I have to figure out how to, um, get past some particularly tricky obstacles."

She nodded, wondering what the obstacles might be. "Okay, me, too."

"Why don't you go up to bed. It's late, and I'll probably be a while."

"No, that's okay, anyway I won't be able to sleep wi—" She stopped short, her words stuck in her throat. *Without you. I won't be able to sleep without you* is what she almost said. The truth of it stunned her, froze her in her tracks. "Um, with having just eaten dessert. Indigestion. Can I keep you company for a while? Maybe I can help."

He looked at her intently, wondering what caused the quick flash of dismay in her eyes, but he nodded, and grabbed her hand, walking with her into the office.

RAINE AWOKE to see Jack still staring intently at the computer, tapping keys, and taking notes, just as he had been hours ago when she had nodded off. Crossing over to him, she wrapped her arms around his shoulders from behind, snuggling into his warmth.

"What time is it?"

"A little after two."

"Time for bed, huh? Did you find anything?"

He grunted. "Nothing notable. Maybe this wasn't the best strategy."

She squeezed his shoulders, and shivered. "It's the best idea we have right now. And I appreciate you doing all this detective work while I fell asleep in the chair."

He craned his head back, and kissed her softly.

"You cold?"

"It's gotten a little chilly in here."

He moved forward, disentangling himself, and stood. "The

fire must have died down—I need to go out and get more wood. It will only take a few minutes to get it warmed up in here, then we can go to bed."

Heat leaped between them as he uttered those completely mundane but deeply intimate words. He found that love made everything, even the slightest moment, richer and more meaningful. He walked to the door, shrugging on a jacket and sending her a warm look.

"Back in a minute."

15

It was bitter cold outside, and Jack grabbed his work gloves as he walked out back toward a large stack of split wood. It was a crisp, moonless night, and he stood for a moment, taking a deep, refreshing breath.

The snow from the recent storm lay like a sparkling blanket on the landscape. He was exhausted—but he was happy, and warm with anticipation of going back to the house to spend the night with the woman he loved. *The woman I love. I love Raine Covington.*

He laughed to himself, feeling a little giddy, like the teenager who'd had a crush on her so many years ago, but this time he wasn't just watching her from afar. She was his now; he wanted it to stay that way.

He leaned over to grab some firewood, and tumbled forward, plunging hard into the dark, snowy corner when something cracked him on the head. He lay there, collapsed against the woodpile, fighting the darkness creeping over his consciousness.

His attacker, just a shadow skulking in the dim light, strode quickly back to the house.

In the den, Raine lost the battle and dozed off. She smiled when she felt a caressing hand on her cheek awaken her. She raised her hands, put them on shoulders that were close to hers and registered immediately that something was wrong. Her hands knew Jack's body intimately, and she knew the broad feel of his chest and shoulders—and this wasn't it.

Too slight. Too narrow.

Alarmed, she cried out, pushing wildly at the shadow in front of her, striking out with her legs and catching him unexpectedly, toppling him over the coffee table.

She heard the resulting crash and a string of vile curses as she bolted over the side of the sofa and ran toward the door. *Jack. Where was Jack?* She screamed his name. Just making it to the door, she reached out to open it, but was tugged back rudely by the hair, her scalp screaming with the force of it. Pain shot up her arm when she smashed her elbow into the wall as she was dragged backward almost off her feet.

"Sit down, dammit!" The voice that yelled at her was high and almost whiny, and she felt herself shoved down into the couch cushions, where she sat and tried to focus on the face across from her. The fire was gone now, and light entered the den dimly from the office down the hall, so it was hard to make out details.

The figure paced back and forth in front of her, grumbling to himself, and she felt a prick of familiarity at the back of her mind—the stature, something in the voice—and she struggled through her fear to place it.

Neal.

It was Neal, though he looked different. Not the quiet, reserved young man who had sat across the table from her earlier in the evening; his hair was tossed about, and his face deathly pale except for the red splotches on his cheeks.

For a moment, she was too shocked to think about her situation—Neal was the one who had been harassing her? He was staring at her now, staring through her as if he was trying to read her thoughts, and she looked away, a new wave of terror overcoming her. She leaped up from the couch, which had him crossing the room, and she spun on him, screaming at him.

"Where's Jack? What have you done with Jack?"

He walked up and grabbed her by the neck, yanking her close to him, and she fought, flailing, but he was surprisingly strong and dug his fingers painfully into the soft skin behind her ear to keep her still.

"Lover boy? Oh, I took care of him. I took care of him but good. I wouldn't be counting on any help from your precious Jack." He grinned, and Raine felt the coldness of it down to her bones. "Besides, what do you need him for? You have me now."

She fought again, not caring about the pain of his fingers in her skin, and finally he drew his hand back and the strong slap against her cheek tumbled her back on the sofa. She felt tears sting her eyes, and looked up at him. He was standing over her, his voice shaking.

"I didn't want to do that! I don't hit women, don't like to hit them—why do you keep making me do these things?" He looked at her, his face contorted with rage. "Bitch. You're all bitches. Every last one of you. I thought *you* might be nicer, different, but you aren't. A whore, just like all of them."

Raine felt weak with fear. "Why, Neal? Why would you do this? I don't even know you—"

His face momentarily softened, then contorted with anger again. "You didn't want to know me. You met me before him—I watched you at work, I tried to get to know you, and you all but ignored me. Vague pleasantries—that's all you ever offered. The things people say when they really want you to leave them alone. But then you found *him,* and you didn't tell him to leave you alone, did you? Sluts—you're all sluts."

He turned on her, spitting mad.

"But you were mine first. He had no right—neither did you. I knew you were meant to be mine. And you would have been if he hadn't interfered. I just needed more time. Now we have the time."

Raine raised her hand to where the side of her face was stinging, and tried to comprehend what he was saying. It didn't seem right—Neal? She thought back to the times she'd dealt with him at work, but she couldn't remember any of their encounters clearly.

"I tried to do nice things, tried to get to know you—the only way I could get around you, or get any information about you was with Gwen—"

Raine's eyes flew open, and she sat forward. "No—you haven't hurt her, Neal, please say you haven't."

He made a disgusted face. "Hardly. I just gave her a little something so she would sleep really sound tonight. She thinks she's in love with me—so stupid. But she was convenient—she liked to talk about you, and she was an easy lay. I figured it was practice until I could get the real thing. I'm good, you know—very good. Gwen even said so." His smile was sly. Raine felt her skin crawl, but made her voice sound as calm as she could.

"You can't get away with this, Neal. Gwen will know. Everyone will know."

"No one knows anything! I'm taking you out of here with me tonight, and no one will know anything." He smiled again, moving closer. "As for your former boyfriend, I figure he'll die of exposure. Sad, but necessary. I can't afford to have him around. They'll just think he fell down getting some wood, smashed his head on a log and died from being out in the cold too long. That's how I planned it."

Raine felt her stomach twist and her whole body began to shake as she realized that Jack was hurt, maybe dying, and she was trapped in here with Neal. She had to do something— had to figure out a way to get to Jack.

She looked up at Neal, the change in his voice alerting her to something dangerous, and she felt shivers run down her back. He was standing closer now, and he looked at her almost— gently? He made a clucking noise and stepped closer to her.

"Oh, I've upset you—don't be upset about him, you have me now. I can take care of you. All I want to do, all I have wanted to do is be with you, take care of you." He reached out to touch her face. "Touch you." She pulled back, and saw the flash of anger in his face, and stopped herself. Swallowing her fear and the vile repulsion that surged through her, she made herself smile as she looked up at him.

"I'm sorry, Neal. I don't want to hurt you—please don't hurt me."

He leaned down over her, and she felt the tears choke her. She only had one shot to save Jack and herself. Neal was focused on her now, stretching out to touch her again, and speaking to her in that nasal-thin, quavering voice.

"I don't want to hurt you—I love you." He strummed his fingers down her arm, and she tried to hold herself steady, not giving in to the repulsion that followed the path of his cold, clammy touch. He braced his knee on the edge of the sofa, his hot breath suffocating her as he leaned even closer, pressing his moist mouth to her temple.

Focusing—focusing hard—she placed her hands on his

shoulders, turning her face to his, and he sighed, obviously pleased, and kissed her. Mustering all her will to kiss him back so that she could keep him distracted, she blanked her mind of the urge to throw up.

She shifted a little farther under him as a groan of desire rattled from Neal's chest. She thought she heard a noise behind her—*Jack*. It had to be Jack! She twisted underneath Neal's groping hands, at once pushing down on his shoulders and bringing her knee up into his crotch—hard. As he sucked in a sharp breath, she dug her fingers into his shoulders and brought her knee up again, for good measure.

"Raine!" Jack staggered into the doorway just in time to see Neal doubled up over Raine and keening in pain. Jack tried to make his body move faster, but the crushing pain in his head was holding him back. When he stepped forward the room spun; he had to stop and grab on to the door frame and catch his breath.

He saw Raine stand, and tried to focus his blurred vision— Neal—it was *Neal?*—Jesus. It *was* Neal. He watched in disbelief as Raine jumped up from the sofa, pushing hard at Neal, causing him to fall backward over the coffee table, his head hitting the floor with a thud. He stayed there, curled up and making strangled sounds. Jack blinked, trying to comprehend what was happening, and steadied himself.

"Rainey…"

"Jack! Oh my God." She rushed to him, and he felt the welcome relief of her hands on him, and her lips touching his face, her wet cheeks against his.

"Raine—God, did he…are you…okay?"

Raine looked back at Neal, lying helplessly on the floor.

"He's not getting up for a while. I'm okay." She felt another wave of nausea as the memory of Neal's hands and lips washed over her. Needing to erase it, she got closer and kissed Jack, and set her forehead to his, trying to catch her breath. Then she stepped away, and picked up a poker from the fireplace, handing it to him, just in case. "Stay here—I'm calling the police."

Jack nodded, his vision cleared again—it seemed to come and go. He had barely found his way back to the house, feared he might have just as easily ended up in the water as he struggled through the dark. His face felt raw from where he had fallen face-first into the woodpile, and his head was spinning, but he kept his eye on Neal, holding the poker firmly in his hand.

Raine came back, took the poker from him and urged him forward to the sofa. Neal was curled up on the floor, whimpering now, mumbling unintelligible things. Jack looked at him and wished they were both standing so he could kick his sorry ass, but then Raine had already done a pretty good job of that. He turned, only to find her gone again, and panicked for a second, until he saw her return, with a wet rag and an ice pack.

"The police will be here very shortly."

She steadied his head so she could wash some of the blood from the cuts on his face, and felt her stomach clench when her fingers felt the stickiness on the back of his head. He winced, going pale. She pulled her hand away and saw blood on her palm, Jack's blood, and choked.

"Oh no, Jack…"

He reached out to hold her, but his voice slurred and she felt her skin turn to ice, unsure of what to do. "S'okay Rainey…he hit me with something…I'm sure it's not that bad…don't worry."

At that moment Raine saw the flashing lights in the window, and managed to get up on her wobbly legs, rushing to the door to let the officers in.

"I need an ambulance, he's hurt! Please, hurry…." She pointed to Jack.

Over the radio, they called an ambulance, and crossed the room to where Jack lay on the sofa.

"Ma'am, can you tell us what happened here?"

She rattled through what happened and pointed to Neal. She suggested they contact Detective Delaney.

"Do you have any proof this is the man who has been harassing you?"

Jack's voice interrupted, a bare croak, but there. "Except for the fact that he just tried to kill us?"

Raine shot the officer a look, and went to Jack, sitting down next to him as two other officers attended to Neal.

"He told me—he told me it was him, and why."

The cop nodded. "Okay, you both need to go to the hospital, we're going to investigate the scene, and we'll contact Delaney—we'll need your statement as soon as you can give it."

Jack nodded, and Raine pushed him gently back against the sofa, murmuring to him as she heard sirens from the ambulances coming up the road. The cops were handcuffing Neal, and reading him his rights even as he lay there on the floor still moaning. Suddenly she started to shake.

She heard the door open again, and she was very cold. It must be from all the frigid air coming in from the door, she figured. There was a lot of noise, and she couldn't seem to stop her teeth from chattering, no matter how hard she tried.

She watched them lift Neal onto a stretcher. blinking, It didn't seem quite real. Someone was kneeling by her and saying something, but she just gazed at him blankly. Somehow understanding that it was over, she let herself slide into the relief of oblivion.

IT WAS A FULL WEEK later when Raine was helping Jack back to his house. She had only been kept overnight in the hospital for observation, but he had sustained some serious head injuries and had been hospitalized for a week. Gwen had also been admitted overnight, after she told the police that Neal had drugged her—fortunately, it hadn't been a lethal dose. It was over now, and they could relax.

It was all cut-and-dried, according to the prosecutors, with the abundance of evidence implicating Neal that the police had uncovered while going through his home and computers. He apparently had a long but previously undetected habit of e-mail harassment and Internet theft. His most serious charge—attempted murder—would send him away for a good long time.

Jack mulled it all over as they pulled in to his driveway, flexing his fist and wishing he could have a go at Neal's face now that he was fully recovered. But it was over and it was time to move on. He looked at Raine and smiled—move on to better things. Yeah.

"Well, let me get your case and we'll go inside—"

"Raine, I'm not an invalid. I'm able to carry my own case. I feel as good as new."

The worry was still apparent in her eyes, and she stubbornly took the case from the back seat, reaching up to slide her hand gently over the back of his head, over the stubbly spot where the doctor had shaved his gorgeous hair and stitched up his wound.

"Yeah, you're a real tough guy. Just let me take it, okay?"

He decided maybe it wasn't so bad to be taken care of,

after all, and grasped her hand as they walked up the steps. The house was cool, but it felt good to be home. As soon as the door was closed, Jack showed Raine just exactly how recovered he was feeling. Sliding his arms around her, he pinned her firmly against the door, fitting his mouth over hers before she could so much as take a breath. She melted into him, heat flaring as he moved his mouth across her cheek, nuzzling her.

"Maybe I will need a little help, you know, getting my clothes off…."

She laughed and squirmed in his hold. "Jack, we just got in, you should sit down…"

He growled against her ear. "I'll sit down if you sit on my lap…."

She giggled, and didn't believe it—she never giggled. Realizing that made her giggle more as he kissed her face, and she playfully shoved him away.

His expression was passionate, but amused, and he backed up, holding her hand. As they stepped into the foyer, he looked into the den, and remembered the last time he had come through this door. Clinging to the door frame, barely able to stand, he'd seen Neal leaning over Raine, watched her fighting him off, feeling sick with helplessness. He shook his head in disgust at the memory.

"Ouch." Raine tugged her hand from his. "You're squeezing too hard."

"Oh, hell. I'm sorry, baby. I just…"

She touched his face. "It's okay. I know, the memory of it hits you when you walk back in. Me, too. I almost couldn't stay here alone the first night, but it wears off soon. Get some food, a fire, and the house feels better."

He pulled her close again. "The house feels better with you in it."

Kissing her soundly, he picked up his case. "I'm gonna take this up and change—wanna help me?"

She grinned. "Later—maybe after I get you some lunch."

"Toasted cheese? And tomato soup?" he angled, figuring if she was in the mood to baby him, he wasn't going to pass it up.

"Sure."

He grinned and kissed her again, and went upstairs. Raine busied herself in the kitchen, and didn't even hear him when he came quietly back into the kitchen.

"Raine?"

She turned from stirring the soup and smiled. "Hey. Almost done here. Maybe you should get a fire going, it's going to be a cold night."

"Where are your things?"

She turned, wrinkling her forehead. "What?"

"Your stuff—your clothes, paperwork, your briefcase— nothing is here."

She felt her muscles tense in response to the edge in his voice, and she kept her voice light and even.

"I took my things home. I stayed here for a day or so, but I was spending most of my time at the hospital with you, and I figured it was safe to go back—"

"You left? Why?"

Truly puzzled now, she turned the burner under the soup off and shrugged. "It was over, time for me to go home. There wasn't any point in me staying here after things were settled."

"Over? No point in you being here? How about the fact that

we are together now, Raine? This is where you are supposed to be." The words really grated as he said them, causing her anger to flare.

"Where I am *supposed* to be? What the hell does that mean? Yes, we are together, but I have my own house, my own life, and I needed to get back to it. We are still together. I don't know what you are so upset about."

"I told you I wanted you with me, every day, every night— in my bed. Not in another house, another town."

She felt the blood drain from her face. "What are you saying? You expected me to live here? With you? Permanently?"

He was so angry she nearly flinched just from the expression on his face. She'd seen him angry before, but this was different. Something else was layered over the anger—hurt? She felt terrible when she realized what he had expected.

"Jack, be reasonable—we have only been together a few weeks, and under stressful circumstances. It was nice for you to let me stay here, and we obviously are together, but—" She paused, hearing the strain in her voice.

"Nice? You think I was *nice* to let you stay here? You want me to be *reasonable?*"

"Stop repeating everything I say."

Crossing the kitchen in a few long steps, he backed her up against the sink, pressing into her, his face close.

"I don't feel like being reasonable, Raine. I can't believe you would pull away from me like this, just…up and leave. What do you want, Raine? How do you feel about me? What do you think this thing is between us?"

His eyes searched her face, and she stammered under the scrutiny, not able to form a reply before he continued.

"Because I'll tell you, my ideas about us didn't include you moving out and going happily on with your life—where did I fit into your plan, Raine? Am I in it?"

His eyes glittered, and she gazed back at him. "Yes, God, Jack, yes! I didn't leave *you*, I just returned to my own home. I assumed we would keep seeing each other, see what it is we have, what we really feel…"

She couldn't finish as he leaned even closer into her. "What we *really feel?* What do you really feel, Raine?"

"I…I, I'm not sure. It has all gone so fast, and there has been so much—how can we know for sure…?"

"I'll tell you what I know for sure. I love you. I love you and I want you here with me, living with me, sleeping with me, sharing everything with me. I don't want to date you, Raine—we crossed that line a long time ago."

She couldn't breathe—he *loved* her? He thought she was just going to live with him, to stay there and never go home? A feeling of uncertainty suddenly overwhelmed her, and she wiggled her way out of his tight hold. She crossed the kitchen, then whirled, turning on him, confused, angry, and a million other things.

"You love me? And what does that mean? That you get to make all the decisions, that you decide what this relationship will be and I am supposed to just go along? I don't think that is how you show you love someone."

"Oh, and you didn't do exactly the same thing, just moving out of here, and never mentioning a word of it? Why didn't you say anything, Raine? You have spent every day with me, but never mentioned a word about going back home."

"I…I guess I just didn't figure it was a big deal."

She felt his chill across the room, and realized she'd put

that badly, but refused to back off now, and lifted her chin stubbornly. He walked to her, slowly, and looked at her deeply

"What exactly do you feel for me, Raine? You want me to ask, so I am asking."

She squirmed. He wasn't touching her, only standing there, looking right through her, and she could only find weak words, started to lift her hand to touch him, but dropped it back to her side.

"I…well, I want you. I care for you—a lot. You know that."

His eyes veiled, and he didn't say anything, just nodded. "You care for me."

She nodded, and felt lost. Small. Sad.

He walked to the window, and leaned on the counter, looking out. "And do you believe I love you?"

She took a breath, trying to find something right to say.

"I know you care about me, too—I don't know about love, Jack—I haven't had any experience with it. And we have been in this horrible situation, so maybe it has made us feel things that we normally wouldn't have—"

He turned, cutting her off. "Please, Raine. We've been down this road. I am a grown man, and I am in love with you. At least accept that much."

She felt sick, and wanted to go to him, but didn't know how to break down the wall that was growing between them.

"I just need some time—we can still be together, still see each other."

"Why? So you can decide if you really feel anything for me or not?"

"No! Stop twisting things. You know I have feelings for you, I just don't know how to handle them, I don't know what they are. I need to figure things out."

His shoulders slumped, and he ran his hand over his face.

"Fine. Okay." He came back to her, placed his hands on her shoulders, pain evident in his eyes.

"I guess that's it, then. I guess we'll just see where it goes. But right now, I need you to go. I want to be alone."

Raine felt the hurt cut through her, and nearly wept. She wanted to say something, but the words weren't there, she didn't know what they were, where to find them. So she nodded as his hands fell away, and she whispered, "Okay," and went back to the hall to get her jacket.

Walking away from the house, she felt her heart break with each step she took, but for reasons even she couldn't understand, she kept walking.

16

HERE SHE WAS. Home. It was what she wanted. The fight with Jack had left her miserable and frustrated—why couldn't he understand? He had had no right to make the assumptions he had. He had no right to be angry at her. She was sure of it.

So why did she feel so awful? So lonely? A knock on the door startled her out of her muddled thoughts.

"Just a second."

A shiver of paranoia ran down her spine, and she breathed in and out slowly, reminding herself there was no one stalking her now: she was safe. She opened the door.

"Gwen!" She smiled with joy at seeing her friend, but the joy faded when she took in Gwen's pale features and sad eyes. She wasn't sparkly the way she usually was, and she was dressed in jeans and a plain gray T-shirt, which was definitely *not* Gwen's style.

Raine slid her arm around her friend's slim shoulders and drew her inside. She had talked to Gwen the morning after everything had happened, offered to be there when the police wanted to talk with her, but Gwen had insisted she was fine and needed time alone. Raine knew she was embarrassed, humiliated and hurt.

"Here, sit down, and let me make us some tea."

Gwen nodded. "Yeah, put something stiff in it if you have anything."

"Sorry, all I have is some good old Earl Grey."

Raine stopped halfway to the kitchen and watched Gwen bury her face in her hands. The tea could wait. She went back to the couch, surprised at how tightly her own heart twisted when Gwen raised her tear-filled eyes to her and spoke raggedly through sobs that seemed to be threatening to take over.

"I…thought…he was it, Raine. I…slept with him…he said things, made me feel so special. I went to the jail to see him—yesterday…."

"Oh, no—you should have called me, Gwen. You shouldn't have done that alone."

Gwen nodded. "I couldn't process it. I needed to hear it from him. And boy did I hear it. He said I was just a slut he was using till he could get what he really wanted. You." The last word came out on a wail, and she fell against Raine wracked in sobs. Raine followed her instincts and hugged her.

Eventually, Gwen's sobbing ceased, and they just sat there, two friends, comforted by having each other. Raine hadn't known until this moment how much she cherished their bond. Rarely in her life had she felt that kind of connection with anyone.

"I feel so stupid. How could I have thought I was in love with that insane *jerk?*"

Raine sat back, and took both Gwen's hands in hers, and squeezed.

"You were not stupid. Not ever, not for a moment. He was more than a jerk, he was evil, Gwen, and you can't be expected to have known that. He fooled you, and used you in the worst possible way. He fooled all of us. It's not your fault."

Gwen didn't quite nod, and Raine didn't know what else to say, so remained silent.

"I told him things, about us, being friends, about you—just general stuff, but he might have used the information to hurt you, I didn't know. If you had gotten hurt, I never could have forgiven myself."

Gwen was on the edge of tears again, and Raine put her hands on either side of Gwen's face, and spoke firmly. "Nothing that happened here is anyone's fault but Neal's. He's sick. I am so sorry you are paying so dearly for this, Gwen. You don't deserve it. You just don't deserve it, hon."

Gwen nodded, sighed, and sat back against the couch.

"I thought you were getting wine."

Raine smiled. "Tea, Gwen. It's only one in the afternoon."

"So?"

"I don't have any wine, but I might have some chocolate chip cookies in here somewhere."

Gwen smiled, the first real smile Raine had seen. They went into the kitchen to sit.

"So how are things with you and Jack? I'm so glad he was okay. I would have come to see him in the hospital, but…"

"He understands completely." She sat, sighed. "Things kind of…blew up the other day. He was mad that I wanted to come home."

"Why would he be mad about that?"

Raine looked sheepishly at Gwen. "Well, I guess I didn't go about it very well. I moved back home while he was in the hospital, and didn't let him know."

"Ouch. Raine, sheesh."

"Well, c'mon! It's not like we were really living together, not like I ever agreed to that. We never even discussed it, he never asked me what I wanted."

"What *do* you want?"

Raine stared out the window.

"I don't know. I guess we'll have to wait and see if what we had was real or just part of the situation. I don't know how to trust what he feels…what I feel."

"What *do* you feel?"

Raine couldn't answer. Words jammed in her throat, feelings in her heart. Gwen smiled again.

"Raine, it's pretty clear that you love him."

"I do?"

"Yeah. And he is nuts about you, too—has he told you?"

"Yeah."

Gwen prompted her eagerly. "And you said…?"

"Um, well, I wasn't sure—how can he be sure he loves me? I care about him, and I want to be with him, I told him that—"

Gwen collapsed back in her chair. "So he spilled his guts to you, and you told him thanks, I care about you? Oh, God, poor Jack. That is the worst."

"What do you mean poor Jack?" It came out in a squeal, and had her up and stomping to the sink again, then back to the table. "He shouldn't have assumed so much, he just had it all so neatly planned, and without talking to me about it at all."

"You didn't tell him you had moved out, either."

"That's different—I never moved in on a permanent basis. He should have known."

"C'mon, Raine—the guy basically laid his life at your feet, and you stomped on it."

Gwen got up to go get the tea, and came back to the table.

"Listen, I know you are afraid, and that it's a risk. Believe me, I know what it feels like to fall down on the wrong side of a risk."

Raine started to speak, but Gwen was on a roll, and continued. "But there's no gain without risk. I jumped too quickly with Neal, didn't know enough about him. But as much as my ego has taken a bruising, losing Neal was not a fatal blow. We didn't have what I see when I look at you and Jack—that connection, that passion—I *wanted* us to have it, maybe so much I missed the signals. If you let go of what you have with Jack, Raine, I think it will be one of your biggest regrets. He's one of the good ones."

Raine absorbed the words, unsure what to say. Her mind was going a mile a minute.

"Raine, stop thinking—just feel how does he make you *feel?*"

She sighed, fidgeted with her cup. "Safe. Cared for. Special."

"Desired? Passionate? Happy?"

Raine nodded, feeling uncomfortable. "Yeah. I know it's not just sex, it's more. I just don't know how much more. I don't know how I am supposed to know. How can anyone know?"

"Well, you just have to trust your heart. And his. Think of how you felt when you knew he was seriously hurt, about the time you spent together at the house, and how you felt when you went to stay with him in that hospital room—every day."

Gwen leaned across the table, squeezed Raine's hand and looked at her intently. "I know I didn't deserve what happened to me with Neal—neither did you. But you *do* deserve Jack. You have to go for it, Raine—admit how you feel to yourself, and then let him know. It could be the only good that comes out of this mess, aside from putting that asshole in prison."

Raine nodded, and sipped her tea, and knew Gwen was

right. Overthinking things wasn't going to make them clearer. She had hurt him. She was so caught up in her own baggage that she hadn't put it down long enough to think about how her actions were affecting him. She had to stop hiding behind her wounds.

She missed Jack—it was the plain truth. The truth she had been struggling with since she had left him. She had hated walking away from that house with every step she took. She had felt empty every second since. She hadn't ever really known love, but she thought, maybe, she was knowing it now. And, at the moment, it hurt.

"I think Jack's due back in town today. I guess I have some Christmas shopping to do."

Gwen smiled, and the old sparkle came back into her eyes for a moment. "Attagirl. Go get him. And remember, I'll want all the details."

They laughed, and Raine felt more alive than she had in her whole life. She knew exactly what to give Jack for Christmas.

HER NERVOUSNESS was all-consuming. She had never done anything like this in her life. Obviously. If she had done things like this before, she would not be so nervous now. She would be cool and calm and ready to go like she always imagined she would be like when she had thought this was a good idea, and in the shops when she had gotten this entire deal together—*stop!* God, she was rambling in her own head. Silence. Relax.

This may not have been a good idea, but it was all set to go now, no backing out, and she had to see it through. God help her.

She'd bought a Christmas tree, decorations and candles.

She had decorated it in Jack's bedroom. She then put one brightly wrapped box underneath. She took the pretty quilt from the bed and laid it out on the floor beside the tree.

She looked at the clock and hoped he would come home before she completely lost her nerve, but not before she was completely ready.

She had called him, left a message on his cell that she wanted to see him and would wait for him at his house, so he knew. Ducking into the shower, she soaped and shaved and shampooed with the fragrant accessories she had bought herself, ignoring the totals that had added up on her credit card. It was Christmas, after all. Time to splurge.

She dried off, applying the exotic lotion she'd bought, and slipped on the bright-red, lace flyaway baby doll she had purchased that afternoon. She looked in the mirror and her eyes nearly popped out—it sure didn't hide much. But she was done with hiding, so she took a deep breath and turned, examining herself in the mirror. Not half bad, really.

The top barely contained her breasts, and parted at the middle to show off her trim waist and inny belly button. The small, triangular scrap of lace that lay over her abdomen made her feel sultry and sexy. Daring, even.

She slipped on a furry white garter and felt a sense of anticipation flow over her. She fluffed and dried her hair, applied a deep red tint to her lips. She didn't need any other makeup, her cheeks were flushed enough with anticipation. She had never seduced a man before. Furthermore, she had never seduced a man she loved before.

It was five minutes to seven. God, she hoped he was still coming home tonight.

Taking a deep breath, she went into the living room and

checked the champagne she had bought, lit the candles she had placed on each stair leading up to the bedroom. She lowered the lights and, finally, put on the satin Santa hat she had bought, just for fun. Then she returned to the bedroom to wait. It was just past seven. She hoped he wouldn't be very late. She had called him at four. Not that he would come running just because she called.

BUT HE HAD. Pulling up to the house, he saw her car, and had no idea what was going on, or why Raine had left the vague message on his phone. But he had listened to it twice, just to hear her voice more than anything else. It had only been a day, but he missed her like hell. He frowned, why didn't she answer the door? Pushing the door open, he only heard silence, and apprehension clutched at him as he turned the knob.

"Raine…where are you?"

He stopped for a moment, surprised, and then caught his breath and grinned like only a man can when he realized what was going on. Lowered lights, candles, champagne—*oh yeah.* He locked the door securely behind him and followed the candle-lit path up the stairs to his room, where the door was partially open, and soft lights blinked out into the hall.

He stopped dead in the doorway, losing his breath completely in the wash of stunned desire that swept over him when he saw her. She was laid out on a green blanket under a Christmas tree. The scrap of red lace that barely covered her gorgeous body turned his mouth dry in seconds. The room was dark except for the blinking tree lights that played over her skin. She tilted her head provocatively, bending one leg up at the knee, tempting his eyes to follow the movement, and smiled at him.

He moved into the room, staring at her, his eyes dark with desire, his voice choked.

"Raine…what? You look…amazing. But…"

"I'm your Christmas present—I hope you like it. I know it's a few days early, but I couldn't wait to…give it to you."

Jack stood over her, felt himself go hard in a flash, and regarded her silently, unsure of what to say. So he just lowered himself to the floor next to her, leaned over and touched his mouth to hers.

He had so much to say, was feeling too much, it all logjammed in his chest. He'd been furious with hurt, but that quickly melted away into desire. He'd meant just to give her a hello kiss, but his soul caught fire just from the scent of her, and the kiss became more demanding. She pulled away, and he groaned, almost falling over to follow her, needing more.

"Uh-uh—you have to open your present first."

"But you are my present."

She smiled, all nervousness gone as she read the pleasure in his eyes, and she let herself absorb the peculiar but wonderful sensation of female control and power. She pushed herself up slowly onto hands and knees, letting him have a full view of her breasts and behind as she leaned over to reach for the box under the tree.

She handed him the box, smiling seductively when she noticed his erection straining against his pants; reaching down, touching him there for just a moment, lightly, her eyes lit with need and mirth.

"Wow, and you don't even know what's in the box yet."

He growled and reached for her, wanting only to tear off her wrapping and enjoy the gift of her hot, sweet body, but she leaned back, and gestured to the box.

"You have to open this first. I have to see if you like it. Then we'll go from there."

Jack's hands trembled as he took the box and ripped through the wrapping paper, thinking only that he knew he would love whatever it was—a watch, a tie, *socks*, for God's sake—anything—he didn't care as long as when he was done he could go play with Raine under the tree.

His body was aching for hers—it had been so long. He lifted the top and wrinkled his forehead as he found the box empty except for a small piece of red stationery in the bottom. He reached down, lifting the paper and unfolding it. He read it to himself, and found emotions clogging in his throat. For moments on end, all he could do was stare at the paper.

This gift entitles the recipient to all the love I have to give. There's more than I could fit in this box, as there is more than I could ever fit in my heart. I love you, Jack. Merry Christmas, Raine.

Raine thought she would die a thousand more deaths if he didn't say something soon: he was still, staring at the note, and she felt as if she would pass out if he didn't just say *something*. Then he looked up, and her breath caught. His eyes glowed with raw emotion, and he set the box and the note carefully aside.

Getting up on his knees, bringing them face-to-face, he drew her into a long, deep, drugging kiss. Pulling back, he looked into her eyes, and felt his world fall into place.

"Rainey—I love you...this is the best gift I have ever had, the best I will ever have. Tell me, though, I want to hear you say it."

She wasn't embarrassed when her eyes swam with tears, and she hugged him tightly to her, telling him over and over and over, until they were both laughing with sheer joy. She drew back, her face glowing with happiness as she looked into his.

"But that isn't all of it."

His eyes went opaque with desire, and he looked at her hungrily.

"I was hoping not."

"Let's get you out of these."

Enjoying her new sense of confidence and control, he let her undress him, only helping minimally, until he sat completely nude and aroused before her. Her breath was shallow, and he raised his hand to cover her breast and pinch her distended nipple through the lace, tugging her down next to him when she moaned.

Love made need multiply exponentially, and Raine gasped when she heard the lace rip. His hands raced hungrily over her skin, touching her everywhere, his mouth capturing hers, kissing her deeply, plundering her while his fingers did the same. She came suddenly in helpless waves as she wrenched against him, moaning into his mouth. She was his, and she gave herself freely. Her hand stroked his cock as she recovered, and he gently pushed her back to the blanket, beginning to position himself over her, when she planted a hand on his chest.

"Let me love you, Jack. Let me take you."

Jack sat back, praying to the universe for control beyond what a mortal man could possibly be expected to have. He laid back on the blanket, and watched her, smiling, her eyes hot and confident, her lush body flushed with the pleasure he had just given her. And wanted to again.

He heard himself curse hotly, not quite believing his own eyes as he watched her standing over him, her legs parted. She dipped a finger into the shadowy crevice between her legs and then trailed it up the firm flatness of her stomach, massaging the wetness from her sex on one nipple, then repeating the process on the other. He licked his lips, his body hard as a rock and frozen still, his fists digging into the blanket.

She looked down at him, wearing only the satin hat, drunk on power and pleasure, her sultry voice every man's erotic fantasy.

"Santa thinks Jack has been a very good boy."

He could barely talk, but tried, his breath heaving. "I have been very good, Santa. I can be even better if you come down here."

She laughed, and the husky sound nearly drove him over the edge. She lowered slowly to one knee, and then to the other, leaning over him, letting her breasts fall forward, swaying in front of his mouth. She trembled with sensation as she ran her wet, hot sex along his erection, teasing them both.

Her own vision blurred when he moved up and drew one breast, salty and delicious with her own taste, into his mouth. He suckled one, then the other as she slid over him, until he lost track of where she started and he ended.

Needing him more than she had ever needed anything, anyone, she took him deep inside of her, glorying in the guttural cry that broke from him with the contact. She smiled, and almost lost herself again when he arched upward, driving himself into her. But she held on, no—not yet. Her breath came out in pants, and she smiled at him, pushing him back, moving her hips slowly. Taking charge.

She watched him, his skin taut, his head arched back,

mouth moving in gasps of shock every time she ground against him. She knew what she wanted, what she wanted to give him most of all, and she knew it was within reach, recognizing the hot pleasure building in her.

She gave him everything—all of her passion, all of her trust, all of her love. She looked down into his eyes, and saw that he was offering her the same, and her heart burst as she lost control, loving him with all that she had.

He brought his hands up, grabbed her hips tightly and moved wildly under her. With him supporting her, she met his rhythm and rode him hard, arching her back as her orgasm consumed her. As the waves of it traveled through her, she declared her love for him when she felt him shudder underneath her, the heat of his climax shooting inside of her. Their voices blended, faded to murmurs; their bodies continued mating, until she fell against him, their hearts pounding, exhausted.

She lifted her head and kissed him tenderly.

"I do love you, Jack. I haven't ever loved anyone, haven't ever been loved. But I want to discover what it all means with you."

He slipped his arms around her, holding her close, cherishing her words.

"I want to share it all with you, too, Rainey, but I have to say, I think we have one problem."

She frowned against his shoulder. "What?"

He laughed softly, burying his face in her hair, inhaling the scent, and feeling—incredibly—his passion stirring again.

"This is only our first Christmas together, and I am not sure you can ever top this gift, sweetheart."

She laughed, too, feeling happiness deep down into her bones.

"Well, I'll just have to keep on trying." She wiggled against

him in a way that made his blood catch fire. "But I don't think
we are quite done here yet."

"Me neither. And by the way, don't ever, *ever* lose that hat."

Laughing and loving, Raine lowered her lips to his, and
made that promise to him. And many more.

HARLEQUIN® *Blaze*™

HARLEQUIN® *Temptation*®

Single in South Beach

Nightlife on the Strip just got a little hotter!

Join author Joanne Rock as she takes you back to Miami Beach and its hottest singles' playground. Club Paradise has staked its claim in the decadent South Beach nightlife and the women in charge are determined to keep the sexy resort on top. So what will they do with the hot men who show up at the club?

GIRL GONE WILD
Harlequin Blaze #135
May 2004

DATE WITH A DIVA
Harlequin Blaze #139
June 2004

HER FINAL FLING
Harlequin Temptation #983
July 2004

Don't miss the continuation of this red-hot series from Joanne Rock!

Look for these books at your favorite retail outlet.

www.eHarlequin.com HBSSB2

eHARLEQUIN.com

The Ultimate Destination for Women's Fiction

**Visit eHarlequin.com's Bookstore today
for today's most popular books at great prices.**

- An extensive selection of romance books by top authors!

- Choose our convenient "bill me" option. No credit card required.

- New releases, Themed Collections and hard-to-find backlist.

- A sneak peek at upcoming books.

- Check out book excerpts, book summaries and Reader Recommendations from other members and post your own too.

- Find out what everybody's reading in Bestsellers.

- Save BIG with everyday discounts and exclusive online offers!

- Our Category Legend will help you select reading that's exactly right for you!

- Visit our Bargain Outlet often for huge savings and special offers!

- Sweepstakes offers. Enter for your chance to win special prizes, autographed books and more.

**Your purchases are 100%
guaranteed—so shop online
at www.eHarlequin.com today!**

INTBB104

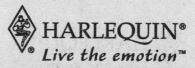

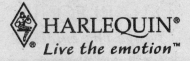